My Book

All Kinds of Love

Also by Carl Reiner

Enter Laughing

All Kinds of Love

Carl Reiner

A Birch Lane Press Book
Published by Carol Publishing Group

A Birch Lane Press Book
Published by Carol Publishing Group
Birch Lane Press is a registered trademark of Carol Communications, Inc.

Editorial Offices: 600 Madison Avenue, New York, N.Y. 10022
Sales and Distribution Offices: 120 Enterprise Avenue, Secaucus, N.J. 07094
In Canada: Canadian Manda Group, P.O. Box 920, Station U, Toronto, Ontario M8Z 5P9
Queries regarding rights and permissions should be addressed to
Carol Publishing Group, 600 Madison Avenue, New York, N.Y. 10022

Carol Publishing Group books are available at special discounts for bulk purchases, for sales promotion, fund-raising, or educational purposes. Special editions can be created to specifications. For details, contact: Special Sales Department, Carol Publishing Group, 120 Enterprise Avenue, Secaucus, N.J. 07094

Manufactured in the United States of America

10 9 8 7 6 5 4 3 2 1

Library of Congress Cataloging-in-Publication Data

Reiner, Carl, 1922–
   All kinds of love / Carl Reiner.
   p.   cm.
   "A Birch Lane Press book."
   ISBN 1-55972-163-4
   I. Title.
PS3568.E4863A79   1993
813'.54—dc20   92-35890
                                            CIP

For Estelle

"Love is the only gold."
—Alfred, Lord Tennyson

I would like to thank the following
people for their work and encouragement:
George Shapiro, Dan Strone, Bruce Shostak,
Barbara Scher, and Mike Zimring.

All Kinds of Love

1

FRED COX had hesitated to inform his wife that he had decided to hire a Japanese tutor. He knew exactly what Sharon's reaction would be, but he could never have predicted the profound impact such an innocent decision would have on their lives.

Sharon reminded her husband that they were going to be vacationing in Japan for a mere eight days, and Fred argued, "Yes, but those eight days could be a lot more fun if you knew the Japanese for 'How much is that?' and 'Where's the toilet?' "

"Fred," she said, sighing, "you know I have no aptitude for languages, and I especially am not interested in *habla*ing Japanese!"

Nobu Yoshi, the proprietor of the Sushi Gardens, had once mentioned to Fred that his cousin was an excellent instructor who gave private lessons to many people in the film industry, but Nobu neglected to mention that his cousin, Hana Yoshi, was a beautiful woman. Sharon discovered this when she opened the front door and found herself looking squarely into the blemish-free face of an atypically tall Japanese woman who easily could have been a finalist in a Miss Universe contest.

Sharon's impulse was to slam the door in her face and shout, "Sorry, my marriage isn't that solid," but instead she smiled sweetly and sang out in a mock coloratura, "Oh, hello, my husband is expecting you. Won't you please come in?"

In the time it took Hana Yoshi to cross the threshold, Sharon made a complete reconnaissance of this elegant, narrow-waisted, long-legged goddess whose breasts were at least a cup size larger than was the norm for most Asian women.

As Hana Yoshi and her heady, exotic scent glided into the room, Sharon considered for a moment whether it would not be wiser to forgo her shopping plans and stay for the lesson.

"Freddie, darling," she sang out, "your tutor, Hana Yoshi, is here."

"Be right down, darling," Fred sang back. "Would you offer Mr. Yoshi a drink?"

Hana giggled into her graceful, ringless hand. "My cousin Nobu must not have told your husband that I am a woman. Perhaps you should tell him."

"Mr. Cox," Sharon assured her, "is very perceptive and will immediately discover that for himself."

Hana Yoshi lowered herself onto the couch and discreetly crossed her ankles.

No one, Sharon thought, not Princess Di, not Audrey Hepburn, could have placed herself on that couch more gracefully or self-assuredly.

Sharon was brought back to reality when Hana Yoshi asked her if she would be taking the lessons, adding, "Nobu said that your husband wasn't sure of your interest."

Until Sharon had seen who was giving the lessons, she was sure she was not interested, but now she was having second thoughts.

"I am interested, but I'm afraid I don't have much of an ear for languages."

Hana Yoshi smiled warmly, parting her lush red lips to display an absolutely perfect set of teeth. They couldn't be real, Sharon thought. Nobody has teeth like that.

She stared at these white, white teeth as Hana Yoshi explained that many of her students who had felt as Sharon did were now speaking fluent Japanese. In fact, she boasted, one of them is now employed as a translator for Columbia Pictures.

Fred Cox bounded down the stairs, confidently announcing his arrival by calling out, "*Mushi, mushi,* Mr. Yoshi!" which brought a laugh from "Mr." Yoshi. Just as Sharon had prophesied, Fred immediately recognized that Hana Yoshi was a woman and apologized for referring to her as Mr. Yoshi. He then repeated his Japanese greeting of welcome. Again, Hana Yoshi laughed, explaining that "*Moshi, moshi*" was the word for

"Welcome" and that he was saying, *"Mushi, mushi,"* which meant "Insect, insect." An embarrassed Fred assured Ms. Yoshi that she looked nothing like an insect, turned to his wife, and admitted, "I might need more than two weeks to master the language."

Sharon managed to smile and wondered how she was going to handle wandering through Bullock's knowing that Captain Pinkerton was home sipping Perrier with a six-foot Madame Butterfly.

Fred had been married to Sharon for almost eighteen years and knew what her good-natured smile was masking. She must have noticed how his face brightened when he discovered Hana Yoshi sitting on his couch. Fred thought it wise to suggest that Sharon stay for the lesson.

"Honey," he reasoned, "you have Bullock's for the rest of your life. Ms. Yoshi will be with us for only two weeks. Stay, darling, you may love the experience."

It was obvious to Sharon what Fred was doing, and she considered upsetting his plans by agreeing to stay.

"No, no, no, darling," Sharon was surprised to hear herself say "You'll progress much faster if I'm not around. Good-bye, Ms. Yoshi. It was such a pleasure meeting you. Fred, if anyone calls, I'll be back in two hours. Have fun!"

When Sharon thought she detected a Cheshire-cat smile on her husband's face, she decided to return in an hour.

Sharon pulled out of her driveway and found herself making a right turn when the shopping mall was to her left. She drove a half mile before she realized her mistake. She shook her head, made a U-turn, then quickly made another U-turn, which in essence was an O-turn, and continued to drive away from the mall.

Where the hell am I going? she demanded of herself.

I don't know, she answered. I could drop in at Miriam's and invite myself in for coffee.

Suddenly, Sharon was struck with a sharp pain in her abdomen. She checked her calendar watch and ruled out mittelschmerz. It wasn't a pain, she decided, but a pang, a hunger pang. She realized that she had no interest in visiting her sister-in-law, Miriam, but had a sudden yen for sushi. With visions of salmon-skin hand rolls dancing in her head, she made a single U-turn and steered her red Miata toward Nobu's Sushi Gardens.

As soon as he heard the drone of his wife's car fade, Fred started a series of nervous, rambling questions:

"Hana, may I call you Hana? . . . Where would you like to sit? . . . Would you like something to drink before we start? . . . Perrier, water, some white wine, perhaps some tea? I have a world-class assortment, including a decaffeinated Oolong-Almond-Rocha blend. . . . Will we be needing any pads and pencils, or do you use an oral approach? . . . I had a French instructor, and she and I just conversed. . . . Would you like to take off your jacket?"

Hana Yoshi smiled and calmed Fred by miraculously answering all of his questions in chronological order.

"Of course you may call me Hana. A glass of cold water will be fine. No, we won't be needing any pads and pencils. Thank you, but I cannot remove my jacket, as I am wearing nothing underneath it."

Sharon arrived at Nobu's Sushi Gardens just as Nobu and his staff were about to sheath their sushi knives for the afternoon. She pleaded with Nobu to delay his closing long enough to make her two orders of yellow-tail sushi and a salmon-skin hand roll.

"For you, Mrs. Cox, anything you wish. But my cousin Hana at your house to teach you lesson, you forget?"

"No, Nobu, I didn't forget. Your cousin is teaching my husband. I'm not very good at learning languages."

"You like me!" Nobu laughed.

Nobu's inflection led Sharon to reply, "Of course I like you, Nobu. Why do you ask?"

"No, no," he explained, "I say, 'I, like you, no good to learn language' . . . but I glad you like me. . . . I like you . . . you very, very pretty . . . you mind I say this?"

Sharon assured Nobu that she didn't mind. In fact, she thanked him and confessed she was very much in need of that kind of compliment, especially today. Nobu was surprised that a woman so beautiful would need to be told so.

It was after four when Sharon retrieved her red Miata and dragged the valet parking sign out of the empty lot. Realizing she was much drunker than she thought, she stumbled out of the car, wrestled the parking sign off the bumper, and swore never again to drink four bottles of warm sake for lunch unless it was absolutely necessary. Sharon found that last thought terribly amusing and started to laugh uncontrollably. As she drove off the lot and down the street, the pitch of her laugh rose higher and higher until she started to retch. She stopped her car, opened the door, and threw up every last bit of the fine lunch Nobu had prepared. She was amazed to discover how much she had eaten.

When Sharon approached her house, she was not happy to find Hana Yoshi's car still parked in the driveway and became unhappier after looking into her rearview mirror and seeing the network of exploded capillaries that she had retched into her face. Not wanting anyone to see her this way, especially Ms. Yoshi, Sharon decided to sneak in through the kitchen and go up the back stairway to her bedroom.

On finding the kitchen door bolted, Sharon started to crawl through the doggie door. She had just pushed her head through when she heard her husband announce, "And this, Ms. Yoshi, is our little kitchen."

Sharon froze when she heard Fred shout, "Nougat!" For a brief, unsettling moment, Fred thought his faithful old golden retriever had come back from the dead. The color of Nougat's fur and Sharon's hair were identical; a subtle shade of honey brown that Sharon's hairdresser, Vittorio, after many failed attempts, had duplicated exactly.

Acting as if his wife crawling through a doggy door were not all that unusual, Fred gallantly pulled Sharon through. When Sharon fainted in his arms, Fred smiled casually, bid Ms. Yoshi sayonara, and asked her if she minded letting herself out.

Fred deposited Sharon's limp body on their oval king-sized bed and began to massage her cold hands. After he had called her name a dozen times, Sharon's eyes fluttered open, and she whispered something that sounded like "Hana."

"Hana?"

"Yoshi," Sharon replied, and fell asleep.

An hour later, she stirred as she felt a hand slipping into her blouse. She assumed it was Fred's. She squinted open one eye and saw a hazy vision of someone who had a long black rubber tube hanging out of each ear.

A stethoscope, she deduced. The hand in my blouse belongs to my brother-in-law, Dick.

She closed her eyes and tried to reconstruct what had brought her to this, but instead started to ruminate about her brother-in-law's name, Dr. Dick Cox. Besides being a redundancy, she thought, it was an undignified name for a gynecologist.

"She'll be fine if she stops the afternoon boozing," Dick advised.

Raising up on one elbow and without opening her eyes, Sharon insisted, "Sipping a little sake while having sushi is not boozing."

As she lay back on her pillow, Sharon thought she detected the faint aroma of Hana Yoshi's perfume. She closed her eyes and concluded that something strange was going on in her life.

2

FRED COX pulled on his blue bikini swim shorts and examined himself in the three-way mirror in their pool house. He loved what he saw, especially the side view that reflected the flattest stomach he had sported since his days as a young lifeguard. He patted it lovingly and turned to his trainer for a professional evaluation.

"Not too bad for a forty-four-year-old fart, eh, Stoney?"

Stoney Sheib, personal trainer to the stars, thwacked his own stomach sharply with a cupped palm, hurriedly tossed his equipment into a well-worn Adidas bag, and prescribed that "for added abdominal definition," Fred do three sets of leg raises after swimming his morning laps.

"Say hello to Mrs. Cox for me, and tell her I hope it's only a twenty-four-hour virus. I hate to see her miss a session. I'm really happy with her glutes. I put the calipers on them yesterday, and she's added a very solid two and a quarter centimeters just where we want them."

Standing at the edge of his swimming pool, Fred tried to visualize how Stoney had used his calipers. Did he measure his wife's ass nude or through her leotards? He decided that Stoney, given his honest dedication to firming up flabby muscles, used his calipers on Sharon's bare skin.

Fred dove into the pool, glided smoothly through the water, and lingered on the image of this bronzed muscleman disinterestedly handling his wife's ass. Within seconds he was swimming his laps encumbered by an unprecedented erection. As he wondered if he could manage his full, twenty-minute morning ritual handicapped this way, his housekeeper, Maria, stopped him at the end of the pool to inform him that a Miss Hana was calling. She handed him the portable phone and glanced into the pool, giving no indication that she saw his erection. However, when she returned to the kitchen, she giggled and told her sister, Carla, that Mr. Cox was well named. Carla, who spoke little English, had to have the joke explained.

Carla and Maria were identical twins who had migrated from El Salvador. Maria had arrived first, securing a green card and a job working for the Coxes. Six months later, Carla arrived but found that she could not obtain a green card because of her jailed husband's political affiliations. It was then that the twins decided to share the same green card and the same job. They alternated keeping house. When one worked, the other stayed home and tended to Carla's infant son, Julio. They were quite content to live this secret life and would have continued had not Sharon noticed that the mole on Maria's cheek would disappear every other week.

As Fred stroked his way through the last five minutes of his swim, he continued replaying the phone call that for almost three laps had prolonged his erection. Was it pure wishful thinking, or did he hear in Hana Yoshi's voice an invitation to a liaison? Why else would she phone to suggest that his next lesson be at her apartment? He recalled now how relaxed she seemed when he escorted her about the house, showing off its newly decorated rooms, and there was her mysterious smile when, in the master bedroom, she caressed a pillowcase and said, "I love sleeping on satin."

As Fred draped a terry-cloth robe around his shoulders and made his way toward the house, he tried unsuccessfully to shake Hana Yoshi's image from his mind. What was there about this girl? As a movie producer, he had met and dealt with his share of beautiful women. His ruminations were interrupted by his wife.

"Fred, I'm in the breakfast room. Do you have a minute to talk?"

"Of course, dear," he said sweetly as he slid his arms into his robe and tightened the belt around his new taut stomach. He strode into the sunlit room, picked up a glass of freshly squeezed orange juice, drained half of it, and asked, "What's up, Shar?"

To avoid any unnecessary vibrations in her head, Sharon spoke very quietly.

"Three things. One, I want to apologize for coming home in the condition I did. For some reason, instead of going to Bullock's, I found myself with this sudden craving for sushi—I think it was having that Japanese girl in our house. Secondly, I think I was wrong not to try to learn a few words of Japanese for the trip."

Against his will, he heard himself say, "If you're serious, darling, Ms. Yoshi just called and asked if we could have our lesson at her place tonight."

"No, darling, you take that lesson by yourself. I think we'd both do better if we took individual instruction. It would be less pressure for me. I'll call Ms. Yoshi and arrange a time for myself."

Fred pretended to object and then admitted, "What a good idea."

"What's the third thing?" he then asked.

"What's *what* third thing? . . . Oh, yes," Sharon remembered. "Your father called and said not to waste money by calling him back. He just wanted to tell you that the check arrived and to thank you for it. I told him you were doing your laps, and he said not to disturb you while you were taking care of your health."

"Is that it?"

"More or less. . . . Your mother's fine, and he asked about Kevin."

"Did you tell him?"

"Me? Tell your father that his only grandson is flunking most of his subjects and walks around in a daze all day? I didn't feel like hearing again how smart you were in high school and how bad a mother I must be. Oh, yes, he also asked if Kevin ever used drugs."

"I hope you told him that he doesn't."

"I did. But he suggested we make him urinate in a bottle and have him tested. . . . It might not be a bad idea."

"Sharon, Kevin is sixteen," he explained, trying not to sound impatient. "His hormones are now in charge of him. They're telling him that there are other things in life besides studying hard and doing homework."

"Like what? Napping all afternoon? He looks terrible, and he hardly sees any of his friends anymore. He even stopped seeing that lovely Liz Layton. She's such an attractive girl. She keeps calling, and he never wants to talk to her. I—I'm beginning to think . . . "

Sharon found it very difficult to say what she thought, but Fred was sure that what she was thinking was so completely wrong that he voiced it as crudely as he could.

"You're beginning to think what? That our son is a fag?"

"You don't think it's possible?" Sharon asked beseechingly.

"Sharon," Fred reasoned, "there has never been a homosexual in either of our families. I guarantee that kid is as straight as you or I."

3

Leon Cox had everything, or so it would appear. He and his wife, Sarah, had been married for fifty-one years, lived in Miami Beach, Florida, and except for a recent procedure on his prostate, bothersome cataracts in both eyes, and a profound hearing loss, Leon had enjoyed a disease-free and injury-free life.

For the past nine years, he and Sarah had lived in the deluxe two-bedroom condominium that their achiever sons "Dickie the doctor" and "Freddie the producer" had bought for them. Leon was fortunate in many ways. He married a woman who loved him deeply and told him so, even though he had never told her that he loved her; not on the day he proposed, not on their wedding day, not even on the day she gave birth did he find it in him to say, "I love you, Sarah." The closest Leon came to a declaration of love was on the morning she delivered their first son. He had stroked her sweaty brow and with a tear in his voice said, "Sarah, you're a fine woman, and I really, really appreciate what you have done here today, and I'll always be grateful. God bless you!"

Leon Cox was also fortunate to have had a slightly paranoid father, who felt that the very early rantings of Adolf Hitler were personally directed at him and his family. Leon remembered his father often boasting, "I, Simon Kakaffsky, am smarter than Sigmund Freud. Why, you ask? Because, in 1934, Simon Kakaffsky got out of Germany. It took that schmuck psychiatrist four years longer to wake up and leave."

Simon, among other things, gave the family its present name. In 1946, when his son Leon was about to open his accounting office, it was Simon Kakaffsky who suggested that "for business purposes, it might be smart to drop the 'sky' from Kakaffsky." When Simon realized that Kakaff, in Yiddish, translated to "shit on," as in the oft-used suggestion *"Gay kakaff 'n Yom!"* (Go shit in the ocean!), he shortened it further to *Kak*, which still meant "shit." He then added an *s*, Anglicized the spelling, and ended up with Cox.

Leon Cox idolized his father, and whenever he felt either Dickie or Freddie were being disrespectful to their grandfather, he would shake his finger at them and shout, "Listen, you cockers, if it weren't for the old Jew with the funny accent, you wouldn't be here!"

On one occasion, Fred thought it would be funny to ask, "Where *would* we be?"

Fred never forgot his father's smiling response: "Where would you be? I'll tell you where you'd be."

Like a cobra, his father's hand darted out and whacked him sharply on the back of his head.

"That's where you'd be, Mr. Wisenheimer!"

"Freddie," Leon complained, "I told Sharon you didn't have to waste a call. I just wanted to tell you that the check arrived and thank you very much. Look, as long as they charge the same for three minutes as they do for a minute and I've got you on the phone, tell me, how are you?"

Fred had given up trying to explain to his father that he could well afford this call.

"I'm fine, Pa, how are you?"

"Don't ask. Listen, Freddie, I don't like to bother you with stuff like this, but your brother's wife—"

"Dad," Fred interrupted, "what about Miriam?"

When his father started with the phrase, "Now, you know that your brother's wife isn't one of my favorite people . . . ," Fred knew he was in for a long call unless he used the one excuse that was always effective.

"Pop, I have a production meeting in five minutes. Can I call you back tonight?"

"Freddie, a woman who lives in our condo . . ." Leon began explaining, speaking rapidly. "I won't tell you her name because she doesn't want to be involved. . . . I'll call her Mrs. P."

Fred knew that Mrs. P was the code name for the condo's resident gossip, Mrs. Pechter.

"Anyway, this Mrs. P heard from her nephew Jim, who owns his own beauty parlor in Beverly Hills. One of this Jim's operators isn't a *faygele*. Coyle, or maybe she said Doyle, it doesn't matter, the point is, he does your sister-in-law's hair and, it seems, other parts of her, too. Freddie, I didn't want to tell your brother, Dickie. He'll think I'm making this up because I hate his wife's guts. Could you check it out? I don't want to start rumors that aren't true. Tell Kevin he should study hard so his Grandpa will be proud of him. I'll call next week. You'll check out about Doyle?"

Fred knew he wouldn't but promised he would.

Sharon clutched her coffee mug in both hands and stared out the window of the sun-filled breakfast room. The willow tree that drooped over the pool house was motionless, as was Sharon. Sharon had many things to do this day, but she could not raise herself from the breakfast table. She kept hearing Fred's voice insist that there had never been a homosexual in either of their families and that Kevin was as straight as they were. She wondered why she had not used that opportunity to tell Fred about her mannish aunt Lilly who, five months after marrying a much older man, was left widowed and wealthy and spent the rest of her life living in bliss with her lesbian stepdaughter. Why hadn't she told him that? And why was she so squeamish about asking her son, Kevin, why he had become an uncommunicative recluse? Her introspections were interrupted as a sleepy-eyed, disheveled Kevin shuffled in, dropped into a chair, and mumbled, "Gmonimim," which Sharon understood to be "Good morning, Mom." Then, with his head resting on the table, he ordered scrambled eggs and toast. Not feeling equipped to discuss with her son the reasons for his recent antisocial behavior, Sharon instead castigated him for his lack of manners.

"Kevin, dear, don't you think it would be polite if, before you ordered your breakfast from Maria, you said good morning to her?"

Kevin raised his head slowly and told his mother that it

would also be polite if, after all these months, she learned that "that was not Maria, but Carla."

Sharon was indeed aware that one of her twin maids had a beauty mark on her cheek but kept forgetting which one.

Climbing the stairway to her bedroom, Sharon attempted to distract herself by checking each tread of the stairway to see if the workman had matched the elaborate pattern in her new and expensive carpeting. Happily, she discovered three badly matched sections. Now here was a problem she could handle. She strode determinedly into her bedroom and went directly to the phone, where she found a yellow Post-it stuck to the base. She picked it off and cursed her husband for writing so small that she could not decipher it without her "damned reading glasses!" Sharon held the tiny yellow memo at arm's length and managed to decode it. It was Hana Yoshi's telephone number and some scribbled words that seemed to read, "If you're really interested . . ."

She quickly dialed Hana Yoshi's number, and to her utter amazement, she heard herself coyly addressing Hana Yoshi in a voice she had not used since her days in high school. She was also amazed to hear how honestly delighted Hana Yoshi sounded on learning of Sharon's desire to study Japanese.

Sharon felt a sudden and strange chill come over her. She drew her satin robe tightly around her body and immediately, and incorrectly, diagnosed it as an oncoming cold.

4

F RED COX was looking forward to this day. As he drove up Wilshire Boulevard toward his office, he thought of all the appointments he had scheduled. None were with people who might disturb his equilibrium. He was particularly looking forward to meeting Jason Hansen, a new young writer whose book, *The Wacaluma Log*, he had planned to option, with the hope of persuading the author to do the adaptation.

Fred was certain that this project was the one that would secure his niche in the industry, put him in with the big boys, and give him a chance to enjoy all the luxuries he already had but could barely afford. Soon he would be able to pick up lunch checks without wincing. For the past few years he had been living off the success of *Alimony, Nougats and Acrimony*, a low-budget movie that had captured best-picture awards at the international film festivals in Cannes, Venice, and Buenos Aires. He had never admitted to anyone how shocked he was to receive an award for producing "an uproarious comedy about infidelity" when, in fact, he had produced what he thought was "a serious drama about the disintegration of the modern family." Fred learned from this experience never to overestimate his ability to judge material. He now left the choosing of properties to his assistant, Walter Quigley, a 120-pound mass of neurotic facial and body tics who had earned for himself the nickname "Squiggler."

In 1984, when Fred Cox chose the name Sky Productions for his new motion-picture production company, he called his father in Florida and asked, "Pop, do you remember how you used to tell us that it was a sin to waste anything?"

"Yes, Freddie, and do you remember that the phone rates go down after seven? So, besides half a dollar a minute, what else are you wasting?"

"Pa," Fred proudly announced, "I took the *s-k-y* from Kakaffsky, and in honor of Grandpa Simon I'm calling my firm Sky Productions."

Leon Cox, moved but anxious that his son not catch him experiencing a moment of honest sentiment, joked, "Don't expect a big applause, son, you only saved one lousy syllable."

Fred Cox was recounting this story to Jason Hansen, who had asked about the genesis of Sky Productions. The young author wanted to know all he could about the company that was about to option his novel. He barely allowed Fred to finish his story before asking, bluntly, how Sky Productions was planning to "fuck up" his book. Fred stared at Jason, then announced dramatically, "Young man, if *The Wacaluma Log* gets fucked up, then you'll have been the fucker!"

Jason was aware of Fred's very obvious ploy but was anxious for the scene to play out. Fred Cox was giving the young neophyte his first opportunity to observe, firsthand, what an older screenwriter had once described to him as "a certain breed of industry hyphenate, the 'producer-schmuck.' "

Feigning naïveté, Jason Hansen inquired as to how he possibly could be the "fucker" of his own book.

"If you allow anyone"—Fred paused dramatically before driving home his point—"*anyone* but yourself to write the screenplay!"

The negotiation was joined. Fred was hoping that a little flattery and the chance to protect the integrity of his work would entice the author to accept any insulting offer that was laid before him. Jason Hansen, on the other hand, to protect his baby from being hacked to death by one of the town's many available hacks, would have done the job for free, but since he had recently married a young lady who had just learned to shop in designer boutiques, he was not about to tell the producer-schmuck how he felt. Instead, when Fred explained about the tightness of the budget and the importance of having enough money to hire the caliber of stars that *The Wacaluma Log* deserved, Jason nodded understandingly and asked how much money Fred was thinking of spending for the screenplay. Fred said that they would get into that as soon as the budget was finalized. Then, offering Jason his hand, he declared, "When the film version of *The Wacaluma Log* is released, I guarantee that I will personally make this industry aware of the name Hason Jansen."

"And *my* name, too," Jason Hansen asked, "as long as you're at it?"

5

KEVIN COX was a master eavesdropper. When the phone rang in the house, he knew intuitively how many times it would ring before someone would answer it, and he would synchronize lifting an extension off the cradle at the precise moment his mother or father did, thus becoming privy to all manner of interesting and usable information.

The conversation he was now monitoring would be of immediate use to him. He had planned to go to school this morning and to return home after his last class, but when he heard his mother ask her hairdresser if, at noon, he could take her for a wash, cut, and coloring, he realized that his plans could change. He crossed his fingers and prayed while Vittorio checked his appointment book.

"Mrs. Cox, you're in luck!"

"And so am I," Kevin mouthed.

To avoid passing his mother's room, Kevin, carrying his schoolbooks and his camcorder, tiptoed down the back stairway. He had learned early on that the less contact he had with either parent, the less opportunity they would have to ruin his life.

Kevin Cox had always been very mature for his age. At thirteen, he had grown enough hair on his face to warrant receiving an electric shaver for Christmas. At fourteen, he had grown the extra inch he needed to be as tall as his father. It always embarrassed him to be told that he was handsomer than his very handsome dad. In elementary school, smitten preteen girls would look for any excuse to ring his doorbell: "Kevin, I didn't get our history assignment for today. Could you . . . ?" or "Kevin, would you help me with my math homework?" or "Did you lose this pen?"

Aware of the attention their son was getting and using the Hollywood formula of measuring success by popularity, Fred and Sharon deemed their son a hit. At thirteen, Kevin had a steady girl, Liz Layton, and even though he spent more time with girls than did most of his friends, Fred and Sharon considered their son normal and healthy. However, one time, after watching Kevin play Juliet in a comedy sketch at school, they were a little taken aback when, afterward, Kevin was voted the prettiest girl in the school and crowned "Miss El Rodeo." Fred pooh-poohed Sharon's concern, but soon afterward, he gifted Kevin with a subscription to *Playboy*.

Kevin skillfully maneuvered his black Toyota Celica out of the school parking lot just as the lunch bell started to ring. He debated whether to stop at Thrifty's and pick up a dozen fresh condoms or make do with the two he had stashed in his camcorder case. His groin dictated the decision, and using the fastest route possible, he sped straight home. His heart skipped a beat, and the growing balloon in his jeans started to deflate when he spied a plumber's truck parked in his driveway.

"Oh, shit, shit, shit!" he growled as he pounded the steering wheel.

Though Kevin never believed in the power of prayer, he prayed hard that by the time he counted to ten, the plumber would leave the house and drive away. When, at the count of two, the man exited the house and drove off, Kevin noted that he might have to reevaluate his agnosticism.

Kevin found Maria at the kitchen sink stuffing breakfast leftovers into the garbage disposal. The noise of grinding grapefruit rinds allowed Kevin to sneak up behind her and cup her breasts. Maria responded by snatching a paring knife from the sink, whirling around, and slashing at his chest. She had assumed the hands on her breasts belonged to the plumber, who had come back to rape her. When she realized that it was Kevin she had stabbed, she fell to her knees and begged, hysterically, for his forgiveness. Apologizing profusely for startling her, Kevin knelt down and ripped open his shirt to show that his wound was superficial. The sight of the small trickle of blood on Kevin's smooth skin only heightened her hysteria. She buried her head in his chest, and while kissing and licking his wound clean, attempted a blubbering explanation of why she had acted so violently. Only after Kevin had lifted Maria's face to his and kissed her deeply did she stop weeping and give thanks to the Lord for sparing the life of the man she loved.

Kevin gently lifted Maria from the floor and carried her upstairs to his bedroom. As Kevin went to lock the door, Maria started to remove her apron but stopped and smiled when she heard Kevin say that he wanted to undress her. She blew him a kiss, seductively retied the bow, and allowed Kevin to disrobe her and have his gentle, loving way with her.

Soon after Maria and Carla had come to work for his folks, Kevin started paying a fearful but willing Maria nightly conjugal visits. He always waited at least an hour after his parents went to bed before tiptoeing past their bedroom door and down the back stairs to Maria's cozy room in the servants' quarters. Kevin had made Maria promise that she would tell absolutely no one of their affair. "Except Carla," Maria insisted. "She would know even if I said nothing."

Kevin slid his arm from underneath Maria's warm body and looked at his watch. When he realized that his mother would not be home for at least an hour, he cursed at himself.

"What? What is it, Kevin," Maria asked tremulously. "Is something wrong?"

"Nothing, nothing," he lied. "My arm was going to sleep."

Actually nothing on Kevin was going to sleep. He and Maria had made passionate love twice, and Kevin was mentally kicking himself for not stopping to buy condoms. When he felt Maria's warm mouth sucking on his earlobe, he knew that there was no way he was going to let a condom come between him and a third round of ecstasy. Kevin had taken seriously the school's classes in safe-sex education and had promised himself that he would never not wear a condom during intercourse; until today, he had kept faith with himself. Kevin gently placed the heel of his left foot on the inside of Maria's right calf and, with the faintest of pressure, invited Maria to spread her thighs and welcome him in. For the first time in his life, he felt the warm flesh of a woman's vagina against his naked penis. It was a sensation that he wanted to last and last and last and last and last.

Kevin and Maria had made love dozens and dozens of times in the months they had been together, but something happened this time that surprised them both. When Kevin's body finally relaxed, he opted not to roll off Maria, but instead tightened his arms about her and held her until she found it difficult to breathe. Only when Maria started to sob softly did Kevin relax his hold. When he tried to lift himself off her body, she threw her arms around him, rolled to one side, and squeezed him with an intensity that was new to both of them. He responded by matching the strength and power of her embrace. He looked at her beautiful face, which was now wet with tears, and gently put his lips against her eyes.

"Maria, I love you!"

He said it not once but over and over again, and the more he said it, the more tearful she became.

When he asked why she was crying, Maria shook her head and then buried it in his chest. Kevin tilted her face up to his, looked deeply into her red-rimmed eyes, and told her that he wished she would marry him so that they could sleep together every night for the rest of their lives.

Maria stopped crying just long enough to listen to Kevin's unquestionably sincere declaration of love. With her lips on his, she began to explain, in Spanish, why she was so miserable. Although Kevin got the gist of what she had said, he asked her to repeat it in English. In a soft whisper, she stammered and whimpered that she, too, was deeply in love but felt that their love was doomed. She reminded him that she was twenty-one years old and he was not yet seventeen; if his parents found out that they were having an affair, both she and her sister, Carla would lose not only their jobs but their sanctuary in this country.

Kevin held Maria's throbbing body close to his and tried vainly to assure her that their love for each other was strong enough to withstand anything his parents or his country might attempt to do to them. To prove the sincerity of his words, he put his lips to the small silver crucifix that lay between her moist breasts and swore that they would never be separated. He then, very gently, entered her and remained there for ten motionless minutes—a genital handshake that, in his mind, sealed forever their promise "to love each other through eternity."

6

S KY PRODUCTIONS owed its tentative but insistent existence in the film industry not only to its president, Fred Cox, but in great part to Fred's fifty-five-year-old executive secretary, Elspeth Bunter.

Elspeth could type 85 words a minute, take shorthand at 150, and because of unfulfilled maternal instincts, actually enjoyed making and serving freshly brewed coffee to her boss.

At five minutes to six, Elspeth entered Fred Cox's office, discreetly placed a note on his desk, and reminded him of his Japanese lesson at six-fifteen.

Fred snaked his newly detailed, shiny black Porsche out of the Century City garage and aggressively shoehorned it into an assembly line of slow-moving cars inching their way toward Santa Monica Boulevard.

As Fred powered along in his sleek, German-engineered racer at nine miles an hour, he computed that the street construction that closed off one lane of the boulevard could make him at least ten minutes late for his appointment with Hana Yoshi.

"God bless that woman!" he shouted when he discovered that the note Elspeth had slipped him was Hana Yoshi's telephone number. As Fred dialed, he was surprised to feel a rush of blood flooding his groin. He was sixteen again, calling Edith Komack from a pay phone in a Bronx subway station. He remembered how, with each ring, his passion for Edith grew and grew, just as it was now growing for Hana.

"Uh, Hana, this is Fred Cox. . . . I seem to be hung up in traffic. I should be about ten minutes late."

"Whenever you come," she trilled, "will be fine."

There was nothing in Fred Cox's life experience that would have prepared him for his Japanese lesson with Hana Yoshi. He parked his Porsche in Hana Yoshi's driveway behind a vintage Bentley that he assumed was hers. As he sprang from his car, he looked up and found a smiling Hana Yoshi framed in her doorway, her hand extended in greeting. Fred removed his sunglasses and shook her cool, delicate hand. He watched her lips and award-winning teeth mouth a greeting in Japanese that she immediately translated.

"Welcome, Fred Cox, to my humble home."

As Fred was ushered into Hana's living room, a sudden calm enveloped him. Everything in the room was geared to soothe: the warm beige tone of the upholstered walls, the pictures that hung on them—delicate watercolors of flowers, soaring birds, deserted beaches, and mist-shrouded meadows—and probably the most important element, the quiet silkiness of Hana Yoshi's voice.

"Well, Mr. Cox, are you ready for your first lesson?"

"Ready, willing, and, I hope, able!"

Fred started to sit, but Hana stopped him, saying, "I wish to try a new method of teaching."

"What do we do, stand?" Fred asked, and laughed nervously.

"Come," she beckoned. "I will show you what we do."

Fred's heart started to race as Hana led him into her bedroom and directly to her bed. On the pale pink king-sized bed lay two black satin kimonos, each with a colorful landscape of Mount Fuji embroidered on the back panel. Before Fred could start to guess at a possible scenario for the evening, Hana, speaking Japanese in a very crisp, clear voice, gave what seemed like a directive that he thought included the word kimono. Hana handed him one of the kimonos and requested that he join her in the Jacuzzi. Fred watched Hana pick up the other kimono, glide gracefully across the room, and exit into a room that, he assumed, housed the hot whirlpool. Fred stood stock-still, trying to imagine what might be in store for him. He thought, Could this be a practical joke that my smiling friend, Nobu, is playing on me? Or maybe Hana Yoshi is a new breed of Hollywood hyphenate: the teacher-hooker.

Fred gingerly entered a dimly lit, white-tiled bathroom,

where he found a smiling Oriental goddess soaking in a large Jacuzzi. Her perfectly sculpted arms, draped over the rim of the tub, showcased her exquisite breasts, wet and gently buoyed up by the hot, bubbling water that lapped them just below their firm nipples. He could not keep an "Oh, my God!" from escaping his lips. At this point, Hana Yoshi informed him that everything he said in English she would translate into Japanese and have him repeat it.

"In this way," she explained, "we will build your vocabulary."

Hana then translated "Oh, my God" into Japanese and had Fred repeat it five times, which he managed perfectly. Her next instruction was more difficult. Hana, in Japanese, bade her pupil to disrobe and sit in the tub, facing her. She translated this into English, and Fred responded immediately by slipping out of his kimono and into a whole new world of academia.

7

SHARON WATCHED Maria, red-eyed and sniffling, move around the dinner table and place a bowl of potato-leek soup in front of Fred. As Maria approached to serve her, Sharon asked if there was anything troubling her.

"No, señora, I am fine," Maria said, wiping her eyes. "It's the onions I was cutting for the . . . salad."

"But Maria, we're not having salad today."

As soon as the words were out of Sharon's mouth, she regretted saying them. Maria apologized for making a salad and quickly took off for the kitchen, trying unsuccessfully to stifle a gut-wrenching sob.

"Touchy little thing," Fred mumbled, a spoonful of soup poised at his mouth. "If it's going to upset her that much, tell her we'll eat the damn salad!"

"It's not the salad, Fred," Sharon whispered. "The girl is upset about something more important, and I think I know what it is."

"Whatever it is, work it out," Fred urged. "I don't want to lose anybody that can cook up a soup like this."

Fred was ravenously hungry and had half-finished his bowl before Sharon took her first spoonful. He was happy that Sharon was distracted by this household problem and was hoping she would forget to ask him about his Japanese lesson.

"I think," Sharon continued, "that Carla wants to go back home to be with her mother."

"What makes you think that?"

"I eavesdropped on a call Carla made to El Salvador a week ago," Sharon admitted.

25

"How the hell do you eavesdrop on a conversation in a language you don't understand?"

"I could tell," she explained, "just by the amount of times Carla mentioned her son Julio's name and the amount of crying that went on. Fred, it would be a disaster if Carla went home with the baby. Maria is bound to leave with her. . . . Twins are like that. I could never replace them in time for our trip to Japan, and even if I could, I wouldn't feel comfortable leaving Kevin with a strange housekeeper."

"I don't see that it would matter that much," Fred argued. "As far as I can see, Kevin hardly has anything to do with either one of those two."

"Perhaps I'll ask Maria point-blank if Carla intends to leave."

"Good. Just be sure," Fred suggested, "that it's not Carla you're asking."

When Maria came to collect the soup bowls and Sharon saw no birthmark on her cheek, she asked tentatively, "Maria? Is there anything you'd like to tell me?"

Maria stiffened and blurted out, "*Madre mia*! No, no, I don't like to tell you anything—I mean, I have nothing to tell. Señora, do you think I have something I should tell?"

"No, no, no, Maria," said Sharon in her most unctuous lady-of-the-manor voice. "I simply wondered if you and Carla are happy working here. Mr. Cox and I have grown very fond of you, and Kevin has, too, even though he may not show it. We hope you and Carla are planning to stay with us."

Maria heaved a loud sigh of relief.

"Carla and I are very happy here," she stammered. "We wish to stay forever."

Sharon patted Maria's arm, smiled, and without missing a beat, said, "Maria, serve the *pollo*—and the *ensalada*, too, as long as you've prepared it."

A relieved and grateful Maria rushed into the kitchen, pulled the tiny crucifix from inside her blouse, kissed it, and thanked Jesus for allowing her happiness to continue.

Fred could tell from the deliberate way Sharon placed her wineglass on the table and directed her patented, joyless smile at him that she was about to talk about Hana Yoshi.

"Sooo, darling," she sang, "tell me about your Ms. Yoshi."

"What would you like to know about her?"

"Well," Sharon said, smiling, "I am curious to know if a girl with legs like hers can be much of a language teacher."

"Honey," he lied, "I don't know about her legs, but I got more from her in one hour than I got in six weeks from that guy at Berlitz. That Ms. Yoshi has a very original and effective method of teaching."

Hoping that Sharon had not called and arranged for a lesson, he asked if she had and feigned delight when he learned that Sharon was driving out to Hana's house the following day.

"Maybe," Sharon wondered, "Ms. Yoshi's original method will work for me. Nothing ever has before."

As Maria placed a plate of savory chicken before her, Sharon asked, "By the way, what is her method?"

"Oh," Fred could not resist offering, "it's mainly oral."

Although Fred and Sharon dined in silence, they were each enjoying separate fantasies about Hana Yoshi. Sharon saw herself in Hana Yoshi's house, being praised by Hana as the most brilliant and gifted pupil she had ever taught, while Fred wondered if Hana would use the same teaching method with his wife. He felt himself getting excited as he pictured Sharon lowering her trim white body into Hana's hot, bubbling Jacuzzi. He smiled as he envisioned Sharon's thick, curly red pubic hair and Hana's straight black pubic hair soaking side by side in the same steamy tub.

8

WHEN FRED arrived at his office the next morning, he was surprised and upset to find Jason Hansen and his secretary sharing a bagel. Jason had called Elspeth earlier and asked if he could come to meet with Fred.

Elspeth agreed to get him in.

Before Fred could object, Elspeth told him that the meeting with his accountant, Marvin See, had been rescheduled for the following morning.

Fred had hoped to read the young man's novel before scheduling another meeting and having to discuss with him the actual contents of the book. He had been in this situation more than a few times and knew exactly what he had to do.

"My boy," he began while patting a copy of the book lying on his desk, "I can't tell you how impressed I am with the quality of the writing in this fine work of yours. Before I get into some of the passages that I have marked, which, by the way, I found particularly brilliant, I would love to hear you speak about the genesis of this *Wacaluma Log* of yours."

Fred leaned back in his chair, accepted a mug of coffee from Elspeth, and listened attentively as Jason explained that Wacaluma was a fictional name he had invented to protect the identity of members of a society of zealots who called themselves Luminescence.

He told how, two years earlier, he had infiltrated Luminescence and lived the communal life for 150 days before stealing away one night armed with a subject for his exciting docu-novel. He worried about publishing a book that might incite some of his former fellow campers to sue, or possibly maim, him. The most fearsome, he felt, was Dr. Hamilton Faust, a former unsuccessful, self-degreed doctor of reflexology and chiropractic and now the strong-willed leader of the cult, given to the purification of man and his planet. To achieve Luminescence, his followers were required to go through a purification process that included drinking pure water, eating pure foods, breathing pure air, and partaking of pure sex with him.

"You know"—Jason smiled—"for a moment I toyed with the idea of titling my book *The Luminescent Log*, but I realized that in some people's minds it might conjure up a halating penis. So to avoid this, and a big libel suit, I settled on *The Wacaluma Log*. I borrowed the 'luma' from Luminescence and added 'waca,' a Latinized version of 'wacky,' which I feel is an apt description of Dr. Faust and most of his sad disciples."

Fred Cox raised up his copy of *The Wacaluma Log*, slapped at the back cover, and announced, "No wonder this little baby reads the way it does. It's based on truth! I'm happy you filled me in on this Hamilton Faust character. It gives me a good take on how to cast the son of a bitch. I love that name Dr. Faust."

"I don't use his name in the book."

"I know," Fred lied.

"Did you realize that Safut is an anagram for Faust?"

"Oh, right," Fred covered quickly. "Dr. Safut . . . I didn't realize it was an anagram for Faust. Clever."

Jason was intrigued that Fred was already thinking about the casting of the central characters and, with juvenile enthusiasm, asked what actor Fred saw playing the role of Jack Hardy.

Fred hesitated and kept a frozen smile on his face as he tried to remember which character in the short synopsis Elspeth insisted he read would be Jack Hardy. Assuming that it must be the leading male role, he asked, "Who would *you* like to see playing Jack Hardy, which by the way is a helluva part for an actor."

Jason, anxious to hear the opinion of the man to whom he was considering selling the rights to his book, insisted on hearing Fred's choice.

"Well," Fred stalled, "to play the role of Jack Hardy, I see any one of a number of stars who could kick the shit out of it."

"Like who?"

"Well, off the top of my head, Tom Cruise, Tom Hanks, Tom Selleck."

"Just Toms? No Dicks or Harrys? Mr. Cox, did you read the book?"

"Of course I read it." Fred feigned indignation. "I hope you're not going to give me a hard time and object to having a big box-office star in our picture?"

"Mr. Cox, Jack Hardy is based on me, and as you can see, I am not a hunk."

"Jason, those were just preliminary suggestions. I've already told Elspeth," he lied, "to check the availability of Woody Allen, Billy Crystal, and Danny DeVito."

"What about the girl?"

"Which girl?"

"The one Jack Hardy becomes involved with, Shirelle."

"Oh, Shirelle . . . Well, I didn't finalize my list yet, but there are a lot of brilliant young actresses available who would make a wonderful Shirelle. Julia Roberts and Michelle Pfeiffer, to mention just a couple."

Jason took a deep breath. "Neither Julia Roberts nor Michelle Pfeiffer is black. You didn't read the goddamned book, Fred!"

"Of course I read the goddamned book, and I'll thank you not to refer to it as a 'goddamned book.' Remember, I'm buying that book, and it's a great book. Look, if you'll just calm down, maybe I can tell you a little about Sky Productions and the philosophy that guides it. No, Julia and Michelle are not black, and by the way, I think these days our black brothers and sisters prefer to be called African-American."

Fred, mistaking Jason's shocked silence as rapt interest, continued. "At Sky Productions, we don't look at the color of a person's skin. We look for talent, and we try to get the best talent for each part, period. I don't give a damn if she's white, brown, black, or Japanese."

"Japanese?" Jason asked incredulously.

"If she has the talent, yes!"

Fred's mind was racing. He fantasized, Oh, my God, what a great thing that would be. I cast Hana Yoshi in a small role, and during production she can continue giving me "lessons."

Jason stared at Fred and then burst out laughing. It was a full two minutes before he could bring himself under control. Fred waited patiently while Jason sputtered and gasped and wiped tears from his face.

Finally, Fred spoke. "May I ask what the hell you're laughing at?"

"I'm sorry," Jason explained, "but I was trying to imagine an American audience accepting a Japanese girl named Shirelle being raised in a Detroit slum by parents who were militant Black Panthers."

Fred cupped his chin in his hand, pretending to think. "What if the girl were adopted? . . . And we don't have to call her Shirelle. That's an easy fix."

Jason nodded. He realized that he was involved in an idiotic but valuable exchange of ideas that someday he would use in an essay to illustrate the ultimate in Hollywood-executive schmuckiness.

9

FROM THE MOMENT Sharon awoke from a fitful night's sleep, she had a strange, unsettled feeling. Four cups of black coffee and one-half milligram of Halcion had no perceivable effect.

Why, she wondered, would taking a Japanese lesson cause me this much anxiety? She had thought of calling her psychiatrist and asking him why he thought she felt as she did, but she knew Dr. Lowenthal would ask her, "Why do *you* think you feel this way?"

She considered calling Hana Yoshi and canceling their appointment, but this idea, instead of calming her, made her twice as jumpy and, of all things, sad.

As Sharon searched her closet for an appropriate outfit to wear to an afternoon Japanese lesson, her anxiety increased. She touched each outfit in her wardrobe but was unable to select one.

If Maria had not come into the room at this moment to make the bed, Sharon might never have succeeded in finding the right clothes. With feigned casualness, she instructed Maria to "pick out a nice outfit for me to wear today and lay it on my bed while I shower."

Sharon arrived at Hana Yoshi's house wearing a thigh-length red jersey sheath, a dress that brought out the very best of Sharon's quite remarkable figure. The millimeter or two that Stoney Sheib had helped her add to her glutes would not go unnoticed by anybody who appreciated a fine behind. The feelings Sharon was experiencing as she walked to Hana's front door were not dissimilar to what she had felt on that first day in grade school. She was again consumed with fear that the teacher would not like her.

When a smiling Hana Yoshi opened the front door and said, "Welcome, Mrs. Cox. My, how beautiful you look," Sharon knew that her fears were irrational and paranoid. She thought, My teacher likes me. Sharon thanked Hana for her gracious compliment, squared her shoulders, and entered the jasmine-scented world of higher learning.

Hana warned Sharon that she might find her method of teaching unorthodox but assured her that it was quite effective. Sharon confessed that she had been unsuccessful learning any language by conventional methods and was open to anything that might help her overcome her language-learning block.

"I find that two ounces of chilled wine and soothing music help one to be more open to new ideas," Hana explained as she offered Sharon a small glass of Chardonnay.

Sharon sipped her wine and listened to Hana discuss how they would converse in English and how Hana would immediately translate everything into Japanese and have her repeat each phrase several times. Sharon was having difficulty concentrating. She became fascinated by the tone of Hana's voice and the grace of her hands as they punctuated her thoughts. Sharon noticed, as she had when Hana had visited her house, the flawlessness of her skin and the luster of her silken black hair. She wondered if Fred had similar difficulty concentrating.

What was it Hana just said? Did she say something about a gentle massage, a state of total relaxation, and following her into her bedroom?

Next to Hana's bed was a massage table draped with a black satin sheet, and on the bed were two white satin kimonos. Hana instructed Sharon to take off all of her clothes and underwear and put on one of the kimonos. Hana's voice was so firm and reassuring that Sharon was happy to do as she was bid. Hana turned her back and slipped out of her dress and into a kimono, allowing Sharon to catch sight of two more of Hana's perfect features, a long, smooth back and firm, round buttocks.

"We will stand face-to-face," Hana dispassionately explained, "and we will look into each other's eyes until we are comfortable with one another."

With that, Hana gently took Sharon's hands, bringing

Sharon's face close to hers. Sharon tried not to tremble but could not stop herself.

"Ms. Yoshi, I don't know if I can do this."

Hana smiled and translated "I don't know if I can do this" into Japanese and instructed Sharon to say it five times.

Each time she mouthed the Japanese phrase for "I don't know if I can do this," Sharon became more and more certain that she would like to try to "do this," even if she ended up failing. Sharon stared silently into Hana's eyes and saw there someone she would like to trust. When Sharon's gaze drifted to Hana's full, soft mouth, Hana broke the silence, taught Sharon the Japanese word for mouth, and had Sharon repeat it five times. She then touched each part of Sharon's face and taught her the Japanese words for them. When Sharon had finished reciting each one five times, Hana took Sharon's hand and led her to the massage table, where Sharon learned the word for table and massage.

From the moment Sharon saw the table, she had expected to be massaged, so it did not surprise her when Hana undid her sash and helped her out of her kimono. Sharon did not like massages, but somehow she did not experience any of the mild revulsion she usually felt at the prospect of having people she did not know rubbing their oily hands over her body. As Hana guided her over to the table and told her to lie on her stomach, an image of her husband, Fred, lying naked on the same table flashed through Sharon's mind. She froze.

"If you are wondering, Mrs. Cox, did I massage Mr. Cox during his lesson, I can assure you that I did not. I have different methods for men and women."

Sharon admitted that she did wonder. Hana Yoshi, in a soft, buttery whisper, then bade Sharon to close her eyes and open her mind. Sharon did, then waited nervously for the lesson to continue. As she felt Hana's gentle hands caressing her body, she learned the Japanese words for oil, hands, neck, back, buttocks, thighs, calves, ankles, feet, and toes. It took more than fifteen minutes to repeat each word in Japanese five times. When Hana suggested she turn over on her back, Sharon was more than ready to learn the words for breasts, nipples, stomach, pubic hair, and clitoris. Sharon had a difficult time learning and pronouncing the word for clitoris, *kuritorisu*, but Hana, very gently and very patiently, went over and over the word. When Sharon finally got it, she exploded in ecstasy, and Hana quickly taught her the word for orgasm. She laughed and cried and reached out for her extraordinary Japanese teacher to thank her for the only language lesson she had ever enjoyed. Hana slipped off her kimono and offered her nude body for Sharon to hug. It was while Hana Yoshi was atop Sharon that Sharon learned the Japanese words for kiss, tongue, cunnilingus, and lesbian.

10

FRED WAS AMAZED at his wife's progress, as was Sharon at her husband's. In two weeks both had mastered hundreds of words of vocabulary, which they proudly showed off to their friends and each other. Neither, of course, displayed *all* the words they had learned.

Fred complimented Sharon on her extraordinary linguistic accomplishments, once remarking how happy and motivated she seemed since she started studying Japanese. Sharon credited Ms. Yoshi with helping her find resources in herself that she did not know existed.

Neither Fred nor Sharon was as eager to fly off to Japan as they were two weeks earlier, and both were reluctant and embarrassed to bring up the subject of postponing or canceling their trip.

At two-thirty on Sunday morning, an aroused Kevin lay awake in his bed, thinking of the idyllic two weeks that would start for him and Maria in twelve hours, when JAL flight 63 took off for Tokyo. There was no way Kevin could wait that long before holding Maria in his arms and making love to her. He made his way to his parents' room, hoping to find them asleep, and gingerly pressed his ear to the door. He was upset to hear them talking and even more dismayed to hear what they were saying.

"Sharon, what do you think about rescheduling Japan for a couple of months from now?"

"You'd be willing to do that?"

"Why not? Japan'll be there in August."

Kevin wanted to shout that an atom bomb was once dropped there in August.

"Fred, I just had the craziest idea." (The idea actually came days earlier, when she and Hana decided that they could not stand being apart for two entire weeks.) "It's really a mad idea, Fred, but before you jump, think about it for a minute. . . . Why don't we invite Ms. Yoshi to come with us to Japan? She could act as our interpreter and continue with our sessions."

Fred did not notice that Sharon had said "sessions" rather than "lessons."

When Kevin heard his mother agree to call Hana, he crossed his fingers and prayed to the same God that made Joe the plumber disappear. God came through again.

As soon as Kevin learned that Hana Yoshi was joining his parents, he tiptoed back to his room instead of to Maria's. It was obvious that his folks would not sleep soundly this night, so rather than risk everything, he decided to suffer one more night of abstinence.

Fred, unable to secure a first-class ticket for Hana, settled for a seat in business class. While they were boarding, Fred whispered to Sharon that if she did not mind sitting with Hana, he would be happy to move to business class, as it would finally give him the opportunity to read *The Wacaluma Log*. Sharon objected just long enough to convince her husband that she was doing him a favor by agreeing to sit with Ms. Yoshi.

"Hana can give you a lesson or two," he offered. "That'll shorten the flight for you. I'll stop by to visit once in a while, and if you don't mind sitting in business class for a bit, I might come up here to grab a lesson myself."

Fred smiled smugly as be buckled himself into his seat. With a little clever maneuvering, he had made it possible to sit with Hana for at least a part of the flight. As the plane taxied to the runway, Fred closed his eyes and thought about how, when they were in Japan, he would have to find a time and place for him and Hana to get in one or two of their "special sessions."

As the plane took off, Sharon, who had a fear of flying, closed her eyes and was happy to feel Hana's warm, reassuring hand slip into hers. Even after the plane leveled off, Sharon held on to her teacher's hand and thought how exciting, albeit bizarre, it was to be sharing with her teacher this wonderful adventure.

When Hana looked over and saw Sharon staring at her, she smiled, pursed her lips, and sent a tiny airborne kiss to her adoring friend. Sharon acknowledged the subtle kiss and sent one back. Hana mouthed, "Thank you," lay back in her luxurious first-class seat, and wondered how long she could keep two balls in the air before dropping one of them.

11

L EON COX was a natural worrier, but today he felt his worrying was justified. In the elevator, on his way up to his apartment from retrieving the mail, he found a letter that unnerved him. When the elevator finally stopped on the eleventh floor, Leon, impatient to discuss with Sarah what he just found in a Sky Productions envelope, started to exit before the doors fully opened. He bumped and bullied his way out and started down the long, plush corridor to his apartment. He had never mentioned to his sons that the elegant four-hundred-thousand-dollar gift they had bought for him was five miles from the elevator and "a pain in the ass when you have to schlep groceries." Puffing noisily, he marched into the narrow kitchen where Sarah was adding a pinch of pepper to a pot of mushroom-and-barley soup.

"Sarah," he announced as he waved the envelope, "something fishy is going on in California."

"Not now, Leon," she countered. "First you'll eat, then you'll curse California."

Leon would not be denied and thrust a check under his wife's nose.

"It's a check from Freddie," she shrugged. "What's the big megillah?"

"The big story," he explained, "is that Freddie sent us a check two weeks ago. This is next month's. He never sends us a check two weeks early. Two weeks late, maybe, but never two weeks early. Something very funny is going on out there in La La Land."

Leon often peppered his speech with jargon he picked up

from the trade papers that Fred sent him. Leon loved scanning their pages and coming upon his son's name and reading about current and future productions.

Sarah carried two bowls of the steaming soup onto a small, aluminum-awninged patio from which, if they looked directly between the two large gray condominiums that faced them, they could see a sliver of ocean. Leon followed Sarah onto the patio and continued to wave the check.

"You didn't look at this check, did you?"

"I looked, I looked," she said, humoring him as she placed the bowls of soup on the table. "Now eat your soup before it gets cold."

"Sarah, we're in Florida, nothing gets cold in Florida. And why do we need hot soup on such a hot day?"

"Because you love mushroom-and-barley soup, and cold, it doesn't taste good."

"You didn't really look at this check, did you?"

"Again with the check," she said impatiently as she looked at it. "This is not Freddie's signature."

"Aha," Leon gloated.

"There's another name here," Sarah said, adjusting her glasses. "I can't make it out."

"Well," Leon announced triumphantly, "I can! It's Marvin See, Freddie's accountant, and I'm asking, Why would Mr. See send out a check that's not due for two weeks and why would he sign it, and I'm also asking, How many more checks did Mr. See sign and did Mr. See, maybe, make a couple of them out to Marvin See and what the hell kind of a name is See, anyway?"

"Maybe it was shortened from something else," Sarah suggested, "like Kakaffsky was shortened to Cox."

"Cox," he bellowed, "is a name, it's a noun! See is a verb! I see, you see, they see. It's not a name. I don't trust that son of a bitch."

"Leon, how can you say that? You never met the man."

"I don't trust anybody who handles other people's money, period."

"All your life you handled other people's money."

"But I never signed my name to any of my client's checks. In California, people give powers of attorney to any crook who asks for it."

"Leon, you're being ridiculous."

"Am I? Call up Doris Day or Kirk Douglas or Debbie Reynolds and ask them if I'm being ridiculous."

"After we have our soup, I'll call them. Now sit and eat!"

"Freddie never lets his accountant sign a check," Leon shouted, waving a finger in his wife's face, "unless he's out of town, and Freddie is not out of town."

"How do you know?"

"I just spoke with him."

"When?"

"When last month's check came."

"Leon, that was almost two weeks ago. Two minutes after he hung up he could have gone out of town."

"He didn't say he was going anywhere. He always tells us if he's going somewhere."

"Never! When he comes back, he tells us he's *been* somewhere."

"Sarah, I was an accountant for too many years not to know when something smells fishy. Someone is screwing my son, and I'm going to find out how!"

Leon went back into the living room and picked up the phone, Sarah trying unsuccessfully to coax him to eat first and call later.

Leon growled as he listened to his daughter-in-law's recorded voice asking if he cared to leave a message.

"No!" Leon shouted as he slammed the phone down. "I don't care to leave a goddamned message!"

Sarah called from the patio, "Leon, come eat your soup, it's so delicious."

"Sarah," he hollered back while circling the phone, "how can you eat soup at a time like this? Where the hell are they?"

"Maybe they're out," Sarah said calmly.

Leon paced the apartment, muttering that he had to find out what was going on. When Sarah quietly suggested he call Dickie, Leon shouted, "I am not calling Dickie."

"Why not, for goodness' sake?" Sarah dared to shout back.

"Because it's Wednesday, and if he's out playing golf, the *nafke* might answer."

"Leon, I know you're not crazy about Miriam, but you don't have to call her a whore."

"I didn't. I called her a *nafke*."

"Leon," she pleaded, "Miriam is your son's wife—"

Leon cut Sarah off abruptly, reminding her, "Miriam is not Miriam, but Mary Kathleen."

"Leon, the girl changed her name to please us."

"Well, 'the girl' didn't please me. Without batting an eyelash, she changes her name to Miriam and converts to Judaism. And why? Because she studied and searched and found Catholicism wanting? No! She saw a young, handsome gynecologist who could someday make a quarter of a million dollars a year."

Leon's voice now took on the sound and fury of Rabbi Rubinoff, the old bearded gent who, an eternity ago, had prepared him for his bar mitzvah. "People who are disloyal to their heritage are people of little substance, and they should all go to hell! I say, if a person can stray so fast from her religion, how could we expect her not to stray from her marriage? Yes, Sarah, your daughter-in-law is a first-class *nafke*. Your neighbor, Mrs. Pechter, told me that Miriam was having an affair with her Beverly Hills hairdresser. Did you know this?"

Sarah reluctantly admitted that she had known about her daughter-in-law's errant behavior for years.

"Why would you keep such a thing from me?" he bellowed.

"Why? Because I remember how crazy you got with Elizabeth Taylor when she 'cocked around' on Eddie Fisher . . . and they're not even family."

Leon was now beside himself. He cursed Miriam, he cursed Marvin See, he cursed Mrs. Pechter, and he cursed the world for allowing immoral behavior to go unchallenged. Sarah considered her options. She could sit quietly by and listen to her husband rant, or she could inform him of something that would instantly defuse his rage but would undoubtedly drop him into a depression that might take a greater toll on his health than the high-decibel screaming he was doing. She decided to let him holler himself out rather than tell him that his "son the doctor," the apple of his myopic eye, was in grave danger of being sued for malpractice. Sarah had kept this dread secret locked in her bosom for more than nine months.

Their son, Dr. Richard Cox, was arguably the nation's single handsomest gynecologist. His rare good looks, a smooth, resonant bass voice, and a grace that he could only have developed by watching old Cary Grant movies understandably made unhappy, frustrated, and adventurous women eager to bed with him. Using his silky charm, he could make a woman believe that she was the seducer rather than the seducee. But to discourage the possibility of real commitment or involvement, Dr. Cox rarely broke his standing rule of dallying no more than three times with any one patient.

Sarah learned this shocking news while watching *Geraldo*, whose subject that afternoon was "Lonely Women and Their Unscrupulous Gynecologists."

Sarah sat transfixed as she listened to women tearfully describe how they had fallen in love and had sex with this tall, blond, blue-eyed gynecologist.

Sarah prayed that they were talking about another tall, blond, blue-eyed gynecologist who practiced in the San Fernando Valley.

Leon suddenly stopped pacing, smacked at his forehead, shouted "Idiot!" and rushed to the phone mumbling, "Kevin."

"Why are you calling your grandson an idiot?"

"Would I call Kevin an idiot? Me, I'm the idiot for not calling Kevin's number. He'll know if Freddie left town."

While Leon dialed, he muttered about how ridiculous it was for "a fifteen-year-old *pisher* to have his own phone number."

"Sixteen," Sarah corrected.

"Sixteen? . . . All right, so I'll call him Mr. Pisher."

Kevin, picking up the phone just in time to hear "Mr. Pisher," informed the caller, "Sorry, there's no Mr. Pisher at this number."

"Kevin! It's Grandpa. I didn't recognize your voice, it's so deep. You got a cold?"

Kevin explained that it was just something that's been happening to it lately.

"For a minute," Leon joshed, "I thought I was talking to your uncle Dick. So how's my big boy?"

Kevin was very fond of his Grandpa, even though he had seen him less than a half-dozen times in his life.

Before asking about his parents, Leon went through his usual list of interrogatives.

"So, Kevin, what have you been doing?"

Kevin wondered how his grandfather would react if he told him that when the phone rang, he was making love to his girlfriend.

"Oh, right now," Kevin said, caressing Maria's leg, "I'm studying for a biology exam."

Though Maria knew Kevin's grandfather could not see her, she scrunched her body into a little ball and slid under the covers.

"Kevin, have you made any more little movies with that TV camera? The one that you sent us, I played for all my neighbors. I like that part where the maid walks into the kitchen with a tray of dishes and then comes right in again wearing an evening gown. Was it trick photography?"

"No, Grandpa, I used twins."

"Oh, you used twins. Well, you fooled me. Beautiful girls, especially the one in the black velvet dress."

Kevin was dying to say, Grandpa, the one in the black velvet dress is the girl I love and plan someday to marry. Instead, he said, "Oh, that was Maria. She and her sister, Carla, work here."

"Is that so . . . twins?"

Leon cupped the phone and asked, "Sarah, did you know that Freddie has twin housekeepers working for him?"

"How would I know?" Sarah shrugged. "Does Freddie ever tell us anything?"

Leon nodded sadly and asked Kevin if he knew where his father was. "I called his number," he explained, "and I got the machine."

"Is it important, Grandpa? Because I have a hotel number for Dad."

Learning that his son was in Tokyo solved for Leon the mystery of the Marvin See–signed check. He thought, Fred forgot to sign the check before he left and told his accountant to do it. Case closed!

"So, Kevin, when are you coming for another visit? You haven't been to Disney World for so long, I'll bet Mickey Mouse won't remember you. Anyway, say hello to the pretty twins and give the one in the black velvet dress a kiss from your grandpa."

Sarah admonished her husband for telling his grandson to kiss the maid for him, but Kevin, happy to hear someone acknowledge the existence of his love, ducked under the covers, found a tightly balled up Maria, kissed her behind, and said, "That's from my grandpa!"

12

FOR TEN GLORIOUS DAYS, Kevin and Maria spent nearly every waking and sleeping minute in each other's company. They were apart only when Maria insisted he not accompany her to the bathroom.

He watched her wash her face, brush her teeth, comb her hair, dress, and undress. They swam, showered, and bathed together and never missed an opportunity to declare their love for each other. During these extraordinary days, the only schoolbook Kevin opened was his Spanish-language book. He taught himself how to say in Spanish all the endearing things he had said to Maria in English. Maria dissolved into tears when, in her native tongue, she heard how deeply Kevin loved her. He would attend roll call at school each morning and loudly announce that he was present. He would then meet Maria in the school parking lot, where she waited eagerly for her daily driving lesson.

On the morning of the eleventh day, when Kevin and Maria had begun to feel depressed about the impending end of their romantic idyll, Kevin received a call from his father saying that they were "having a really spectacular time," adding, "If you're not too lonely, son, Mom and I would like to extend our trip for another week or two."

"Stay for a year!" Kevin exploded. "Just kidding, Dad. I think it's great that you and Mom are having such a great time. I'm fine here. I'm studying hard, and I'm doing really good in Spanish."

His and Maria's unbridled happiness was reigned in later that day when, while they were splashing around in the pool with Carla and little Julio, the phone rang. Kevin, dripping wet, answered and heard a man speaking excitedly in Spanish, asking to speak with Carla.

When Carla heard the man's voice, she shrieked, "Domenico!," burst into tears, and kissed the phone. Maria echoed, "Domenico!" Simultaneously, the twin sisters crossed themselves and thanked God for sparing the life of Carla's husband. Maria then held Julio's ear to the phone to let him hear his father's voice.

Kevin was touched by the joyous reunion Carla and her husband were having, but a selfish pragmatism took over as he tried to evaluate how this windfall of good fortune for Carla would affect his relationship with Maria. As he listened to Carla effusing in nearly incomprehensible Spanish, it somehow became clear that Domenico was asking her to join him. After hanging up, Carla and Maria conversed in Spanish quickly and animatedly and then suddenly stopped. They turned their twin faces toward Kevin and looked at him imploringly with four big, beautiful, wet brown eyes. The looks of consternation on their faces informed him that Domenico's phone call had, along with its joy, brought problems. Neither twin would speak. Finally, Maria explained that her brother-in-law had escaped from an El Salvadoran political prison and wanted Carla and Julio to join him in Puerto Rico. Maria, holding her tightly clenched fists to her bosom, prepared herself to say something that Kevin knew would break his heart.

"Kevin," she stammered, "Carla wants me to go with her."

Tears welled up in Kevin's eyes as he nodded that he understood. He held his breath, knowing that Maria's next words must be "She is my sister, and I must go with her." He heard instead, "I cannot go with her, but I told her that I would try to help her get enough money to fly with Julio to Puerto Rico and to—"

Before Maria could finish listing all the things her sister would need, Kevin picked up the phone and dialed.

"Marvin See, please. Kevin Cox calling."

Maria stood by and saw a side of Kevin she did not know existed. Using his news-anchorman-type voice, he informed Marvin See that there was a bit of a "household problem" that he was sure Marvin would have "no trouble solving."

"Marvin," he asked, knowing what the answer would be, "did my mother remember to call you about an advance on

Carla's salary for her dental bill? . . . Oh, damn it, she asked me to remind her, but in the rush of packing for their trip, she must have forgotten."

"Listen," Marvin philosophized, "everybody forgets. Your father forgot to sign his father's check. I'll send it out, no problem."

Kevin thanked Marvin for his understanding, and told him that Carla would pick up the check on her way to the dentist.

As Kevin drove to the airport, he was juggling a myriad of emotions. He felt happy for himself and little Julio, who was sleeping peacefully beside him in his car seat, and for Carla and her husband, who would soon be reunited, but he also felt a deep sadness for the twin sisters, who now sat quietly in the backseat. They held hands and did not say a word for the thirty-five minutes it took to drive to the airport.

As Kevin unloaded Carla's things from his car, he was struck by how little she owned. All her earthly belongings were crammed into two worn canvas suitcases and a cardboard carton that once held cans of Dole pineapple juice.

Inside the terminal, Kevin stood by, holding Julio until the hugging, weeping sisters silently signaled each other that the moment had come for them to part.

On the ride back, Maria started to weep quietly and continued sobbing on and off until the following morning, when Carla called from Puerto Rico and told her how happy she was and how much Domenico loved his son. When she hung up, she threw her arms around Kevin's neck and kissed him feverishly. Between kisses, as they pledged to love each other forever and ever and ever, they sank to the living room floor and started to undress each other.

While lying atop Maria, Kevin became aware that they were now truly alone and free to make love in any room in the house. Although it was a very large house, they managed handily. They found Fred's den particularly to their liking and even used it once just to read. Kevin had found a copy of *The Wacaluma Log* on his father's desk and read it, along with Jason Hansen's accompanying letter that described how *The Wacaluma Log* was based on his personal experience living in Salton, Oregon, as a member of a cult called Luminescence.

13

FRED, SHARON, and Hana Yoshi spent the last week of their month long cultural and sexual adventure traveling to small, primitive islands. On Kyamura, a tiny, remote, phoneless, faxless picturesque fishing village, Hana managed to locate friends and distant relatives who had known her mother and grandmother.

From their stories, Hana was able to reconstruct those parts of her background that had always been a mystery to her. She discovered that during the Second World War most of her male relatives were killed in combat fighting the Americans. When Hana related this to Fred, he shook his head embarrassedly and offered a belated apology for his country's part in the death of her family.

On a small farm in the interior of Kyamura, Hana had found Cho, a seventy-five-year-old great-aunt, who, like Hana, was unusually tall. Hana had always wondered about her un-characteristic height and learned from her great-aunt Cho that her paternal great-grandfather had not been Japanese but a Chinese sailor who came from a region in northern China where tall people still abound.

Hana learned, too, that at fourteen her great-grandmother, whose name was Suki, was sold to a "house of pleasure" in Tokyo to work as a "love geisha." Her very first client was a tall, handsome sailor who took from her her virginity and, ultimately, her sanity. Sharon was especially moved when Hana reported the sad beginnings of Suki's tragic life. Hana, however, chose not to tell the Coxes all she had learned about her great-grandmother. She did share with them how deeply

49

her great-grandmother grieved for the sailor who never returned and how, after his child was born to her, she went mad
and committed suicide. Hana thought Fred and Sharon might
not enjoy hearing about how, on the day of her suicide, in
a psychotic frenzy, her great-grandmother Suki randomly
searched out three of her regular clients, stabbed them to
death, and then castrated them.

During the six days on the islands, with Hana caught up in
researching her heritage, Fred and Sharon found that their time
spent together was becoming increasingly uncomfortable. Early in their marriage they had tried, unsuccessfully, to find
something in which both could become interested. Today, as
they sat in their hotel room reading, they were totally unaware
of the common interest they now shared. Sharon was anxious
to get back home and discuss with Dr. Lowenthal why, for the
first time since they married, she was not feeling some kind of
anger or resentment toward her husband. Was it, she wondered, connected to her newfound sexual identity? She quickly
decided that she would not ask her psychiatrist's opinion about
this because she had promised herself never to discuss, with
anyone, her relationship with Hana.

14

KEVIN TRIED not to think about Sunday. At four-thirty that day he would be awakened from the delicious dream in which he and Maria had lived for three and a half weeks. He could not imagine going back to his old reality and losing the freedom to stand on the dining-room table in his underwear every night after dinner and shout at the top of his lungs, "Maria Francesca Degrut, I loooove youuuu!"

This morning, he had awakened early and sneaked out of bed. When Maria awoke, she would read the note he had left on his pillow: "Maria, my love, if you follow the scent of frying bacon, it will lead you to the two things you love most in the world, huevos rancheros and me!"

As Kevin lay slices of bacon on the griddle, he quietly hummed "Maria" from *West Side Story*, a song he had never hummed before and did not realize he knew.

Kevin's plan was to cook Maria's favorite breakfast and have it on the table when she stepped into the kitchen. He had just placed four slices of perfectly crisped bacon onto a paper towel when a very pale and drawn Maria rushed past him and vomited in the sink. Kevin held her forehead and tried to comfort her as she spit up watery gobs of greenish-yellow bile. Between heaves, Maria struggled to apologize for being unable to eat the beautiful breakfast he had prepared for her.

When the siege subsided, Kevin held an ice cube against the back of her neck and suggested that she may have food poisoning from "that fucking roast chicken I bought last night at the convenience store."

"No, Kevin," she protested, "I have felt this way for three

mornings now, but you were asleep when I vomited in the bathroom. My sister was this way when she was pregnant with Julio.''

"Pregnant?" he gulped. "How could you have become—?" he started to ask, but answered himself. "That time in my bedroom when I ran out of condoms. Holy shit!"

Kevin sunk into a chair and stared at Maria, whose big, sad eyes were starting to pool up. She began to blubber an apology, but he tried to reassure her that she had no need to apologize for anything. Kevin reached across the table, took Maria's trembling hands in his, and spoke slowly and quietly. What Maria heard surprised her, but no more than it did Kevin. He had never given any thought to what he might do if confronted with the situation in which he now found himself. After hesitating briefly, he heard himself say, "Maria, will you marry me?" Maria gasped, and Kevin rushed to continue. "I know that you're Catholic and religious and I'm Jewish and not, and even if you weren't religious, I want you to have this baby. . . . I mean it. I've seen you with little Julio and you'd be great with a kid. And even though I'm only—almost seventeen, I think I'd be a good father." He had no idea why he said, "Look, Romeo was only fourteen," but he quickly stopped and changed the subject, hoping that Maria did not know how Romeo and Juliet solved their problem.

"I have some money in the bank," he continued. "I have a car, and we love each other, don't we?"

Maria nodded her head sharply three times and kissed her crucifix.

15

O N THE long flight from Tokyo to Los Angeles, Hana unsuccessfully attempted to calm her two impatient, nerve-racked
clients. Their anxiety was kindled when Fred contacted his
office on the air phone to ask Elspeth to arrange for a limousine
and to find out why Kevin's line was always busy. It was then
that Fred learned that Sky Productions was having a problem
securing the rights to *The Wacaluma Log*. Elspeth had also tried
to assure the Coxes that their son was fine and had probably
done nothing worse than played hooky from school.

Sharon was juggling feelings of disappointment, anxiety, and
fury when she and Fred walked up the ramp at LAX and saw
only Elspeth and the limousine driver waiting to welcome them
home. When Elspeth informed them that she still had not been
able to contact or locate their son, Sharon became hysterical
and refused to be calmed, even by Hana, who held her hand
and whispered words of comfort to her.

"Sharon," Fred reasoned, "he could be staying at a friend's
house or gone fishing."

Between sobs, Sharon reminded Fred, "Kevin has no
friends, and he hates handling worms." Fred offered to drop
Hana at her house, but she volunteered to take a taxi. Sharon
pulled herself together just long enough to appreciate the two
gentle kisses that Hana placed on her flushed cheeks.

As the limousine rolled to a stop in their driveway, Sharon
bolted and raced to the front door.

"For God's sake," Sharon shouted as she set off the security
alarm, "somebody, what's the damned code?"

Fred quickly punched it in, and Sharon ran through the house calling Kevin's name and praying that she would not find his body lying in a pool of blood.

She automatically hesitated before Kevin's door and knocked before entering. The bed was unmade, and there were magazines and books strewn about. Sharon slid open the closet door and gasped. "Bare hangers!"

Sharon grabbed a wooden hanger and flung it out the door. As it flew toward his head, Fred, approaching from the hall, ducked to avoid the cedar missile and announced, "Kevin is nowhere in the house, and neither are Carla or Maria." Sharon pointed to Kevin's bare closet and shouted, "Your son has run off."

Sharon started to throw another hanger but was checked when a respectful Elspeth poked her head in.

"Mrs. Cox," she said, holding out a piece of folded notepaper, "I found this. It's addressed to you."

A ransom note! Sharon worried as she unfolded it. Realizing that she did not have her reading glasses, she handed it to Fred, who was also without glasses. Holding the note at arm's length, he read, "Dear Señora Cox, I feel bad that I leave and not say good-bye. I enjoy you let us to stay in the house and to swim in your beautiful pool. Kevin is very kind to me and Julio and the money he lend me to go to my husband in Puerto Rico, I pay back as soon as I get a job. *Muchas gracias*. God bless you and Señor Cox. Carla."

Sharon snatched the note from her husband and shouted, "Well, we know where Carla is, but where the hell is Maria?"

"Puerto Rico!" Fred deduced. "Maria went to Puerto Rico with her sister. Twins do that sort of thing. I'll bet Kevin drove them to the airport and that's why his car wasn't out front."

Sharon unleashed a fresh burst of hysteria when she realized that Kevin's car was gone. She bolted from Kevin's room and ran through the house, opening every door to every room and closet in hopes of finding some clue to her son's fate. She ran across the lawn toward the maid's quarters and let out a blood-curdling scream when she saw, lying at the bottom of the pool, a large clump of dead bougainvillea leaves. Fred tore across the lawn and dove into the pool just as Sharon shouted for Fred, who was in mid-dive, to stop.

Sharon watched the strangely emotionless face of her Armani-suited, Gucci-loafered husband as he rose up from the bottom of the pool. As he swam to the ladder, she explained how much, at first glance, the clump of dead leaves looked like their son's body.

Fred dragged himself out of the pool, discarding his seventeen-hundred-dollar "Dry Clean Only" all-silk outfit. Elspeth collected the wet clothes and followed Sharon and Fred into the pool house, averting her eyes as Fred peeled off his soaked red briefs and reached for a terry-cloth robe.

In an attempt to calm two very anxious people, Elspeth quietly offered, "Why don't I call some of Kevin's school chums. One of them might know where he is."

A distraught Sharon, knowing how unlikely that was, suggested that Fred call the police.

"And what, Sharon? File a missing person's report? We're not sure he's missing yet."

"I am."

"Sharon, before you send his picture to the milk company, why don't we examine a few more possibilities."

"Like what?"

Fred picked up the phone and started dialing. "He might have called my brother and told him where he's off to."

"Kevin never calls Dick!"

"In an emergency he would!"

Fred became infuriated when his brother's new secretary informed him that she could not "disturb the doctor while he was in with a patient." Fred restrained himself from shouting, "In with a patient?" More likely *in* a patient."

Dr. Cox, at the moment, was examining Mrs. Barbi Feldman, former lingerie and underwear model and present wife of the very old, very wealthy, and rapidly deteriorating divorce attorney Hal Feldman. Dr. Cox had been Barbi's gynecologist for more than a year before she decided to approach him sexually. At the time, even though the good doctor had overcommitted himself and was suffering from a mild form of prostatitis, Barbi Feldman's petite, overall blond loveliness so obsessed him that he broke his long-standing rule and met with her for many more times than the three proscribed assignations.

By the time Dick returned Fred's call, Sharon already had

gone through Kevin's phone book and called all of his friends and schoolmates, including Liz Layton. No one could shed any light on where Kevin might be "hanging." Liz was the only one who seemed concerned that Kevin might be in trouble. Sharon's worst fears were confirmed when she heard Dick Cox tell her husband, "I was really surprised, Freddie, when your son called me. I thought something happened to you and Sharon. Anyway, he tells me that he couldn't get in touch with your accountant and he needed some money to pay for a C.O.D. package. He said he didn't know what was in it but assumed it was the new computer attachment you were waiting for."

"Computer attachment?!"

"You do have a computer, don't you?"

"Yes, but I never learned to use it. It's still in the box. Why the hell would I buy an attachment for something I never use? How much did you give him?"

"I don't know, four hundred and something dollars. . . . Look at the bill."

"Dick, there *is* no bill, and there is no computer attachment."

At this point Sharon insisted, "Fred, Kevin has run away. Call the police!"

After thanking his brother for his help, Fred dialed another number and explained to Sharon that he wanted to explore one more possibility before bringing in the cops. When Sharon heard her husband say, "Hello, Pa," she shouted, "Why are you calling your father?"

"Hello, Freddie. Why shouldn't you call your father? Why did she ask such a question? Freddie, is something wrong there?"

"Oh, no, Pa." Fred glared at Sharon as he spoke. "What she meant was, Why are you calling your parents *now?* She knows how upset you get when I call before the rates go down."

Fred then chatted about Japan, the exotic food they ate, and their teacher, Hana Yoshi. "Freddie," Leon interrupted, "you'll tell me later about the sushi and the Yoshi. Tell me first about my grandson. How is he?"

When Fred admitted that Kevin was not at home, Leon launched into one of his patented lectures on responsibility and respect.

"You come home after being away for a month and your son is not at home to greet you? What is that? Is that how you taught him, Freddie? Is that what we taught you? If your grandfather Simon would go away on business for a couple of days, we would make a Welcome Home, Papa sign and hang it on the door. What happened to responsibility? Kevin told me he was going to meet the plane and drive you home."

"When?" Fred screamed. "When did he tell you this?"

"Freddie, whatever hearing I still have, I would like to keep. Why are you screaming in my ear? What's going on there? Is Kevin in some kind of trouble?"

Fred admitted that he feared that Kevin had run away. Leon mulled over his son's words and offered a very considered "Aha!"

"Dad, why did you say, 'Aha'?"

"I didn't know I said, 'Aha.' I was thinking 'Aha' and wondering if that's the reason Kevin asked me about nice places to visit."

Sharon, who was now on an extension, asked sharply, "What else did he say?"

"Not too much. I asked Kevin if he made any more of those videos with those two cute twins. Freddie, I didn't know you had twin housekeepers."

"We don't anymore. They've left for Puerto Rico."

"Only one left. Maria, the one in the video with the black velvet dress, she didn't go."

"Dad, how do you know this?"

"How? She told me."

Both Sharon and Fred pounced. "You spoke with her?"

"Yes. I even said a few words in Spanish. She said she was happy to meet me because Kevin had told her so much about me."

Sharon was beside herself. After quickly saying her good-bye to Leon, she turned to Fred. "Kevin told her so much about your father? My God, he never said two words to either of those girls."

Fred found himself smiling. "Well, dear, it seems like your heterosexual son's gonads and his Toyota Celica have driven him to some cheap motel for a weekend of wild sex."

"For a weekend of wild sex," Sharon fumed, "you don't take

every piece of clothing in your closet. And whenever Kevin leaves the house for any length of time, he always leaves me a note."

"What kind of note would he leave? Mother, if you want me, I'll be at the Motel Sleaze for the weekend screwing my brains out?"

Elspeth stood outside the Cox's bedroom door and discreetly eavesdropped on their conversation. Her boss was never able to handle more than one ugly situation at a time, but she felt it imperative that she discuss with him the serious problems that were besetting Sky Productions. Elspeth knocked gently and in her most obsequious manner requested a moment with her boss.

When she was alone with Fred in his den, Elspeth poured a drink of brandy for him, which, she felt, he would need. On hearing that Jason Hansen's new agent was negotiating with M-G-M and Paramount for the rights to *The Wacaluma Log*, Fred hurled his crystal brandy snifter against his paneled wall of signed celebrity photographs and damned all the sonuvabitchin', bloodsucking agents in the world.

_16_

A MILE OR so before every freeway exit Kevin would ask
Maria if she was hungry or needed to use a rest room. These
polite exchanges constituted the bulk of their conversation, and
the farther they drove from his home in Bel Air, the more silent
they became.

In his parents' garage, just after loading their belongings into
his car, Kevin had taken a trembling Maria into his arms and
assured her that if they stayed at home, his parents would do
everything in their power to destroy the beautiful thing they
had built together. He insisted that he had a wonderful plan for
their future. When Maria asked what the wonderful plan was,
Kevin smiled, kissed her on the cheek, and asked that she trust
him. As they drove onto the San Diego Freeway, Maria asked
again, and again he smiled and asked her to trust him. Each
time he asked to be trusted, she became less and less sure that
Kevin had any plan at all.

Except for the thirty-minute pit stops in San Luis Obispo,
Santa Rosa, and now, in Ukiah, Kevin had been driving for
eleven straight hours. As he sat in a restaurant booth watching
Maria use a french fry to draw little circles in a dollop of
ketchup that lay beside her half-eaten hamburger, a wave of
love swept over Kevin, and he told her how much he adored
her. Maria smiled and offered him her potato stick, which he
wolfed out of her hand. Then, making bearlike growls, he
sucked the ketchup off her thumb and forefinger and kept
licking her palm until she laughed.

He considered, for a moment, that it might be the proper
time to tell her of their destination. It was ironic, he thought,

that his father, the man from whom he was running, was responsible for his finding the place where no one, including his father, would ever think of looking. Tonight he planned to stop at a Motel 6, and after making love, he would tell her about the book he had read in his father's den and describe only the positive things the author had to say about communal life in an Oregon forest.

On the drive to the motel, Kevin discussed with Maria the problems that might arise from their decision to act as man and wife. To avoid being traced and until they could get good phony ID cards and arrange to get married, they agreed to change their names. Because Kevin had dark hair and a somewhat swarthy complexion, he suggested they use Spanish aliases. She was touched when he chose to call himself Carlos in honor of her sister, and she laughed when he said that she should call herself Evita in honor of him.

"Just the *e-v-i* from the middle," Kevin explained.

They were trying to decide between Lopez and Gomez for their last name when Kevin spied the shamrock-shaped logo that warned of the approaching exit for Motel 6.

Despite all of his problems and anxieties, Kevin's heart started to pound when he realized that in just minutes from now he and Maria would be lying in a bathtub filled with hot, soapy water. In a millisecond, Kevin's penis went from limp repose to a fully extended throbber. If there were an Olympic event for this phenomenon, Kevin undoubtedly would hold a new world's record.

When Kevin parked his car in the crowded Motel 6 lot and made no move to get out, Maria became concerned that he might be having second thoughts. She asked, "Why are you sitting there looking funny?" Since he had been a little boy, Kevin had always been embarrassed by his frequent and insistent erections and had never discussed them openly with anyone until now. Hesitantly, he admitted that for the past few minutes he had been fantasizing about lying with her in the motel bathtub.

"I'm sitting here," he explained, "waiting for my dumb penis to disengorge."

Maria giggled, reached over, and found that he was not only being serious but was understating his problem. Kevin suggested, "If ever I'm to walk upright again, you will have to remove your hand and yourself." Maria, feeling very much loved and needed, laughed and ran off to find a ladies room.

A few minutes later, Kevin found himself at the registration desk being asked by a wizened old clerk if he and his wife had reservations. Kevin always had an ability to detail a lie and make it sound like the truth.

"Gee, I think so," he began. "My parents arranged this whole trip. It's our honeymoon, and my dad said that he would call in all the reservations. We're driving up to Salton, Oregon. So far, Dad hasn't let us down."

Maria marveled at his ability to tell such lies with a straight face. It did not occur to her to wonder whether Kevin might also be lying about his commitment to marry her and be a father to her child. The clerk picked up his reservation list and asked, "Last name?"

Not having agreed on their alias, Maria blurted out "Gomez" just as Kevin shouted "Lopez!" Without missing a beat, Kevin explained, "It's Lopez-Gomez. My wife is an actress. Evita Lopez is her professional name, but when we married, she decided to use both names, Lopez-Gomez. Lots of career women are doing that now."

Reservations or not, the clerk had no intention of denying a trysting place to two such beautiful young lovers. Kevin was to learn that the no-frills policy Motel 6 advertised so proudly meant that their rooms had no bathtubs. For now, Kevin's fantasy of lying with Maria in a hotel bathtub would go unfulfilled. However, he did learn that night that a tiny, prefabricated, plastic stall shower, used creatively, is a very exciting place to be with someone you love.

17

B Y NINE O'CLOCK the following morning, Elspeth reluctantly was handing Fred his third cup of strong black coffee and warning him how bilious he would become if he insisted on drinking it. Fred, in no mood to heed the advice of anyone on his inept staff, defiantly took a giant swallow of the boiling hot coffee and instantly sprayed it all over the memos and messages that were neatly laid out on his desk. He had not once, in all the years Elspeth had worked for him, ever swore directly at her, but this morning, every foul word that he could remember exploded from his mouth. Behaving as if Fred were six years old and had wet his pants, Elspeth very quietly and methodically went about sopping up puddles of coffee from the memos that would be needing his attention as soon as he finished swearing. When Fred finally wound down, he apologized profusely for his behavior.

Fred had been trying since early this morning to scrape off some of the heavy shit that had hit the fan while he was having what he thought was the vacation of his life. One pleasure-filled afternoon in Japan, after leaving Hana's hotel room, he actually thanked God for smiling down on him. Now he felt that God was no longer smiling at him but laughing hysterically.

Elspeth smoothed out the coffee-puckered memos as Fred dialed Lieutenant Huddley, hoping for some news of Kevin. There was none. Fred slammed the phone down, walked to his celebrity wall, and asked an autographed photo of Jack Nicholson, "How the hell can a modern police department with sophisticated computers not be able to locate a teenaged boy driving a registered black Toyota Celica with a Spanish maid next to him?"

Elspeth answered for Jack Nicholson by clucking sympathetically and then gingerly informing Fred of the other unpleasant reality of his life, a ten o'clock meeting at which he would hear from Clarence Burroughs, his four-hundred-dollar-an-hour legal brain, why he was losing the rights to *The Wacaluma Log*.

"As I see it, Fred," Clarence Burroughs explained carefully, "we have a very strong legal right to the property, and I have no doubt that we would win a court case handily—"

Fred knew a "however" was coming, and he sped it along by saying, "However . . ."

"However," Clarence obliged, "a court case could drag on, and even if the decision was in our favor, and there is no question in my mind that it would be, a lot of money would have been spent, and the actual production of the film would be delayed for at least a year or more. By that time, you may have lost some of your enthusiasm for the project, or *The Wacaluma Log* might no longer be as viable a subject for a major film as it is today. I've seen this scenario too many times."

Fred checked his watch as Clarence Burroughs smiled beatifically and left the office. Fred was livid. He thought, Not only have I lost the rights to the book, but I have to pay that oily shyster four hundred dollars for bringing me the shitty news.

18

WITH MARIA and Carla gone, Sharon decided not to replace them but to rely on part-time help. The days the maid did not come in were the days that Sharon would invite Hana to visit. These late-morning/early-afternoon meetings—sitting in the sun parlor, drinking mint tea, and snacking on some exotic goodies that Hana provided—were keeping Sharon sane. Unless Fred asked, Sharon would not volunteer any information about if or when Hana would be visiting their home, except, of course, for the nights when she would invite Hana to join them for dinner.

On their first meeting, Hana inquired about Kevin, and Sharon unburdened herself by tearfully describing her helpless feelings of frustration. She asked over and over again if Hana thought that Kevin had fled from her because she was a bad mother. Hana assured her that she was a sweet and loving person and could not imagine anyone wanting to flee from her. At these moments of insecurity, which actually started in Japan, Hana would take Sharon in her arms, gently stroke her head, and deliver butterfly kisses to her cheek and neck. Most times, Sharon preferred that Hana massage her, but every once in a while, Hana sensed that Sharon would enjoy acting the masseuse.

When Hana now felt Sharon's hand slide under her skirt and clutch at her buttocks, she knew that today was her day to be oiled and kneaded. Hana draped herself on the couch and allowed her friend's trembling hands to explore her body. Sharon excitedly removed all of Hana's subtly perfumed clothing, brought each piece to her face, and deeply breathed in its mysterious scent before tossing it aside. The length of the massage was as long or short as the one being massaged required it to be. When Hana massaged Sharon, they were understandably a good deal shorter, since Sharon's arousal started even before Hana laid a gentle hand to her. Hana, on the other hand, enjoyed having her nonerogenous zones caressed for as long as the caresser had the strength. But this would not be a day for a long, luxuriant massage. Sharon, when she started to rub oil on Hana's buttocks, had an uncontrollable urge to put her head on the firm, glistening mounds and massage those cheeks with her cheeks, an urge she was able to control for less than three interminably long seconds. So deeply was Sharon committed to being cheek to cheek with Hana Yoshi's heavenly bottom that she was unaware that the phone had rung four times before she reacted to it.

If Kevin were safely at school, Sharon would have never given up her place on Hana's body to answer it. She had been a mother much longer than she had been a lesbian, and her strong maternal instincts told her that this phone call concerned Kevin. With the tips of her oily fingers, Sharon lifted the phone off the cradle and tentatively said, "Hello?"

An equally tentative voice asked, "Señora Cox?"

Sharon's heart leaped. She grabbed the phone firmly with both her slippery hands and shouted, "Maria! Is that you, Maria? Do you know where Kevin is?"

"Uh, what time is it there?" asked a very small, confused voice.

"Maria, what the hell difference does it make—It's eleven-thirty!"

"Then, señora, Kevin is in school, and he will come home at two-thirty. I am sorry to disturb you, but can I speak with my sister? It is very important—and I am Carla, not Maria."

"Carla," Sharon ordered, "where are you calling from?"

"From Florida. Remember I tell you in my note about how I go to Puerto Rico with my husband?"

It was an anxiety-laced conversation that Sharon and Carla engaged in for a full ten minutes before they were both clear on what each other's problems were. Carla was very upset to discover that her sister was no longer living at the Coxes' and was equally disturbed to hear that Kevin was not there, either.

Sharon finally gave in to her worst fears and faced the probability that Maria and Kevin had run off together.

Sharon learned nothing about Kevin's whereabouts, but she did learn, from Carla's reluctance to talk about her sister's relationship with Kevin, that there indeed must have been one.

Carla was trying very hard to answer Sharon's questions as honestly as she could without betraying her sister's trust. She was panic-stricken that the señora might ask her if Maria was pregnant with Kevin's baby. Maria had spoken of the possibility of extradition or jail, or worse, if anyone found out that she was involved with the sixteen-year-old son of her employers. Carla was now torn between getting off the phone as soon as possible or staying on long enough to get the help from Mrs. Cox that she was seeking from her sister. The panic in Carla's voice was obvious, so Sharon asked, "Carla, are you in some kind of trouble?"

"My husband had to leave Puerto Rico," Carla rushed to explain, "and we're now in Florida without money. I call to ask my sister for a loan. Julio has a bad ear inside and needs a special doctor."

Sharon immediately volunteered to wire her some money, adding, "I'll give you my father-in-law's number in Miami Beach." Leon Cox was not Sharon's favorite person in the world, but she did appreciate how sincerely her father-in-law enjoyed giving people help and advice, whether they asked for it or not.

19

DRIVING HOME after a three-hour, head-clearing drive up to Santa Barbara and back, Fred Cox dwelled on how very little he had to look forward to these days: The prospects of his company's mounting a film this year were nonexistent; his only son obviously hated him enough to run away from home, and to further depress himself, he discovered that the very insignificant pangs of guilt he once felt about having an extramarital affair were now threatening to become significant pangs of fear. The time he had spent with Hana Yoshi were the only moments of unadulterated pleasure in his life, and he did not want to lose them.

As he pulled into his driveway and parked behind Hana Yoshi's black Bentley, he wondered what the hell it was doing there.

Fred turned off the motor, glanced at the dashboard, and noticed that it was four o'clock. Had he forgotten some arrangement Sharon had mentioned to him, or had something gone terribly wrong? He was sure Sharon had said nothing about inviting Hana to dinner tonight, and if she had, why had Hana chosen to drive herself instead of coming by taxi and asking him to drive her home? Wasn't that what they had agreed upon? Did this mean that Hana was trying to tell him something, or worse, was she telling Sharon something?

Before Fred could slip his key into the lock, the front door swung open, and an extremely agitated Sharon wanted to know where the hell he had been. Fred had not been anywhere that should have made him feel guilty, but all the residual guilt that had accumulated in the past several weeks made him behave as if he were caught red-handed committing a capital crime.

Sharon did not really want to know where he had been but to tell him about Carla's call.

Relieved to learn that his son was alive and heterosexually active, Fred smiled and collapsed into a chair.

"Dammit, Fred," Sharon screamed, "what are you smiling about? I just told you that your son ran off with one of our Spanish maids!"

"Calm down, Sharon. Kevin is young, he's flexing his muscles."

"He could have flexed them right here at home."

"And you would have loved that!"

"No, but I certainly would have allowed it."

"Allowed it? Did you expect him to ask your permission? 'Hey, Ma, is it okay if I take one of your maids into the pool house and boff her?' "

As soon as the words escaped his lips and he saw the disapproving look on Hana's face, he apologized profusely to Sharon, explaining that he was in an emotional state and was absolutely furious at Kevin's total disregard for the anguish he was causing her.

Fred complimented Sharon for suggesting that Carla call his father, adding, "Who knows . . . if she calls Dad, she may drop a clue."

Hana stood by quietly and witnessed a familial and mutually respectful interaction between her two clients that she had never before seen. Their concern for the safety and well-being of their son profoundly touched her. Small beads of perspiration suddenly broke out on her flawless face. It surprised and disquieted her. What, Hana thought, is this sudden flash of heat coursing through my body? She suddenly felt disoriented. She took a small sip of wine as she watched Fred dial his office. Fred seemed to be unaware that he was holding Sharon's hand, but Hana was very aware of it, and it unnerved her. Totally involved in arranging to meet and interview two private investigators, Fred and Sharon seemed to be oblivious to her presence. For the first time in her relationship with Fred and Sharon Cox, Hana felt redundant. She picked up her purse, quietly excused herself, then ran out of the house and down the driveway to her car. Why was she reacting so hysterically to a man holding his wife's hand at a time of stress? Why was she feeling this deep rage? Who was she raging at? Fred? Sharon? It was Sharon. It must be Sharon. Not one time, after Fred came home, did Sharon try to make eye contact with her. Heretofore they had always managed to reassure each other with a secret wink or a nod that acknowledged their special relationship.

Hana opened the car door and slid in behind the wheel. She sat silently, trying to sort out the conflicting emotions. She started to weep when she realized that the rage and anger she was feeling were for no one but herself. Against all the rules of her game and against her soundest judgment, she had fallen deeply and hopelessly in love with a married woman.

20

"B<small>IG</small>" B<small>ILLY</small> B<small>ALTHAZAR</small> and J. J. Quicky were the two highly recommended private detectives that Elspeth had scheduled for Fred and Sharon to interview. Their faith in "Big" Billy Balthazar was shaken when this human hippo arrived late for his appointment and explained why he had trouble finding their home.

"These dumb Bel Air roads are so damn confusing—I followed your directions, Mr. Cox, but you must have left something out. I drove round in circles and kept ending up on Sunset Boulevard."

J. J. Quicky, on the other hand, was tall and ruggedly handsome, arrived on time, and immediately guaranteed Fred and Sharon that he would have Kevin back home in no time. This was their man.

J. J. Quicky had an enviable reputation. At thirty-four, he was at least two cuts above most of his competitors. In his twelve-year career, he had successfully located dozens of missing cats and dogs, a pet puma, a cockatoo, a baby boa constrictor, and eleven lost children, five of whom had run away and two of whom were abducted by fathers who had lost their custody cases. He thought it wise not to include in his bio a teenaged girl who was molested and murdered before he found her. He was particularly proud, however, of locating the "Seven Hiding Husbands" who were trying to avoid paying child support and the two Alzheimer victims who had wandered from their homes.

For the next few hours, J. J. Quicky subjected Fred and Sharon Cox to more probing questions about their family and

friends than they cared to answer. They had trouble respond-
ing honestly to questions about how they related to Kevin and
to each other. J.J. also asked that they each write a list of all
their friends and relatives, people in their employ, and anyone
else with whom they recently had contact. Fred and Sharon
each considered including Hana Yoshi's name, but neither did.

Aware of his brother's fear of investigations, Fred had tried
to convince J. J. Quicky that Dr. Cox was not likely to have any
information on Kevin's whereabouts. Fred could not know that
J.J. always contacted first all the people who were least likely to
be of help. He had found that unlikely sources often provided
him with his best leads.

Following his spurious modus operandi, J.J. drove his mint-
condition 1979 white Mercury Cougar onto Dr. Dick Cox's
impressive, red-bricked, tree-lined driveway and toward an
even more impressive, three-story, matching red-brick house.

He parked his car in front of the mansion, ran his pocket
comb through his wavy, dirty-blond hair, and ambled toward
the house.

J.J. pressed the doorbell and smiled when he heard the first
few bars of the Beatles's "Michelle." Michelle, ma belle . . . Ma
belle? he thought, my door*bell*.

As he wondered whether the song was chosen for that reason, he was interrupted by a friendly woman's voice coming
through the high-fidelity speaker.

"Yeeesss?"

In his most professional manner, J.J. started to explain who
he was, but while he was still saying his name, the throaty
voice asked, "Wait right there."

Miriam, who had just stepped out of the shower, crossed to
the bay window and made a quick appraisal of the well-built
stranger who waited on her doorstep. What little she could see
of him definitely deserved a closer look. She wrapped her
towel tightly around her body, stepped into a pair of white
satin high-heeled mules, and started down the long marble
stairway to the foyer. She stopped briefly at one of the mansion's antique mirrored walls and carefully adjusted her towel
to display an improper amount of cleavage. Miriam opened the
door and apologized profusely for her state of "deshabille,"
explaining that she was all alone in the house.

Before asking J.J. to state his business, Miriam ushered him into the library and began her mating dance.

"Now," she said, wiggling her finger at him, "you look like a man who could use a drink. My guess is that you're an Absolut man. Right?"

Before J.J. could tell her that he was a beer man, Miriam had already poured him a healthy shot of vodka.

"Are you on the rocks or straight up?" she asked, posing seductively. "My guess is that you're straight up!"

After watching this woman with the half-exposed tits stirring the ice in his drink with her forefinger and then suggestively sucking it off while announcing, "A *perfect* drink for a *perfect* stranger," J.J. concluded that he had just been invited to a matinee.

It was not in J. J. Quicky's philosophy or personality to allow for business and pleasure to mix. Notwithstanding the pressure that he knew would be forthcoming from this desirable nymphomaniac, he intended to keep his integrity intact. He realized he was facing a formidable challenge to his professional ethics, and to show he meant business, he put his drink down on the malachite coffee table. "Mrs. Cox," he apologized, "I'm sorry for busting in on you like this, but if you would answer a few questions, I'd be most appreciative."

He was slightly taken aback when she asked, "Who are you?"

"Oh, I'm sorry," he fumbled. "My name is J. J. Quicky. I work for Fred Cox, and I was hoping you might be able to tell me something about Kevin."

"Oh, you mean L.B. I first met him when he was eleven, and you have never seen a sexier eleven-year-old, unless you were lucky to get a load of me at thirteen. Guess what L.B. stands for."

"Lover Boy?" he asked.

"Very good, detective. Now let's see how good I am," she said, adjusting her towel to expose more of her chalk white bosom. Your last name couldn't be your real name because you don't look like a quickie to me."

She took a sip of vodka. "Now, let's see," she cooed, "if I can guess what J.J. stands for. . . . Don't help me! That pretty blond hair of yours, that square jaw and those big shoulders

. . . Hmmm, I'd say there's a big Swede or a swordsman in you somewhere. Did I say swordsman? I meant Nordsman. Let's see now," she said, taking his large hands in hers and hefting them as if she were trying to guess their weight. She nodded knowingly, then handed J.J. back his hands.

"With your Norwegian-Swedish background and those large, strong hands," she explained, "it is obvious that the J.J. stands for *Jumbo Joint*. Right? If you say I'm wrong, you will have to prove it!"

J.J. knew of no way to respond without embarrassing himself.

"So, Mr. Jumbo," she added, "I expect that you will give me the courtesy to see for myself just how right I was."

Miriam, sensing that J.J. was about to bolt, asked, "What is it that you want to know about my husband's nephew, J.J.?"

Miriam was shocked to discover that he was missing. Dr. Cox, of course, knew about Kevin's disappearance but had neglected to tell her about it. It was understandable, considering that he had also learned from the district attorney's office that same morning that a class-action suit for malpractice was being brought against him by eight of his former patients. Miriam was less shocked by that disclosure than she was about Kevin's running off with a maid.

Miriam and Dick were a perfect symbiotic pair. Being married gave Dr. Cox an aura of stability that made it easier for him to function as a stud, and for Miriam, marriage afforded her the wherewithal to pursue in comfort her successful career in nymphomania. Unlike her husband, Miriam did not inflict on her subjects years of intolerable guilt and pain, but instead gave them treasured moments of unbridled ecstasy and years of erotic memories.

J.J. could not know that in two hours he was going to come away from this house with a very usable clue for tracking down Kevin and firsthand knowledge of how to make full use of the Kama Sutra without having his balls fall off.

As J.J. pulled out of the driveway, he was upset that for two hours he had lost all sense of himself, some of his integrity, and all of his propriety. With each orgasm, his body was racked by equal parts of ecstasy and guilt.

He giggled now as he remembered how hard he tried to persuade Miriam that he really did not have the energy for one last big one. If she had not persisted, he would have missed picking up his first big break in the case. Of the nine orgasms recorded that afternoon (three were his), Miriam's last one was of volcanic proportions, and J.J. actually felt the room vibrate when, at the height of her rapture, Miriam, pulling on the bedpost, screamed, "Lover Boy, Lover Boy, Lover Boy! . . . I should have a plate made for youuuuu, tooooo, J.J.J.Jaaaaaaay!"

While J.J. dressed himself, he had wondered if Mrs. Cox would think him boorish if he asked her to explain what she was yelling about during that last orgasm. It became unnecessary to ask when Mrs. Cox, lying nude and spent on the rumpled, pink, satin-sheeted bed, quietly announced, "Mr. Quicky, I am *not* going to give you a plate for your heroic performance in bringing me to a personal-best climax, not that you don't deserve one, but I'd hate to make my darling nephew jealous."

J.J. was putting his trousers on and stopped in mid-zip when he realized that the "plate" Mrs. Cox was referring to was a *license plate*! Sharon had told him that Kevin's license plate was BL 91 something and that it was a gift from his Aunt Miriam on his sixteenth birthday. He thought, By inverting the letters LB to BL, she gave me the same incorrect license-plate information that she must have given the police. No wonder they couldn't track the car.

Within hours after obtaining Kevin's actual license-plate number and delivering it to the police, J.J. received a call informing him that Kevin Cox's car had been spotted going south on the Pacific Coast Highway and was stopped by the Highway Patrol just outside of San Francisco. J.J. giggled for the second time that day when he received this news. Had he ever made the right choice today! By going to the least likely source, he had found the key to the case and had made a fine new friend.

Before calling his clients and telling them the good news, he inquired after the well-being of the two runaways. The officer informed him that they both seemed frightened and insisted that they had done nothing wrong. J.J. asked that they be made comfortable until the boy's parents could get there, which he assured him would be on the next plane. J.J. was not surprised to hear the officer report that the young man driving the car stated that his parents were dead.

"Officer, did he also deny that he was Kevin Cox?"

"Yes, sir, and he also claimed that the girl traveling with him was his cousin."

"Did they look like cousins to you?"

"That's hard to say."

J.J. shook his head at the apparent stupidity of the officer. He tried not to sound too snide when he asked, "Did you happen to notice that the girl was Latin and the boy Caucasian?"

The patrol officer recognized the snideness in J.J.'s voice and matched him with "Nooo, but I did notice that they were both African-Americans. Their names are Kareem and TaTa Tasha, and neither of them looked like a teenager."

After listening contritely to the patrolman explain why Kareem and TaTa Tasha were driving around in Kevin's car, J.J. felt that it was something he should report personally to his clients.

J.J. was greeted at the door of the Coxes' home by a shockingly beautiful Asian woman wearing a short white kimono. He winced mentally and thought, Another one? Oh, God, don't let her offer me a drink! He introduced himself and discovered that this apparition was Sharon Cox's masseuse and that he had interrupted her in mid-massage. When Sharon heard J.J.'s voice, she flew out of her room and down the stairs, wrapping her white kimono about her while asking for news of her son. Keeping his eyes off the exciting Japanese woman who was standing inside his peripheral vision, he managed to tell Sharon what he had learned from the Bay Area police.

"Kevin apparently sold his car to a young African-American man who was traveling with his cousin. The registration was signed over by Kevin, and everything seemed to be in order."

Before Sharon could react to this as if it were bad news, J.J. insisted that it was good news. "Knowing the area he's in should make things a lot easier for us. With a little luck, we could have him home in a few days."

J.J. apologized to Mrs. Cox for interrupting her massage and then asked permission to use the phone to inform Mr. Cox of this new development. As he dialed, his eyes followed the lissome masseuse as she and Mrs. Cox mounted the stairs to the bedroom. He marveled how, at thirty-four, after a morning of unconstrained sexuality, the sight of two leggy women in short kimonos going into a bedroom could provoke the activity in his groin that it did.

21

JUST HOURS before being flagged by the Highway Patrol, Kareem Tasha and his cousin TaTa had been seated in a booth at the Country Kitchen Restaurant in Ukiah, enjoying a platter of breaded shrimp and onion rings while eavesdropping on the intense conversation of the young couple that was seated in the booth behind them. Their interest peaked when they heard the handsome young man say, "Maria, we have to sell the car. By now the police have a description of it."

"Couldn't we paint it?"

"Yes, but we can't change the license. It's really better if we sell it. We could use that money for whatever we need, you know, bus fare, maybe plane fare."

"Why do we need plane fare?"

"Well," Kevin explained, "if Wacaluma doesn't accept us or we don't like it there, we'll have money to operate with."

Kareem Tasha understood everything but the word "Wacaluma." He understood that if a young man was worrying about being nailed by the police, he was looking for help and might dump his Toyota Celica for a price. Kareem tapped Kevin on the shoulder and apologized profusely for listening in, adding quickly, "Might be a good thing we did. Get to solve everybody's problems."

Kareem explained that he and his second cousin TaTa had just gotten married, sold a small diner they owned in Portland, and were moving to Los Angeles to put in with their Uncle Adam, who had just opened a successful new rib joint. "Adam's Ribs and Eve's Sauce? On South Robertson Boulevard. You hear of it?"

Kevin found himself nodding even though he had never heard of Adam's Ribs and Eve's Sauce.

"How 'bout this?" Kareem said, pointing out the window. "You see that pretty white pickup truck out there? It's in perfect condition and doesn't have a lot of miles on it. Here's the deal. You give me the Toyota, and I give you my pretty pickup and four thousand dollars."

Kareem picked up TaTa's purse and patted it. "I got it right here, in cash. Whaddya say?"

Kevin reasoned that if he had tried to sell the car to a legitimate dealer, his age might have provoked questions and a call to his father. Kevin took the four thousand dollars from Kareem and stuffed it into his pockets. They signed over their registrations, exchanged car keys, and promised each other to apply for new plates that day. Kareem was on his way to do just that when he was flagged by the Highway Patrol.

Meanwhile, Kevin was checking his map and finding the least traveled back roads to Salton, Oregon.

Kevin had a difficult time explaining to Maria that the commune they were hoping to join—and which he kept calling Wacaluma—was a place he had read about in a book called *The Wacaluma Log*, and although Wacaluma did not really exist, it was similar to an actual camp whose name he could not remember but thought it was something like 'L'Essence' or 'Luminous Essence.' Kevin attempted to describe to Maria all the positive aspects of living in a commune, but he could not avoid relating some of the negative observations that Jason Hansen had written about the camp's leader and the manner in which he operated. The more Kevin tried to rationalize why he thought it would be a good, safe place to live during her pregnancy, the more unsure Maria became about the excellence of Kevin's plan.

Maria, who had never really accepted the idea of living in a commune, became increasingly apprehensive each time Kevin stopped to ask for directions to the camp. They learned from a seemingly pleasant old man that the proper name for the camp they asked about was not Luminous Essence but Luminescence. They also learned that pleasant people suddenly turned unpleasant when asked for directions to Luminescence. One gray-haired woman responded by spitting on the hood of his car and kicking dirt at his tires. Because he had no alternate plan, Kevin tried to calm Maria by pointing out that older people had no tolerance for new and radical life-styles.

Trying to accentuate the positive, Kevin called Maria's attention to the great natural beauty that surrounded them: the giant fir trees, the sweet aroma of the damp earth, and the soothing sound of bird songs. In truth, Kevin was also trying to convince himself that he had not made a major mistake in dragging Maria to Oregon. He was nervous about starting a new life in a place that elicited such universally negative reactions.

To avoid arriving at Camp Luminescence at night, Kevin suggested that they stop somewhere soon, sleep out under the stars, and start out again early in the morning.

He found an idyllic clearing beside a babbling brook where they spread their blanket, ate the ham-and-cheese sandwiches they had squirreled away, and shared a can of Sprite—and, later, a single sleeping bag. They giggled at the implausibility of attempting to make love in a straitjacket but soon found that it was not only possible but quite exciting and, in a strange way, bonding. After climaxing, they found themselves locked in an embrace that neither seemed to want to break—two sweating nude bodies pressing against each other with all the passion and force that was in them. Kevin kept his lips on Maria's cheek as he told her how proud he was that she was carrying his baby and how he hoped it would be a girl and be as beautiful as her mother.

At daybreak, Kevin and Maria were rudely awakened by the sound of wailing sirens and speeding fire trucks that rumbled by within fifty yards of where they lay. They were young enough to be interested in watching firemen fight a fire, and so they hurried their toilette and drove off. After they negotiated a long and tortuous mountain road, the road straightened, and in the distance they could see billowing clouds of smoke rising above the horizon. By following the gray-and-white flumes, Kevin realized he was also following the directions to Luminescence that were given him the night before.

Luminescence was nestled in a ten-acre valley surrounded by rolling hills and a forest of giant spruce trees. When Kevin approached the top of the hill, he was stopped by a fire marshal and told that he could go no farther. Kevin parked his pickup truck at a vantage point overlooking the charred remains of the compound. As they scanned the dozens of smoking and gutted barracks, Maria started to cry and pleaded with Kevin to find out if anyone had died in the fire.

Kevin climbed to a clearing where a young state trooper was calming a group of concerned locals. Kevin learned from the sympathetic officer that a large number of the camp members were being treated for shock and smoke inhalation and a few for superficial cuts and bruises. The officer told the worried group, "Far as I know, there were no fatalities."

"That's not true, Officer! At least three people died. My best friend, Bonnie Sue Prueitt," a young, near-hysterical woman sobbed, "just came to camp last month, and tonight she went berserk after having her first sexual purification with Dr. Faust. She ran into the woods screaming that she had been improperly purified and the only way she would become clean again was to burn the evil out of herself. She opened the valve on the gasoline storage tank, lay down in a puddle of gas, and set herself afire." In her self-purification process, Bonnie Sue burned up the entire camp and the two fellow campers who had tried valiantly to dissuade her.

Kevin decided to tell Maria only about the superficially hurt, and when he saw Maria cross herself and thank God for His compassion, he was glad he had withheld the information about the immolation. He was gladder still when Maria revealed to him that she had prayed hard that they would not have to live in a commune. She had not wished specifically for a fire to befall Luminescence, but in a small way she felt responsible for the disaster.

22

As the last wisps of smoke curled up from the remains of Luminescence, Maria and Kevin sat in the cab of their pickup, watching the exhausted fire fighters roll up their hoses. The two lovers sat quietly, each waiting for the other to suggest their next move. Kevin spoke first and recommended that they find a place to get a proper breakfast, and Maria nodded in agreement. While they were driving toward Portland, she touched Kevin's arm and said, "Kevin, I feel bad that your mother and father must worry about you. I know you do not want to call them, but maybe you can call your grandfather and tell him to tell your parents that you are fine."

Kevin kissed Maria's cheek and told her what a good person she was.

Now that Plan A had self-destructed, Kevin realized that the cash he carried in his money belt might have to last them a long time. With economy in mind, he searched out Salton's nearest McDonald's. While they ate, Kevin considered just how much he would tell his grandfather about his situation with Maria. Kevin, eager to make the call, wolfed down his Egg McMuffin, grabbed his bag of french fries, excused himself, and went to a pay phone just outside the restaurant's front door. Kevin hesitated before dialing. He was not sure if he remembered his grandparents' number correctly. He started to dial it and hung up after dialing half the number. He thought, I'll call collect. If I dial the wrong number, the party won't accept the call. If I'm right, I'll save a couple of bucks.

Kevin had let the phone ring a dozen times and was about to hang up when he heard a very annoyed and out-of-breath voice bellow, "Hello!"

Kevin was sure he had dialed a wrong number when he heard the raspy, unfriendly voice shout, "Damn it, I can't talk now. Who's calling?"

Leon Cox was annoyed that he had to climb off his wife to answer the phone. For fifty-one years, Leon and Sarah Cox, had managed to remain sexually active, and Leon was not ashamed to admit it. He made his sexual prowess known to Dr. Eve Feinstein, a Kinsey-type researcher, who had been invited to their condominium to lecture on "Sex and the Senior Citizen." Much to Sarah's embarrassment, Leon raised his hand proudly and actually waved it when the pretty young doctor asked if there was anyone present who was over eighty and had sex once a week. When she asked, "More than once a week?" Leon kept his hand in the air. Sarah could not restrain herself from setting the record straight by gently pulling his arm down. But Leon was fortunate that Sarah enjoyed making love as much as he did.

When Leon discovered that it was Kevin calling, he happily said good-bye to his erection.

"Kevin, where are you calling from? Have you called your folks yet? How is what's-her-name? . . . Maria . . . Are you and this Maria still having your adventure?"

Kevin was thunderstruck. "Grandpa, how do you know about—?"

"Boychik"—the old man laughed—"the whole world knows! Your father knows, your mother knows, I'm sure the police and the FBI know, and they're all worried about you. Even Maria's twin sister called to ask if I heard from you."

Maria, who had been watching Kevin from inside the restaurant, knew from Kevin's body language that he had heard something important. She ran outside just in time to hear him say, "You spoke with Carla?"

"Carla? Who spoke with Carla? Your grandfather?"

Kevin nodded, and Maria ripped the phone out of his hand and asked Leon if he really had spoken with her twin sister.

"Sure, we're friends. Yesterday my wife invited her whole family over for a nice, roast chicken dinner—her husband, the baby. We had such a good time. That little cockaroach grabbed my nose and wouldn't let go."

Maria burst into tears and handed the phone back to Kevin.

Kevin asked his grandfather to hold for a moment while he calmed Maria. Leon was nonplussed. "Sarah!" he called. "Why should a girl burst into tears when I'm telling her what a nice meal you made for her sister?"

"You never heard of tears of joy? She's happy that she found out where her twin sister is. Here, Leon, put on your bathrobe. It's not nice talking to a young lady with your *shmekl* hanging out."

Leon took the robe and muttered, "She can't see me."

"Grandpa," Kevin asked, "do you have Carla's telephone number? Maria is anxious to get in touch with her."

Kevin dumped out the remaining fries and managed, with difficulty, to scribble Carla's telephone number on the greasy empty bag. Even more difficult was trying to make his grandfather understand why he could not tell him where he was.

"Kevin, darling, don't keep saying I won't understand. I have heard a lot of things in my eighty years, God bless me, and most of them I understood. Look, if you won't tell me why you can't tell me, I'll tell you. You fell in love with that cute little *shiksa*, and who can blame you, and she fell in love with you, these things happen. You want to be together, and you're afraid that your parents will send you to a reform school. Kevin, your father is not crazy about the situation, but he'll understand, and if he doesn't, I'll remind him that when he was your age, he fell in love with Kim, the daughter of our Chinese laundryman, and if you saw this Kim, you'd know why. After school, just to be with her, he volunteered to help deliver the old man's laundry. Your grandmother and I didn't think it was a good match, but we didn't butt in, and it all worked out fine, and it'll all work out fine for you, too, you'll see."

Kevin was tempted to ask, "If Kim was pregnant and Dad was going to marry her, would you have not butted in then?" He decided that his grandfather would have.

"Grandpa, would you call my folks and tell them that I'm fine. I'll call them as soon as I can."

"How soon is that, Kevin?"

"I can't tell you right now. Just tell them that I'm okay and tell Grandma I said hello."

Kevin hung up and turned to see Maria at the adjacent

phone, trembling with frustration as she tried to decipher the number that Kevin had scribbled on the oily paper bag. Kevin dialed the number, which he, too, was barely able to read but fortunately could remember. Maria jumped up and down as she listened to the ringing of the phone. The longer it rang, the less energized Maria's jumps were. Finally, Maria stood stock-still, hung up, and questioned Kevin's memory. He assured her that between what he could read and what he remembered, the number was correct. Maria begged him to call his grandfather to check. He called but found the number busy.

After Leon had hung up on Kevin, he immediately checked a number on a notepad and dialed. When he finished, Sarah said accusingly, "You only dialed seven numbers. You're not calling Freddie! Who are you calling?"

"I'm calling Carla, Mrs. Sherlock Holmes."

"Why are you calling Carla?"

"Because that poor girl is worrying about her sister. As soon as I tell her I spoke with Maria, I'm going to call Freddie."

"Leon, you're calling your son's maid because she is worrying about her sister? Don't you think that, maybe, your son worrying about his son is more important than his maid worrying about her sister? Now hang up and call Freddie!"

Ordinarily, when given a direct order by anyone, especially his wife, Leon would never comply, so when he hung up and dialed an eleven-digit number, Sarah was both shocked and delighted. In truth, he had reached Carla's number and had let it ring until he decided that she was not at home. Leon saw the exaltation in his wife's face and knew that she was thinking, My stubborn mule of a husband finally listened to me! He thought, Let her think; what does it hurt?

Leon had expected that Fred would behave like a concerned parent and ask after his son's well-being; instead, he behaved like an FBI agent who was dealing with an incompetent underling.

"Pa," he barked, "you mean you didn't ask him where he was calling from?"

"I didn't ask because I knew he wouldn't tell me."

"How do you know?"

"Because I asked and he didn't tell me, that's how I know."

Fred spent the next ten minutes describing the police procedure for tracing Kevin's next call. Leon listened patiently and promised he would cooperate, even though he had no intention of running to a neighbor's phone to help trace the call. Leon would not tell his son, but the romantic in him was rooting for Kevin to prevail. When he and Sarah first learned that Kevin and Maria had run away together, Leon joked, "For my money, that little *pisher* picked a better partner than either of my smart, sophisticated sons."

While Fred was on the phone explaining to his father how to go about tracing Kevin's future calls, Kevin had been trying to get through to his grandfather. His third try followed immediately after Fred had elicited a promise from his father that he would follow the phone-tracing procedure. Kevin apologized for calling back and explained that he needed Carla's phone number again. Leon repeated it, and while Kevin was thanking him, Leon, driven by loyalty to his son and his own grandfatherly guilt, interrupted. "Kevin, darling," he said apologetically, "I respect your privacy, and I appreciate what you're going through. Believe me, I know what it is to be in love, and I'm telling you that if you two are really in love, then letting your parents know where you are is not going to change anything. They can't tell you not to be in love; no one can tell anyone that, and if anyone tries to, tell him to go shit in the ocean!"

"Grandpa, if I let my parents know where I am, they'll try to separate us. I know them."

Kevin also knew that if he told them Maria was pregnant, they would immediately offer to pay for an abortion. Fueled by this fantasy, Kevin angrily told his grandfather that if he got into a discussion with his parents, it would just end with his telling them to go fuck themselves. Maria gasped, crossed herself, and silently asked God to forgive Kevin for breaking one of His commandments.

After apologizing for cursing and promising to call again soon, Kevin hung up and immediately dialed Carla's number. When he heard Carla say, "Hello," he shouted a "Hello" back and handed the phone to Maria. For the next five minutes,

Kevin watched Maria laugh and cry and speak thousands of Spanish words into the phone. He could hear, filtering through the receiver, Carla matching Maria sob for sob and giggle for giggle.

Aware that she was excluding Kevin, Maria turned to him and quickly capsulized the conversation. "Carla, Domenico, and Julio are well; they live with Domenico's aunt and uncle. Domenico works in his Uncle Pedro's fish market and drives a cab at night. Carla works at a McDonald's, and Domenico's aunt Teresa helps take care of Julio."

At this point, Maria took two short breaths and informed Kevin that they had been invited to live with Carla and Domenico in their Uncle Pedro's big white house on the water.

A sudden, sentimental desire to take Maria to Disney World made Kevin's decision an easy one. He smiled and shrugged. "Sounds good to me."

23

WITH THE help of a paid mole at the telephone company, J. J. Quicky had no trouble tracing Kevin's collect call to his grandfather. He learned, too, of Kevin's call to the home of a Pedro Sisneros in Miami Beach, Florida, and immediately phoned Fred Cox to ask if he knew of this Pedro Sisneros. Fred did not, and J.J. offered that Pedro Sisneros might be a relative of Carla and Maria's and that he would get on it immediately.

Fred Cox appreciated the speed and efficiency with which J.J. was handling the investigation and found himself complimenting J.J. for the fine job he was doing. As soon as the words were out of his mouth, Fred wondered why he had done that. Why, at a time like this, would he compliment anybody for anything? His life was a shambles, his only son was missing, his company was foundering, and since their return from Japan, his relationship with his wife was deteriorating at an alarming rate, as was his involvement with Hana.

Fred's conclusion—and he hated himself for coming to it— was that Hana had cooled toward him because she was having an affair. He had done the unthinkable. He had allowed himself to fall in love with someone who either could not or would not return his love. Fred suddenly realized why he had complimented J. J. Quicky. He needed a friend who might lend him more than just a sympathetic ear. Fred was consumed with Hana Yoshi and had to know if there was another man in her life. With this possibility gnawing at him, he asked J.J. if he could take on another assignment that was not related to finding Kevin.

When J.J. hesitated, Fred assured him that finding Kevin was

the first priority. J.J., who was more than a little adept at sizing
up his clients, asked, "Does this assignment involve surveillance?"

Fred admitted that it did, and after a few halting attempts to
explain, J.J. offered, "Mr. Cox, is it your wife's comings and
goings you're interested in?"

With not a little embarrassment, Fred explained that it was
not his wife he wanted observed but a young Japanese-
language instructor named Hana Yoshi. J.J. realized from
Fred's description that he was talking about the heavenly masseuse in the short white kimono whom he had lustfully
watched mounting the stairs to Mrs. Cox's bedroom. In his
most professional voice, J.J. promised, "I'll get on her immediately."

At seven the following morning, Fred and Sharon were
awakened to learn from J.J. that he had succeeded in tracking
down Kevin and Maria. J.J. explained to Fred that he had called
Pedro Sisneros's home and, by asking to speak with Carla or
Maria, learned from Aunt Teresa that Carla was at work and
that Maria and her boyfriend were not due to arrive till the
following day. "Oh," J.J. had asked, "are you sure? I thought
they were arriving today." Aunt Teresa obligingly set J.J.
straight by reading off the correct date, airline, and flight number that Carla had written down on a memo pad.

J.J. computed that if Fred hired a private jet, he could arrive
at Miami International Airport at least an hour before Kevin's
plane was due.

"I'm sure that when your son gets off the plane and walks
into the terminal to find that his loving and concerned parents
have flown all the way from Los Angeles to ask him to come
home, he'll be more than ready to listen to reason."

In spite of his faltering financial condition, Fred did not
hesitate to hire a private jet. He assumed that J.J. would accompany them, but J.J. warned, "The presence of a private investigator is just what you don't want. If I'm needed," he assured
Fred, "I'll be a phone call away. In the meantime, I can get
started on that surveillance matter we discussed . . . unless
you've had second thoughts about it."

"No, I have no second thoughts about it."

While putting on her robe, a trembling Sharon asked, "What don't you have second thoughts about?"

"Oh . . . uh, about spending the money for a private jet," he lied. "We're going to fly to Miami and collect your son."

While on the phone with the charter airline, Fred heard his wife call Hana Yoshi and cancel their dinner date. Even though he was excited about the prospect of finding his son, he regretted that he would miss the opportunity to drive Hana to her home for one last try at recapturing the excitement and passion they had enjoyed together. He hoped that while he and Sharon were in Florida, J.J. would find that there were no other men in Hana's life.

24

W̲ʜᴇɴ Cᴀᴘᴛᴀɪɴ Dᴏɴ Sʜᴀᴘᴘᴇ, the sole owner of Shappe Charter Airlines, heard the nature of the Coxes' trip and their need to be at the Miami International Airport at least a half hour before United Airlines flight 230, he assured them there would be no problem.

As Captain Shappe stowed the stairway into its cubby and secured the door lock, he glanced up to see Sharon cross her very attractive legs a foot from his face. Aware that they were being appraised, she pointed her toes and displayed them at their shapeliest. Sharon was quite proud of the firm body she and her trainer had worked so hard to create. She wondered, though, why, when she climbed into the plane, she had felt compelled to wiggle her behind in the young copilot's face. She could see that Fred was annoyed that the handsome co-pilot could look up her dress and made a note to ask Dr. Lowenthal if he thought it was sick to enjoy exhibiting her body to strangers.

Sharon did not have to wait for Dr. Lowenthal to get an opinion. Soon after the copilot had served an afternoon snack of delicate English tea sandwiches, Fred made his thoughts known by asking, "What the hell has gotten into you?" Sharon knew exactly what he was talking about but still asked, "What the hell are you talking about?"

"I'm talking about wiggling your ass in that copilot's face."

"I'm sitting on my ass, Fred, or didn't you notice?"

"I'm talking about when you got on the plane."

"Stoney calls my derriere a piece of physical art," she said, trying to lighten the moment. "I was just exhibiting my art."

Fred shook his head sadly and muttered something unintelligible.

An unexpected wave of compassion came over Sharon. It had not been a good time for either of them, but Sharon felt that Fred had been dealt a particularly bad hand. In a short span of time he had lost his movie project, his son, and his wife. At least I have Hana, she thought.

"Sharon," Fred said, getting back to the current problem, "I'm thinking about calling my folks and asking them to meet us at the airport." Before Sharon could object, Fred bulled forward. "Look, I know how you feel about them, but Kevin is crazy about his grandfather, and he's more likely to listen to reason if it came from him rather than from one of us."

Steeling herself to suffer her father-in-law's long-winded lectures and her mother-in-law's disapproving glances, Sharon accepted that Fred's idea was a good one.

While Sarah and Leon were dressing, Sarah, worrying about her husband's cataracts, casually suggested that instead of his driving to the airport, they hire a taxi. Sarah could have bitten her tongue for adding, "They know the way."

Leon picked up the gauntlet. "And I don't know the way?"

"You know the way," Sarah cajoled, "but they know it better."

"Sarah, how can one person know the way better than another person who also knows the way?"

"Leon, all I meant is that if a taxi driver is driving, there's less of a chance he'll get *farblondjet.*"

"When did I ever get lost driving to the airport?"

"The last time we went to pick up Kevin."

"I was not lost. I was just trying out a different route. We got there on time, didn't we?"

"Kevin was outside with his baggage, waiting for us. I don't call that on time."

"Sarah, at an airport somebody is always waiting for somebody. A boy can wait two minutes to see his grandparents."

"Twenty minutes."

"Two minutes, twenty minutes—at his age, what's the difference?"

As they approached the airport ten minutes late, Leon argued, "I would have made it on time if I didn't have to stop for you to use a rest room. Why in heaven's name didn't you use the toilet when I stopped for gas?"

"Because when you stopped for gas, I didn't have to go."

"But you knew that sooner or later you would have to. That's what's wrong with you, Sarah, you never think ahead!"

Leon did not speak again until he was in the terminal and was being greeted by his son and daughter-in-law.

"Fred," Leon asked while brushing his lips to his daughter-in-law's cheek, "shouldn't we go to the gate so we can meet him when he comes off the plane?"

Fred explained that there was no rush; the plane had been delayed in Chicago and would be twenty minutes late.

The four of them walked down the long corridor toward the satellite. Sharon was annoyed that she had to slow down her regular speed-walking pace to accommodate her in-laws, while Leon and Sarah were proud that they could walk at twice their normal speed without fainting. They arrived at the gate ten minutes before the plane landed, and Fred and Sharon strategically positioned themselves so there would be no chance they could miss Kevin and Maria when they deplaned.

Fred, assuming that Kevin flew economy, cautioned everyone not to expect him to be among the first coming off. The Cox family stood by impatiently and watched a parade of happy, tired people trudging up the ramp and falling into the arms of their waiting relatives or friends.

Carla had not planned to meet her sister's plane, but while shoveling a large order of fries into a cardboard sleeve, she realized that her place, at that moment, was not behind the counter at McDonald's but at the airport.

When Carla arrived at the gate, she was shocked to see her former employers and Kevin's grandparents standing at the exit ramp. Intuitively, she felt that it would be unwise to be seen and quickly hid herself behind a pillar. The Coxes disappointedly watched 140 assorted passengers exit. None was Kevin or Maria. Fred asked a gate attendant if all the passengers had disembarked and was heartened to learn that there were seven still on board—it had been a turbulent flight, and all of them were airsick for the entire trip. Because Kevin had never, in his whole life, been sea-, car-, air-, or even roller-coaster sick, Fred assumed that Maria was one of the nauseated ones and Kevin had remained aboard to tend her. Fred approached the gate attendant again, and while he was asking for permission to help his son, a sorry-looking Chinese family staggered down the ramp. Fred quickly counted the family and realized that they were the sickened seven the attendant had mentioned.

Demanding to know where his son was, Fred was told by an annoyingly calm flight attendant that his son had most likely walked right by him. "It couldn't happen!" Fred exploded.

"It happens all the time," she assured him. "What with the crush and the excitement, you must have missed him."

"Missed him? How the hell could we miss him? There are four of us here, eight eyes, all looking for one person!"

"Ten eyes," Carla whispered to herself from behind the pillar.

The flight attendant remained calm and asked, "Was your son expecting to be met?"

"What difference does that make?" Fred fumed. "The point is that my son didn't come off your damned plane. Now where the hell is he?"

"Mr. Cox," the unctuous attendant explained, "most deplaning passengers don't expect to be met at the gate and usually proceed to the baggage-claim area, where, I daresay, you'll find your son, unless he wasn't on this flight."

The flight attendant scanned the passenger list and assured Fred that his son's name was not on it.

Fred was miffed. He concluded that either Aunt Teresa's flight information was incorrect or Kevin and Maria had missed the plane.

Sarah suggested that they all drive back to the condo, where she had "nice cold borscht and fresh tuna salad" waiting for them.

Carla had heard most of what had transpired and was as confused as the Coxes. Carla knew that Kevin and Maria were traveling under assumed names, but that wouldn't explain how they could walk off the plane without being seen. People with assumed names don't become invisible. Carla would wait. Being a twin, she intuited that Maria was somewhere nearby.

One of the two maintenance men who were servicing the cabin of flight 230 was aptly nicknamed Lucky because of his ability to find something of value when he went about cleaning up. In the pocket of the first seat he vacuumed Lucky found some change and sang out, "Luis! Sixty-eight cents! How you doin'?"

"A girl and a boy!" Luis shouted back.

Lucky laughed. "That beats me."

Earlier, when flight 230 was turning to position itself for arrival at the gate, Kevin and Maria were looking out of the small window at Maria's seat to see if, by chance, Carla might be there. For the short moment that the jet was parallel to the satellite, Kevin caught sight of a group of people he thought looked like his family. When he recognized someone wearing his grandfather's favorite Samoan sport shirt, he knew he was trapped.

As calmly as he could, he picked up all of their hand luggage and beckoned for Maria to follow him to the rear of the plane. When he was sure they were not being observed, he quickly opened the door to one of the toilets and bid a reluctant and frightened Maria to join him. Kevin realized too late that the sanctuary he had chosen had been patronized by the nauseated Chinese family. It was fifteen minutes later that Luis mercifully opened the door and found Kevin leaning on the sink and Maria seated on the toilet. Both were sweating profusely and on the verge of emulating the Chinese family. Kevin explained to the startled maintenance man, "My wife is not feeling well and had to throw up." When Maria realized that the man did not understand English and was a South American compatriot, she decided that he would be simpatico. She guessed right. Luis dispatched Lucky to check the waiting room and see if the Gang of Four that Maria had described were still there. Lucky returned quickly and reported to Maria, "The only one there is a beautiful McDonald's girl who has the same face as you."

A moment later, in the aisle of the jumbo jet, Kevin, Lucky, and Luis were privileged to witness one of the happiest and most tearful reunions ever. As he watched Maria and Carla kiss and hug and wipe tears from one another's cheeks, Kevin was overcome by an uncontrollable urge to become a part of the joyous reunion. Kevin jumped up and embraced the embracing sisters, hugging them as hard as he could and releasing them only after one of them burped and the other passed wind. In a wink, the happy, tearful reunion exploded into one of happy, hysterical laughter. Lucky and Luis joined in when they realized whence the earthy sounds emanated.

When the insane laughter subsided and Kevin considered it safe, they went down to the baggage-claim area, where they learned that their bags were let off at Chicago. Because he was not certain that staying at Pedro Sisneros's house would be safe, Kevin suggested that their baggage be sent to Carla, care of McDonald's.

25

WHILE NO ONE seemed to be doing anything about finding Kevin, Sharon felt that lunching with her in-laws on their outdoor terrace was the last place she wanted to be.

She toyed with food that was not on her diet and behaved as politely as she could while Fred was on the phone reporting to J. J. Quicky how frustrated and disappointed he was at not finding Kevin. Fred described how, when he had called the Sisneroses' house and asked to speak with Maria, he was told that Maria had changed her plans and would not be coming to Florida. "I don't buy it," J.J. insisted. "I know Maria and Kevin are in Florida, and I'll find them. It's just a matter of time."

Leon was on his way to the bathroom when he overheard Fred ask, "So, J.J., did you start on that other matter?" Leon guessed that the other matter was not about Kevin and also not something he was supposed to overhear.

"What do you mean, interesting, J.J.? Is she seeing another guy, or isn't she?"

Before Leon had a chance to make his presence known, Fred ended the mysterious conversation and hung up. Fred was startled to hear his father's voice shout, "Why did you hang up so fast? I wanted to get a professional opinion from your detective."

"About what?"

"About if he thinks it's a good idea if somebody watched Carla's house. Freddie, what was that other matter you were talking about? Who do you think may be seeing another guy?"

Fred was so taken aback by his father's direct questions that he could only start to sputter a cover-up.

"Son," Leon pressed on, "is Sharon the one who you think is seeing another guy? Talk to me, Freddie. I'm your father. I guess you know that Sharon isn't my favorite person in the whole world, but I can't imagine that she would do something like that. Your sister-in-law Miriam is another story. Only a couple of weeks ago a Mrs. Pechter told me about . . . "

Leon's babbling gave Fred the time he needed to come up with a plausible story.

"It's Maria," Fred confided. "I'm having Maria investigated! I thought that if we can show Kevin that she's been fooling around with another guy, he may come to his senses."

"Freddie, you're wasting your money. That girl and her sister are two of the nicest young women. You want to know something? I don't think you were talking about Maria with your detective. You whispered so soft, I could hardly hear. Why would you whisper about Maria? So tell me, what's going on with you and Sharon?"

Fred Cox had never really availed himself of his father's counsel and felt a very strong need to talk to him. He looked into his father's eyes and saw a sadness and wisdom that moved him to make his father his confidant. Leon listened as his son passionately described the debilitating obsession he had developed for his Japanese-language teacher. Leon had always found Asian women attractive and could understand his son's feelings.

He would not have been at all upset if Freddie divorced Sharon and took unto himself an exciting Oriental beauty. Eager to know more about this possibility, Leon asked, "If you find out this girl has another boyfriend, what'll you do?"

"I guess I won't do anything. I'll just try to forget Hana, although that may be a bit difficult."

"Hannah? That's a Jewish name. Is she half Jewish?"

"Sorry, Dad."

"Don't be sorry. A hundred percent Japanese is fine by me."

"What I was about to say is that it's going to be difficult for me because Hana and Sharon have become good friends. Hana still gives Sharon Japanese lessons."

Leon shook his head and clucked. "Freddie, my boy, unless

this Hannah Kasha can fall in love with you like you did with
her, you better forget her!"

Sharon and Sarah came into the living room to find out what
J.J. had to offer, and Fred told them that J.J. was confident that
Kevin was in Florida and he'd have more to report later that
night. Both Sharon and Sarah recognized by their husbands'
demeanor that they were withholding something. "Fred,"
Sharon asked, "what is it you're not telling us?"

Fred looked to his father for help and said, "If there was
something to tell, we'd tell."

Leon shrugged. "I was going to suggest to Freddie that we
drive to where Carla lives and watch the house to see if maybe
Kevin and his girlfriend show up there."

Sharon thought it a good idea but added, "I'd appreciate it,
Leon, if you didn't refer to Maria as Kevin's girlfriend."

"But that's what she is," Leon stated, "whether you appreciate it or not."

"Well, I don't," Sharon shot back. "Do you?"

"I like it," Leon countered. "I have no problems with race."

Hana Yoshi's straight black hair and her beautiful almond-
shaped eyes flashed through Sharon's mind, and neither she
nor her father-in-law expected the shrillness or the volume of
her reply. "Dammit, neither do I!"

Sharon, defending her deep feelings for Hana, could not
restrain herself from adding, "For your information, one of my
dearest friends is Asian."

Fred wondered if Sharon would think as highly of her dear
Asian friend if she knew that she was not only screwing her
husband but at least one other guy.

On hearing his daughter-in-law say that one of her best
friends is an Asian, Leon readied himself to deliver one of his
studied sermons on racial bigotry. "One of my dearest friends
is an Asian?" Leon began. "Do you realize what you were
saying, Sharon? Are you aware that you were repeating an
apologia that anti-Semites have used for years? 'Some of my
best friends are Jews.' Jew haters have always used that phrase
to convince themselves that they were not anti-Semitic. Every
time I hear anyone say, 'My best friend is a this or a that,' I am
angered, but when I hear it coming from a Jew, I am ashamed
. . . deeply ashamed."

Leon was gearing up to continue when Sarah cut in. "Leon, Sharon flew here to find her son and not to find how ashamed you are of how some Jews talk. Now, everyone, why don't we all relax, eat a little something, and then you could maybe drive over to Carla's house and see what's what."

_26_

$\mathbf{B}$ECAUSE KEVIN had a strong presentiment that his father might show up at the Sisneroses' house, he felt that it would be safer if he and Maria stayed at a motel. As he said the word *motel*, he looked at Maria, whose embarrassed smile informed him that she, too, was thinking of their uninhibited night of lovemaking at Motel 6.

Three blocks from McDonald's, where they had lunched with Carla, they found The Rest Haven Motel, a two-story, pink-stuccoed motel whose management was never concerned about renting a room to a luggageless couple. An unshaved desk clerk with a who-gives-a-shit attitude pretended to listen to Kevin explaining that the airline had lost their bags. Mr. and Mrs. Lopez-Gomez held hands as they walked down a dimly lit corridor on a soiled and threadbare carpet to room 201. Kevin smiled lasciviously when he discovered in the bathroom an old-fashioned, oversize bathtub. Maria went directly to the bathtub and proceeded to fill it with steaming hot water as Kevin started to undress, first himself and then his acquiescent partner. When the tub was less than half full, Maria slipped into it and stretched her arms out toward Kevin, beckoning him to join her. Straddling the porcelain tub and using the sides as if they were parallel bars, Kevin slowly and carefully lowered himself onto a happy young woman. For the better part of an hour, they laughed and lathered away the smoky smells of Luminescence and the rancid odors that they had absorbed from the airplane's toilet.

The anxiety-laden events of the past days and the underwater orgasms they helped each other achieve with masturbatory foreplay left both Kevin and Maria with neither the strength nor the will to drag themselves out of the bathtub and into bed. With the warm, soapy water lapping at their half-submerged chins, the debilitated young lovers, locked in a gentle embrace, fell soundly asleep.

Kevin woke only twice, once, when his cooling body told him that the bath needed an infusion of hot water, and a second time, when a phone rang. It was a very agitated Carla calling to inform him that his parents had just left her Uncle Pedro's. "Kevin, I am very, very worried."

When Maria realized that Kevin was speaking with Carla, she sprang from the tub and joined him. Sharing the earpiece, they listened attentively as Carla told her story:

"When I come home from work, I see a big black car in front of Uncle Pedro's house. I see it is Mr. and Mrs. Cox, and I am frightened, but I make believe that I am happy to see them. I tell them that I am sorry Maria did not come to visit me. To make them think I tell the truth, I invite them to come into the house for tea. I think they will say no, but they say yes. My uncle Pedro also says that he is sorry that you and Maria do not come to Florida to visit. I think they believe that you are not here, but then the most terrible thing happened. The doorbell rings. . . . Oh, I feel so bad. It is my fault."

"That the doorbell rang?" Kevin asked.

"No, that I offer Mrs. Cox more tea. They would have left two minutes sooner and not see my friend Amalia bring the luggage. She say she did not want to leave it at McDonald's. Mrs. Cox scream when she see that one of the bags is Kevin's, and Mr. Cox call us damn liars."

Carla then described how Mr. Cox yelled at them that if they did not tell him where Kevin was, he would turn the case over to the authorities.

Fred could not know the terror he struck in Carla's heart when he went on to mention Immigration. Domenico, who was an illegal alien, would surely be deported to a country that was eager to put him back in jail, or worse.

Carla was begging now that Kevin do something before Mr. Cox called Immigration.

Kevin assured Carla that he would contact his father before morning, and he guaranteed that his father would not call the Immigration and Naturalization Service. Kevin kept Maria tightly wrapped in his arms while he considered what he must do. He knew that a face-to-face confrontation with his parents was inevitable, but where? Certainly not in the Rest Haven Motel. He felt that if they met at his grandparents' apartment and his grandparents heard how much he and Maria loved each other, they might become his allies.

As he held Maria's naked body against his and knew that in her belly his child was growing, the word *asunder* kept rolling around in his head. He had never used the word or heard it used except by kindly ministers in old movies on TV. I Will Let No Man Put Maria and Me Asunder became his rallying cry. He weighed telling his folks that Maria was carrying his baby. Would they think differently about putting asunder an expectant father and mother, or would they become violent? He was not looking forward to finding out.

As he watched Maria putting on her brassiere, he became frightened that he might lose her. He considered for a moment asking Maria to accompany him to his grandparents', but he knew that he would not want her to hear the hurtful things his parents were bound to say. The place for Maria was definitely not at his side but visiting with her sister at the Sisneroses'. Maria started to cry. She felt that she and Kevin were being driven apart by forces too powerful for them to combat, and Kevin's assurances that he would not let anyone come between them did not seem to calm her until he took her in his arms and declared, in a stentorian voice, "What God hath joined together, let no man put asunder."

Maria had no idea what *asunder* meant, but she realized that Kevin had, for the first time since they had been together, invoked the Lord's name. Now, with His help, she felt they had a chance.

On the stairs leading up to the Sisneroses' house, Kevin stood one step below Maria to give her the six-inch advantage she needed to look right into his eyes. He kissed her gently and whispered into her ear, "What God hath joined together . . ."

This time the effect on Maria was even more powerful, for during the taxi ride from the motel, Kevin had told her what *asunder* meant.

At least three times on the ride to his grandparents' Kevin had considered ordering the cabdriver to take him back to Maria.

He wondered if Carla had correctly interpreted his father's attitude when he threatened to call in Immigration. It could have been an idle threat, in which case he was being foolish to rush to meet with the enemy. He could see nothing good coming out of the meeting. On the other hand, if his father did carry out his threat and Carla's husband ended up deported or dead, he would never be able to face Maria or himself. Since he had fallen in love, he found himself becoming increasingly more conscientious. He felt downright heroic as he rode to do battle against the forces of parental evil.

As the taxi turned into the street where his grandparents' condominium was located, his newfound strength of character suddenly deserted him at the sight of his father steering his shiny rented Cadillac into the condo's underground garage. His first instinct was to run from a confrontation that could only add to everybody's pain. But his second instinct, which he acted upon quickly, was to pay the driver and beat his folks to his grandparents' apartment. He was about to enter a lion's den, and somehow he felt that welcoming the lions into the den might help defuse some of their rage. Since he had no car to park, he would easily win the race to the apartment.

A group of elderly condo dwellers who were making their way to the recreation hall stopped to watch Kevin running, at breakneck speed, from the street, up the long front walk, through the lobby, and toward the elevator. As Kevin sped by them, an eighty-year-old man ordered, "Sam, next time I pass out, that's the boy I want to run for the doctor."

Kevin could not believe his luck. The elevator was waiting for him, but as he went to press the button for the eleventh floor, the arrow signaled that the elevator was going in the same direction as his heart: down!

While Kevin had been running up the walk to the condo, his father had slipped his car into a stall directly in front of the elevators and had managed to push the DOWN button a tenth of a second before Kevin pushed the eleventh-floor button. Kevin was trapped. The Lion's Den was now the Lion's Elevator. He would not have his kindly and loving grandpa and grandma at his side when he faced his bounty-hunter parents. Kevin considered climbing through the ceiling trapdoor and hiding himself on top of the elevator, but before he could implement this cowardly plan, the elevator stopped at the garage level, and the doors opened slowly to reveal his parents as he had never seen them, openmouthed, bewildered, and dumbstruck, his mother without her full glamour makeup and his father without his hair neatly blow-dried. Fred, who knew just exactly what he was going to say to his son when he met up with him, now could not remember what it was. Sharon stood transfixed. She saw a mature young man who looked nothing like the teenaged boy who drank milk from a carton. All three remained riveted to their spots until the elevator doors started to close. For Sharon, it was a cue to burst into tears and run to Kevin. Fred made no move to follow her in. He knew that the emotional reunion in a moving elevator between Sharon and her baby boy was something he did not care to witness.

For the entire ride, Sharon held Kevin in a tight embrace and wept silently, which surprised him, as he had no idea that his mother liked him that much. When the elevator reached the eleventh floor, Kevin, hoping to be released from his mother's steely grasp, kept his finger on the DOOR OPEN button and suggested that she ride down and get his father while he went to tell his grandparents that they were here.

"Why don't we both ride down together, Kevin?" Sharon said sweetly, still holding his arm in a vicelike grip. "Daddy didn't get a chance to say hello to you."

He knew it was not the case, but the elevator seemed to be descending much faster than it had ascended.

A few short months ago, Fred controlled everything in his life, and now, as he stood waiting to confront his son, he could control nothing, not even his breathing, which was becoming labored. The soft whooshing sound of the descending elevator suddenly became unbearably loud. His face flushed, and his heart started to pound as he felt the sound resonate through his body. Then, abruptly and blessedly, the whooshing stopped.

As the elevator doors opened, Sharon, knowing her husband's volatility, expected that his reaction to seeing his son would be fairly emotional. What she did not expect was to see him lying on the cement floor of the garage, writhing in pain and gasping for air. Sharon had seen him this way once before, during a game of charades, when he attempted to act out the whole title *Death of a Salesman*. This time, the accumulation of spittle around Fred's mouth was clear evidence that he was in the middle of a real-life charade. Sharon, momentarily stunned, took one reflexive step backward and then ran to him, shouting for Kevin to call for an ambulance. On the ride up to his grandparents' apartment, the elevator stopped at the first floor, where Kevin kept two elderly women from boarding, explaining that his father was in the garage dying and he had to get to a phone.

The older of the two women, an eighty-year-old retired practical nurse, shouted, "Call 911 and don't worry, they're excellent. We use them all the time."

Even though Sarah expected her grandson, her reaction to seeing him was far out of her normal range.

"Oh, my God in heaven!" she screamed. "Leon! Leon, he's here! Kevin is here!"

While Kevin was trying to tell her why she should temper her joy, Leon shouted, "Hello, Mr. Casanova!"

Kevin managed to cut through the high-decibel reunion with a piercing, "WE NEED AN AMBULANCE FOR DAD!"

Thirty-five minutes later, thanks to a young, expert crew of paramedics, Fred Cox was lying in a bed at the I.C.U. of Memorial Hospital and being examined by a silent, young black resident whose name tag informed Fred that he was Dr. Theo Goldberg. The only time Dr. Goldberg spoke was to answer Fred's question. "No, Mr. Cox," he explained, "we're not related. Whoopi *took* the name Goldberg. I was given mine by my father, Dr. Hyman Goldberg, chief of cardiology."

The next time Dr. Goldberg spoke was to assure Fred that the urinary catheter was necessary and temporary.

Later, in the waiting room, Dr. Goldberg informed the family that Fred had had a not-so-mild heart attack and was being moved to intensive care. Everyone present, except for Dr. Goldberg, felt personally responsible for bringing on this disaster. Sharon knew that God was punishing her for falling in love with a woman; Kevin knew that his running away with a Spanish maid stressed his father's heart to the breaking point; Sarah knew that it was all the hot dogs she had allowed Fred to eat as a child, and Leon felt responsible for having Rifke for a mother. It was from her side of the family that Fred inherited his "rotten genes." Grandma Rifke birthed six sons and daughters, and only Leon and his sister Ida escaped dying of heart attacks before reaching fifty.

In two days, with the help of the good medicine practiced by Drs. Hyman and Theo Goldberg, Fred's condition went from serious to guarded to stable, and all of the Coxes were permitted a short visit with the patient. No one member of the family had ever seen another member of the family dehumanized, as Fred was. Only his father, Leon, was able to behave as if it were normal for a person to have oxygen tubes in his nostrils, an IV stuck in his arm, a bunch of metal EKG discs pasted to his chest, and a catheter reamed up his penis. Leon, with the lightest, most conversational tone he could muster, spoke first. "So, boychik, how do you feel?"

Fred nodded his head toward the network of tubes that was tethering him to his bed and answered weakly, "Like I'm ready to swim fifty laps. Hello, Kevin. We didn't get a chance to say hello. How are you?"

Relieved to hear his father's voice devoid of sarcasm, Kevin answered ingenuously, "I'm fine, Dad."

His father's next question had the tone Kevin had come to know and hate. "And your little friend, Maria, is she fine, too? Or did she come to her senses."

"Perhaps this isn't quite the appropriate time to discuss that subject," Sharon suggested.

Fred thought it an excellent time. "Isn't that why you came to Grandpa's, to tell me that you're not going to see the girl anymore? Why else would you come there?"

Sarah was distressed to hear her son speak. His usually deep, resonant voice was now thin and raspy, and she knew that the energy he was expending would not be helping his recovery.

"Fred, darling," she said brightly, changing the subject, "we spoke with that nice Dr. Goldberg, and he says that you shouldn't talk too much. Now, Freddie," Sarah said, touching her son's hand, "Papa and Kevin and I will say good night to you. Sharon, we'll wait for you in the hall."

All said quick, efficient good-nights and were gone.

Sharon wished that she, too, could have left. Never before in all the years she had known Fred had she seen him look so helpless and pitiable. It made her feel all the more guilty for having, that day, written a long and emotional letter to Hana in which she explained how she could no longer go on as she had and was planning, that night, to tell Fred everything. Sharon looked up at the beeping EKG screen and had a horrible fantasy of watching the machine record Fred's fatal heart attack after hearing that she and Hana had fallen in love. She was startled to hear Fred's hoarse voice ask, "You know who I'm thinkin' about?"

She was tempted to say, "Hana," but asked, "No, who?"

"Stoney."

"Our trainer? Why are you thinking of him?"

"When he hears," Fred rasped, "that his prize pupil is lying in a fuckin' hospital bed with fuckin' tubes stuck in him, he's going to shit."

Fred's face suddenly contorted, and he started to weep uncontrollably. Sharon was able to hold back all but one tear as she watched Fred regain control of himself. She tried to calm him by suggesting, "You may not have had a heart attack."

"Oh? What did I have?"

"Well, Fred—she smiled—do you remember once, just after we were married, you woke up in the middle of the night and thought you were having a heart attack and I got Dr. Ambler out of bed?"

Sharon, sensing that he wanted to deliver the punch line, gave him the opportunity.

". . . and"—he wheezed—"just as Ambler started to examine me, I farted!"

"Right! It was gas, Fred! Maybe this is—"

"No, no, this is not gas. I just farted, and I feel worse."

Fred's face started to contort again, and she went to the only positive thing in this life. "Kevin seems to be in fairly good shape, Fred—mentally, I mean. I really think that he's ready to listen to reason."

Fred, through a series of short, staccato coughs, observed, "Yeah . . . and it only . . . took my having . . . a heart attack."

As Fred's cough grew in intensity, Sharon's eyes went to the monitoring screen, and she watched, in panic, as the EKG line was making seismographic-style patterns. Before Sharon could ring for a nurse, one appeared and mercifully informed

Sharon, "Time for Mr. Cox to have his little sleeping pill and go nighty-night."

Sharon planted a light kiss on Fred's forehead, and by faking a smile and assuring him that he was going to be fine, she managed to hide how unpleasant it was for her to put her lips to his clammy brow.

27

O N THE CAB RIDE back to the condo Kevin sat in the back-seat, sandwiched between his mother and grandmother, while Leon rode up front with the driver and lectured him on the sorry state of medical research in our country.

"Those bastards," Leon began, "they have all the money they need to build what *they* want—bombers, space shuttles, nuclear arsenals—but for what people want—roads, bridges, research for AIDS, for cancer and genetic heart disease—they have no money! Why? Because there's bigger profits in killing people than in curing them!"

When the taxi arrived at the condo, Kevin, anxious to tell Maria about his father, helped his grandmother out of the cab and, while Leon was paying the fare, announced loudly to the driver that he needed to be driven somewhere.

All of the Coxes were stunned that Kevin, moments after seeing his father lying in an intensive care room, would consider leaving. Leon spoke for all when he summarily dismissed the driver, telling him that his grandson had made a mistake.

Kevin knew better than to argue with his grandfather, who, at that moment, sounded and acted very much as his father would have.

In the elevator, Sharon felt Kevin's impatience and decided that this was the time, if not the place, to start talking about his relationship with Maria. The manner in which she said his name made Kevin know that a challenge was in the offing.

"Kevin," Sharon asked politely, "you were going to visit Maria, weren't you?"

"No, Mother," he said, being equally polite. "I was not going to *visit* Maria. I was going to *be* with her."

"Kevin, do you think it's appropriate to *be* with this girl while your father is lying in a hospital bed?"

"Yes, I do, Mother, and especially *this* girl, who happens to know Dad and would be concerned about what happened to him."

"Would she also be concerned," Sharon chided, "to know that the reason your father is lying in a hospital is because she thought nothing of shamelessly seducing—"

"Sharon," Leon interrupted, feeling that his daughter-in-law was being unnecessarily harsh, "I know you're very upset about Fred, but you can't go around blaming his condition on a young girl who—"

Before Sharon could deliver the broadside blast at Maria that she was priming to do, Sarah reminded everyone that the place for such discussions is inside the apartment, not in a moving elevator.

As the family walked down the hall to the apartment, Sarah suggested, "A nice tall glass of iced tea maybe will cool everyone off a little. And I'll make some nice cut-up strawberries and sour cream, for whoever wants."

Gulping down a full glass of iced tea did nothing to cool off Kevin. He shouted angrily at his mother that it was stupid of her to accuse Maria of seducing him and even stupider to say that Maria was in any way responsible for his father's heart attack. Sharon sat impassively sipping her tea as she listened to Kevin's harangue. By the time he had finished, she was livid. That her son would dare to use the tone of voice he was using was not acceptable, and she demanded that Kevin apologize for calling her stupid.

Sensing that his grandson was not about to do any such thing, Leon jumped into the breach. "A man is lying in intensive care! I would think that this man's wife and son would be thinking about praying for his recovery instead of insulting each other and arguing about whether a sweet, innocent, young girl could, in any way, be responsible for—"

The moment the words *sweet* and *innocent*, were out of her husband's mouth, Sarah, in an attempt to placate her outraged daughter-in-law, offered, "How about a nice dish of refreshing, cut-up strawberries with fresh sour cream? They're so sweet, Sharon, I didn't even have to sugar them."

"Sarah," Sharon lashed out, "will you stop with your god-damned tea and strawberries? And you, Leon, a twenty-five-year-old maid who goes around the house shaking her ass at a sixteen-year-old high school kid is not what I call an innocent young girl. Slut would be more like it!"

"SLUT!?" Kevin screamed.

"Kevin, darling," Sarah explained, "your mother is upset; she didn't mean it."

"I did mean slut, Sarah, and please stay out of this!"

Sarah, seeing the fire in her grandson's eyes, begged, "Leon, say something!"

"Kevin," Leon tried, "I know you must be angry. I would be angry, too, if someone called my Sarah a slut."

"Leon, this is not what I had in mind!"

Sarah turned to her grandson. "Kevin, I beg you not to say something to your mother that someday you'll be sorry for."

"My mother's the one who should be sorry, Grandma. And Mother," he said, pointedly, "the slut's name is Maria, and she is not twenty-five but twenty-one, and I'm not *just* sixteen. I'm *almost* seventeen. And you were right, Grandpa. Maria is a sweet girl, a very sweet girl, and I love her, and she loves me, and as soon as we can get a license, we're going to be married!"

The stunning silence that followed Kevin's announcement was shattered by Leon's shouting out, "Mazeltov!"

"Mazeltov?" Sharon screamed. "You're congratulating your only grandchild for ruining his life? Sarah, how the hell can your husband say Mazeltov at a time like this?"

"It's a natural reaction. When someone says they're getting married, we always say, 'Mazeltov.' "

Sharon shook her head back and forth, searching for the words to describe how she felt about her in-laws. She finally found them. "You people are impossible!"

"No, no, no, no," Leon said, wagging a finger in Sharon's face. "Sarah and I are not impossible. You! You're the one who's impossible! What kind of a mother are you? Instead of celebrating that your son has the capacity to feel such a wonderful emotion like love, you tell him that he's ruining his life and that the girl he wants to marry is a whore?"

"Slut," Sarah corrected. "She called her a slut."

"Slut, whore, *nafke*, it's all the same. I'm telling you, Sharon, if that girl is a *nafke*, then I'll kiss your behind in Macy's window."

Sarah stamped her foot and shouted, "Leon!"

"All right, all right, I know, I made a dumb challenge, but the sentiment is correct. Sharon, listen to me, why don't you ask Kevin to bring Maria here so you can talk with her. Maybe you'll find that your judgment isn't always so perfect."

Sharon stood up, grabbed her purse, and announced, "I no longer care to be insulted."

"I'm not insulting you personally," Leon explained, "just your behavior, your way of thinking, and your thickheadedness."

Sharon glared at her father-in-law and swallowed a mouthful of words that were bound to drive Kevin further away. She turned her back on Leon and addressed her son. "Kevin, dear," she said, fighting to stay in control, "rather than staying with your grandparents tonight, drive back with me to the hotel. Dad has booked a room for you. We could continue discussing this whole matter calmly, and first thing in the morning we'll drive out to the hospital and visit your father."

Kevin stared at his mother. It's incredible, he thought. She's behaving as if I'm still her little boy and everything is now back to normal. "I'm sorry, Mother," he said, aping her civilized tone, "but I've made other plans."

The eerie politeness continued.

"With the Sisneroses, I imagine."

"No, Mother, with a motel. I've rented a room."

"Will *she* be with you?"

Bette Davis could not have invested the word *she* with more vitriol than Sharon did. It infuriated Kevin, but he was not going to let his mother get to him.

"Her name is Maria, Mother. You know her, the one without the mole?"

Sarah and Leon were both amazed and fascinated by the daytime soap opera that was being played out in their living room. Before Sharon could answer Kevin or slap his face, which she was considering, Kevin gallantly pecked his mother on the cheek and said gaily, "See you at the hospital." He then waved, bid an affectionate good-bye to his grandparents, and was out the door as his mother was shouting, "I forbid you to leave!"

Sarah was surprised at the goodly amount of empathy she felt for Sharon. She saw the obvious frustration in her face and knew the pain she had to be feeling at losing control of her child. Sarah had, very early in her sons' lives, lost her power to influence either one of them. Freddie would, at times, listen to his father, but Dickie listened only to his penis.

The moment Sharon finished delivering her admonition to the door Kevin had just slammed, she turned to Leon and asked to use the phone. Leon thought that it was a good idea to check with the hospital, and he berated himself for not thinking to do it earlier. He offered her the phone on the end table, and when he saw her hesitate, he said, "If you'd prefer talking to Fred privately, you can use the one in our bedroom."

Sharon had not intended to call the hospital, but now she felt obliged to do so. Learning from the floor nurse that Fred was resting comfortably, she relayed this to Leon and Sarah and left.

28

SINCE FRED'S COLLAPSE Sharon had been desperate to speak with Hana, but the opportunity never presented itself, and now that her son had blatantly rejected her, she needed to hear that Hana was still there for her. Sharon drove out of her in-laws' garage and immediately started to look for a public phone. She spotted one in front of a convenience store, drove up to it, and then drove away. She could not see herself standing in an open phone booth, pouring her heart out to Hana, while strangers walked by, chomping their nachos and sipping Slurpees.

As Sharon opened the door to her suite, she fantasized that she would find Hana lying in her bathtub under a mountain of bubbles. The image had become so real that Sharon raced to the bathroom, half-expecting to see Hana lying in the tub. Wanting to continue her delicious daydream, Sharon kicked off her shoes, tore open a packet of bubble-bath gel, and emptied it into the bathtub. While the tub was filling and the volume of bubbles grew, Sharon, with a girlish anticipation that surprised her, slipped out of her clothes and into the hot tub. As the water level rose past her navel, she reached for the wall phone and dialed Hana's number. When the phone rang for the second time and Hana had not picked it up, Sharon pleaded, "Oh, please, please, dear Hana, be home!"

On the third ring, Hana picked up and was overjoyed at hearing her friend's voice.

"Oh, Sharon, this is so wonderful. You will not believe it, but I am sitting in the Jacuzzi thinking of you, and here you are! Where are you?"

"Still in Florida, and would you believe it, I'm sitting in a bubble bath and wishing that you could be with me."

"I can, Sharon. I can be with you."

"How? How can you be with me?"

Hana very slowly and carefully described the process.

"Sharon, are you holding the phone with your left hand?"

"Yes, I am."

"So am I. Now you must close your eyes and imagine we are together. Imagine, too, that your right hand belongs to me, and I will imagine that my right hand belongs to you. Now, very lightly, my hand is going to caress your lovely cheek, and then I will let my hand move down your pretty neck until it comes to your breast. Do you feel it?"

Sharon, moving her hand as directed, emitted a soft cat-like purr.

Sharon was so caught up in this new erotic adventure that she never thought of it as an obscene phone call or masturbation but as a long-distance, romantic interlude with the woman she loved. It was not until after her fourth orgasm that she remembered to tell Hana that Fred had had a heart attack and was in intensive care.

Earlier that day, J. J. Quicky debated whether breaking into Hana Yoshi's home to bug her telephone would be worth the effort. He never dreamed that the small risk he took would reap the dividends that it did. Besides hearing of Fred's unfortunate heart attack, J.J. also heard Hana and Sharon's very erotic conversation, which he found enjoyable and not unarousing. He made a note to look up the word *kuritorisu*. He was amazed and a little envious at the number, and the quality, of orgasms they were able to have by telephone and how seemingly simple it was for them to achieve them. J.J. questioned the wisdom of informing his hospitalized client of the conversation he had just overheard. He decided to withhold all potentially heartbreaking information until Fred Cox was well enough to withstand the shock it was bound to deliver.

At four o'clock that morning, Fred Cox awoke from a drug-induced sleep and in his confused state called out to his secretary, "Elsepth, goddammit, get me J. J. Quicky on the line immediately. We'll find out about that dirty bastard once and for all!"

The night nurse, who had just finished checking Fred's vital signs, advised her patient to go back to sleep and wait till morning. Fred had no intention of going back to sleep and risking a continuation of the nightmare that had plagued him most of the night.

It had started out as a pleasant dream—he and Hana naked, sitting at opposite ends of an enormous Jacuzzi. Hana waved for him to swim to her, but the longer he swam, the farther away Hana seemed to be. He swam faster and faster until his heart started to pound. The pounding became stronger and stronger as he approached Hana, who was now smiling and beckoning him to come to her. As he was about to touch her, a beeper went off, and his brother, Dr. Dick Cox, dressed in a white hospital coat, rose from the bottom of the pool, grabbed Hana in his arms, and carried her to his examining table. Fred tried desperately to climb out of the pool, but his arms went limp, and he fell back into the swirling hot water and started to drown.

The dream was so disturbing and so real that he feared the dirty bastard with whom Hana was having an affair might be his brother.

The last person J.J. would expect to be calling him in the middle of the night was his hospitalized client, but there he was, on the phone and sounding panicky.

"J.J., it's me, Fred Cox. I'm in a hospital in Florida. They think I may have had a mild heart attack, but I'm okay. I've got to know if you found out anything about Hana. I know it sounds crazy, but I had this dream . . . "

J.J. needed a moment to gather himself and decide how he could maintain his reputation as a skilled private investigator without jeopardizing the life of his client. He took a swig of warm, flat Pepsi from the can on his nightstand.

"Mr. Cox, you hired me to observe a Ms. Yoshi to ascertain if she's involved with another man. Well, sir, after a pretty thorough investigation that, I may add, included a phone tap, I have concluded that she is not, I repeat, *is not* having an affair with another man. You are the only man in Ms. Yoshi's life, and as far as I'm concerned, the investigation is over."

With the telephone still in hand and the phone cord entwined with his IV tube, Fred lay back on his hospital bed and closed his eyes. With J.J.'s words "You are the only man in Ms. Yoshi's life" reverberating in his head, Fred started to contemplate his life after recovery. He knew now that he would recover. He would have to. He would have to be there for Hana. He would declare himself to Hana, divorce Sharon, start a new film project, and lock Kevin in his room until he was twenty-one. As he dozed off, a young Hispanic nurse tapped him on the shoulder. "Mr. Cox, I'm going to have to take some of your blood." Giddy from the news about Hana and from the drugs that were dripping into his veins, Fred smiled and mumbled a line from a Dracula script he had once optioned.

"My dear, take all the blood you want. Just leave me enough to blush."

29

AFTER RETURNING to the motel, Kevin spent most of the night trying to convince Maria and himself that his father's heart attack would not force them to change their plans. Kevin assured Maria that he would never abandon her, even if, for a while, he had to cater to some of his parents' needs.

"Maybe, Kevin," Maria suggested, "because your father is not feeling so well, it might make him happy to know that he will soon be a grandfather. And your mother—"

"Maria, my mother works out seven days a week so she won't look like a *mother*. To hear people tell her that she doesn't look like a *grandmother* would kill her."

By six o'clock that morning, having talked themselves out, Kevin and Maria fell into bed. For an hour, snuggled in each other's arms, they slept the sleep of innocents. Kevin awoke at seven and realized that if he hurried, he could get to the hospital before any of his family arrived.

On entering the intensive care room and seeing his father as he rarely allowed himself to be seen, unshaved and unkempt, Kevin, for the first time since he was a little boy, worried about the death of one of his parents. As a four-year-old, it was an imagined and unsupported fear of being left alone, but today it was a fear fully supported by reality. Fred's eyes were closed, but the EKG screen told Kevin that his father was still with him.

"Dad, are you asleep?"

"With all this outdoor plumbing stuck in me?" Fred said without opening his eyes.

Kevin had hoped that he and his father would be able to come to some kind of understanding before his mother arrived. On the cab ride over he had rehearsed just how he would open the discussion and was about to when Dr. Goldberg popped in to ask his patient how he was feeling. Before Fred could tell him, Dr. Goldberg explained that he was recommending that an angiogram be done. He assured Fred that it was a relatively risk free procedure that caused only minimal discomfort. "Dr. Chong," he added brightly, "will be stopping by with the consent forms." Before Fred could ask a question, Dr. Goldberg had made a quick and graceful exit. "If this angio-shit is such a no-risk thing," Fred railed, "then how come I have to sign a consent form? Never mind. Look, before they wheel me off to stick more things in me, let's talk about you and this girl."

"Maria!" Kevin insisted through gritted teeth.

"All right, Maria! Now don't interrupt anymore. I don't have much energy. Kevin, I want you to promise me that you'll give her up. She's not for you. You're too young to get involved in this sort of thing. You'd better come to your senses before it's too late."

Kevin dared to interject that he was in full control of his senses but chose not to add that it was too late not to become involved because Maria was pregnant. Fred bulled forward.

"Have you thought of the consequences? Do you know about this girl's background? Do you have any idea how many guys this girl has slept with?"

Kevin was on the verge of exploding.

"I'll bet you never thought to have her checked to see if she has AIDS? Don't look so shocked. Maybe she's okay, but do you know for sure? And what if you made her pregnant? Do you think she'd have an abortion? No, sir, because she's Catholic and she thinks your family is loaded with money."

If Fred were not lying in bed with an oxygen tube stuck in his nose, Kevin would have punched him right there. He was bursting to rebut this ugly attack on his fiancée, but again his father waved him off.

"Let me finish," Fred continued, his speech punctuated by coughing and sputtering. "You tell that girl that she's wasting her time, because this family is broke! Don't look at me like that. If you had taken any interest, you would know that Sky Productions is on its ass, and now, with this fucking myocardial whatever it is I have, we're looking Chapter 11 right in the face. You can say good-bye to your Toyota Celica—Oh, yeah, I forgot, you already sold it for a lousy four thou and a used pickup truck. How stupid can you get!"

At this point, Kevin's rage was so blinding that he did not stop to wonder how his father could know about the details of the deal he made for his car. He was concerned only with how he could restrain himself from telling his father to go fuck himself. But it was difficult for Kevin to sustain his anger as he listened to his father fall prey to another series of gut-wrenching coughs. Fred, gasping for breath, gestured wildly toward a plastic bowl, which Kevin brought to him. He snatched it out of Kevin's hands and proceeded to retch into it but could bring up nothing but his blood pressure. Kevin stood by helplessly as a nurse, who had seen Fred's erratic EKG at the monitoring station, dashed in, quickly diagnosed that there might be a problem, and called for assistance. It came immediately in the form of Dr. Goldberg and a very large male nurse carrying a small portable fibrillation machine that he dropped onto Fred's bed, hard enough to cause Fred to curse loudly between hacking coughs. "Goddammit, that was my foot!"

Kevin winced in empathy as he watched Dr. Goldberg efficiently check his patient's vital signs while issuing orders for his nurse to prepare a hundred cc's of something. A moment later, the nurse delivered the shot into Fred's pale, tense behind. Once again, Fred interrupted his coughing to interpolate two ouch-ouches! Within minutes, the cough suppressant did its job, and a red-faced and totally spent Fred fell back onto his pillow and asked, "Kevin . . . you still here?"

Kevin took a step into the room and said that he was.

"Me, too." Fred nodded. "I'm still here, too . . . but just. Damn, I never . . . coughed that way . . . in my life. What the hell was that, Doctor?"

Dr. Goldberg gently patted Fred's hand and said knowingly, "I don't know."

For the next nine days, with the capable ministrations of Drs. Theo and Hyman Goldberg, the long-distance consultations with Fred's beleaguered brother, Dr. Richard Cox, and Dr. Norman Briskin, Beverly Hills internist to the stars (whose notices for annual checkups Fred had ignored for the last three years), Fred's condition continued to improve. The consensus was that Fred would be able to avoid expensive open-heart surgery.

During this period, at the behest of Sarah Cox, a truce between Kevin and his parents was dutifully but begrudgingly observed.

Sharon continued to stay in the hotel suite that Fred had thought would be for an overnight visit. Fred had chosen not to burden his wife with information about the bleak state of their finances. He fervently hoped that his health insurance policies would cover his stay at the hospital.

Concerned about their own diminishing nest egg, Kevin and Maria traded their seedy hotel room for an equally seedy, but cheaper, furnished room leased from Carla's friend Amalia. Every morning, Kevin would visit his father at the hospital and stay just long enough to tell him how much better he was looking. For the rest of the day, he and Maria would spend their time rehearsing for their upcoming role as parents by baby-sitting Julio.

30

EVERY NIGHT before retiring Sharon and Hana would speak on the phone and reaffirm their love for each other. One night, the idea of pledging themselves to one another in a formal ceremony came up, and Sharon started to giggle. "Can you imagine hearing some minister say, 'Hana Yoshi and Sharon Cox, I now pronounce you wife and wife,' or 'woman and woman'! Or"—Sharon laughed loudly—" 'Jap and Yid!' "

Sharon quickly realized that she was laughing alone. Hana was not amused and informed her friend that she did not appreciate racist jokes. Hana then spent the rest of the phone call instructing Sharon why it was not funny to refer to people as Japs, Chinks, yids, spicks, or wops.

Whereas Sharon had been scrupulously honest with Hana and withheld nothing from her, Hana had not been as forthcoming. She had not told Sharon that, the night before, she had received a very unusual call from Fred.

For two consecutive nights, after learning from J. J. Quicky that Hana had no secret boyfriend, Fred had a series of dreams about Hana and himself snapping pictures of Hana's wrinkled old great-grandmother, who kept snarling at him and threatening to break his camera. Fred Cox never accepted that dreams had any function other than to awaken people when their bladders were full. On the second night, he awoke from his reverie and realized that a full-blown film project was swirling around in his head.

He checked the wall clock and realized that it was 5:00 A.M. in California and an indecent hour to ring anybody but Walter Quigley, who, among other things, was a bona fide insomniac.

Quigley answered the call on the first ring and was overjoyed to hear his boss sound so strong and positive. Fred described his recurring dream in detail and insisted that it was the basis for a wonderful screenplay. Walter had never heard Fred talk about his dreams being the basis for screenplays, so he had to assume that his boss was on medication. However, as Fred continued to outline what was a very human and touching story, Walter started nodding and soon offered suggestions as to how they ought to proceed.

"I'll be damned," he said. "This dream of yours could bring Sky Productions back from the brink!"

With his old-time energy, Fred then started barking orders. "Call Marvin See and find out how much money he can raise by borrowing, stealing, or selling off our available assets, including the television, cable, and video rights to *Alimony, Nougats and Acrimony* and my house.

Immediately following the call, Happy Hilda, a buxom, dour night nurse, bounded into the room to find out why his heart rate was so elevated. While she was taking his blood pressure, Fred begged her, "Put down real good numbers, Hilda baby, and I'll give you a major role in my new film."

Once Hilda took off the blood pressure cuff, Fred dialed Hana Yoshi's number. Just listening to the ringing of Hana's phone made Fred's heart race wildly. The longer it went unanswered, the more excited he became. On the ninth ring, Fred heard Hana sleepily mumble something incoherent.

He had not spoken with Hana since his heart attack. When he said it was him, Hana sounded genuinely pleased.

"Hana, I'm about to make you an exciting proposition, a proposal, if you will, and I'm hoping you won't refuse."

"What kind of exciting proposal?" Hana was now bolt upright in bed.

"Hana, honey," Fred said in his professional producer voice, "how would you feel about working on a film project with me?"

"I know nothing about films," Hana sighed, relieved that Fred was not asking her to become his mistress.

Fred got out of his hospital bed and, limited by the length of his IV catheter, paced back and forth as he made his sales pitch. "Hana, I want to tell the story of your great-grandmother from the standpoint of her great-granddaughter, a young, beautiful, modern Japanese girl who feels unfulfilled and empty and goes on a voyage of discovery to a remote island in the Pacific where she finds her roots and, in the process, all the answers. Now, you wouldn't have to write it. You'd tell it to this brilliant young writer that I'm negotiating with. He'd put it all down, word for word, and he'd add nothing but what he felt was necessary to improve it."

Fred suddenly stopped pacing and shouted, "Hana! You! You should play yourself in the film!"

Hana was intrigued. She had acted many parts in her life—a waitress, a model, a flight attendant, and most recently, a successful language teacher of extraordinary unconventionality. She offered meekly, "I am not an actress."

"Hana, you don't have to act. You'll narrate. Your own sweet, honest, gorgeous self will narrate your own story."

"Fred, I will have to get back to you on this."

"I'll get back to you?" This from the woman who had taught him Japanese while making love to him in a Jacuzzi?

Fred was devastated. He could not accept the obvious truth, so after much convoluted reasoning, he was able to convince himself that Hana had lost interest in him only because he had made no move to extricate himself from his failed marriage. With this bit of illogic and a mild sedative, Fred was able to sleep fitfully for a half hour before somebody came to steal more of his blood.

After delivering her gratuitous dissertation on racism and hearing Sharon's emotionless "Good night, Hana, dear," Hana felt empty. It did not take her long to realize why she had reacted so sharply to her friend's playfully calling her a Jap. Rather than attacking herself for withholding from Sharon the fact that Fred had offered her a most exciting job, she chose to censure Sharon for using racist language. Hana thought of a perfect way to make amends, and she laughed at her solution. She dialed Sharon's number, and as Sharon picked up the phone, Hana asked, "Shar, instead of Jap and Yid, how about, 'I now pronounce you Sharon-san and Kosher Yoshi'?"

Sharon burst out laughing. Not because it was all that funny but because Hana knew of Sharon's anguish and called to comfort her. Sharon repeated, "Sharon-san and Kosher Yoshi."

Hana apologized for behaving like a zealot and admitted that she was angry at herself for not telling Sharon about the very seductive offer she had received from Fred. Hana rushed to describe Fred's proposal and explained, "I did not accept his offer and would only *consider* to consider it if I was sure that it would in no way strain our relationship."

Armed with Sharon's blessings, Hana got back to Fred and told him that she would be proud to be involved in a project that brought to life her great-grandmother's tragic story. She admitted that when originally recounting it, she omitted some of the more dramatic details.

"What dramatic details are we talking about?"

"Oh, about how my great-grandmother cut the testicles off three of her clients after stabbing them to death with a sushi knife. Do you think," she asked naïvely, "that this is proper material for me to tell to your writer?"

"Proper material?" he bellowed as he leapt to his feet, over-turning his bowl of oatmeal. "Hana, these are the kinds of details that writers break their brains to come up with. It's the stuff classic movies are made of. How many guys' balls did you say she chopped off? Three? Three, thirty-three, what's the difference, it happened and it's visual. If we get the right director, we'll have people squirming in their seats—and of course moved to tears by the tragic and degrading life your great-grandmother was forced into. Hana baby, you've given me gold, pure gold. What we've got here is a woman's picture loaded with nongratuitous, honestly motivated violence, violence that women won't turn away from because it's violence against ugly, brutish men who use women as sex objects. It's the kind of satisfying comeuppance violence that will have audiences cheering and weeping. It'll make millions!"

31

O N THE DAY he was to leave the hospital, Fred phoned his father and asked if he might borrow from him a fair sum of money that he promised to return very quickly. Fred was certain that within days after returning to California he would be able to raise a substantial amount of seed money for his new project.

"Son, how much do you need?" Leon was happy to be able to say. "Name it and you got it."

From small, safe, nonspeculative investments, his and Sarah's Social Security checks, and the checks his sons insisted on sending for years, Leon had managed to accumulate rather respectable savings. He had deposited his sons' checks in a special account that he kept "in case some member of the family got caught in a heavy rainstorm." Leon assumed that Fred's hospital bill was his rainstorm. He was surprised, though, to hear Fred ask for twenty-five thousand dollars. He was absolutely appalled. "That much? Boy, that hospital saw you coming!" Fred explained that his insurance took care of the hospital bills, but he did not explain why he needed the money.

"I'll tell you tomorrow, at the condo," Fred promised.

"Tell me what?"

Fred smiled and said, "Tomorrow, Dad!"

As Fred entered the apartment, Leon waved an envelope in the air. "Here it is, Freddie boy, a cashier's check for twenty-five thousand. If you need more, the bank is right around the corner. You look good, Freddie. Sarah, considering what he went through, doesn't he look good?"

"He looks pale, and he's lost too much weight. Freddie,

126

you're always running," Sarah lectured. "That's why you ended up in the hospital. I hope you learned something from this experience."

Fred, eager to talk with his father, agreed that he had learned a lot.

"No, Freddie," she insisted, "I don't think you learned. I can see already that you can't wait to get back to working too hard, and what, all of a sudden, made you run to Japan for a vacation? For what? To eat raw fish? That's why you got sick, running around and eating uncooked fish. Why do you want to eat raw fish?"

Fred started to protest.

"And don't tell me about lox. Lox is not raw; it's cured and smoked and salted, and we don't eat it anymore, anyway, because salt isn't good for your father's condition. And in your condition, Freddie, you shouldn't have driven here. We could've brought you the money. So tell me, Freddie, if the money isn't to pay the hospital bill, then what's it for?"

Fred explained, "It's for something I want Pa to do for me."

"Freddie," Leon asked, "you're not in trouble with the mob? This isn't for a gambling debt, is it?"

"Dad," he said, looking at his watch, "this is about Kevin. A few days ago at the hospital, he and I had a very bitter and upsetting conversation. I tried to reason with him, but he would not hear what I was trying to tell him. That girl has made him crazy. It's like she's hypnotized him or something. He will absolutely not come home with us. He wants to be with her, and there is no more discussion."

"I agree"—Leon shrugged—"he is hypnotized. The boy is in love, and at that age, when you're in love, you're in a trance. Or don't you remember Selma Singer? You were even younger than Kevin."

"Fifteen, and it was Springer," Sarah corrected, "not Singer."

"You sure?"

"I'm sure."

"I always thought her name was Singer."

Fred, having no time to waste, shouted, "Springer! Her name was Springer, Dad! And what you're getting at is not relevant."

"What is this, a court case? What I am saying, Freddie, is that the Singer girl had you walking into walls."

"I never walked into walls."

"It wasn't a wall," Sarah agreed. "It was a lamppost. I'll never forget the lump you got on your forehead; it was the size of a walnut."

"What's the difference? A wall, a lamppost—you were smitten, just like your son is."

"But I didn't run off with Selma *Springer*, Dad, and refuse to come home."

"But," Sarah said, "you stayed out till three in the morning worrying us to death."

Fred shut his eyes, trying to close off reminiscences of the past. When he opened them again, he spoke slowly and clearly. "What you're saying is true, and I don't argue that Kevin is in love with this girl, or thinks he is, but I know that *this girl* will dump him as soon as she gets what she wants out of him."

Leon and Sarah were aching to interrupt, but by raising his voice, Fred was able to keep them in check.

"Let me finish, please! This is very difficult for me. . . . Dad, I'm going to ask a favor of you. I want you to do something for me that, if it were possible, I'd do myself. Dad, I'd like you to have a talk with this girl."

"C'mon, Freddie, *this girl* worked in your house. Her name is Maria. Goddammit, show a little respect for people."

With his goal at stake, Fred did not want to risk antagonizing his father. "You're right, Dad. I'm sorry. I guess I'm not myself yet. Look, Kevin knows that you like Maria, and I'm sure he wouldn't object if you asked to speak with her. I'm going to invite Kevin out for a cup of coffee and try talking to him. Who knows, maybe I'll say something that'll wake him up."

Leon, old accountant that he was, put two and two together and came up with an answer that was too abhorrent to contemplate. Leon stared at his son, afraid to ask if the purpose for his meeting with Maria was as foul as he thought.

"Freddie," Leon said, shaking his head sadly, "are you asking me to be Germont?"

Sarah and Fred spoke at the same time.

"Germont?"

"Who's Germont?"

"I'm talking about what I think you're asking me to do. It's terrible, and I won't do it."

"Leon, what's so terrible? All Freddie is asking you to do is talk to that nice young girl. I don't see what's so terrible."

"Oh, my God!" escaped from Fred when it dawned on him who Germont was.

Leon Cox was an opera buff and never missed a Saturday afternoon Metropolitan broadcast. Among his favorites was *La Traviata*, the only opera that he had ever taken his wife and sons to see. Germont, Fred now recalled, was the old baritone with the paunch who came to Camille's house in the country to offer her money and to tell her that if she really loved his son the tenor, then she should do something nasty to drive him out of her life. Fred couldn't believe how much his plan sounded like the plot of *La Traviata*, and even more unbelievable was how suddenly obsessed he became with the need to remember the name of Germont's son. At this moment nothing was as important as recalling the name of Camille's boyfriend. He furrowed his brow and bit his fist as he dug deep into his memory. Leon misread the pained look on his son's face and worried that his son was having another heart attack.

"Alfredo! Germont's son's name was Alfredo!" Fred shouted triumphantly as he punched the air with his clenched fist.

Leon, relieved, punched the air and shouted back, "That's correct, but Maria is not Camille, and I will not be Germont and offer Maria money to give up Kevin, and I'm disappointed and ashamed that you would think that I would be a party to such a demeaning act."

"Dad," Fred began contritely, knowing that his purpose would be better served if he did not confront his father head-on, "I know how you feel, and you're right. I should be ashamed of what I'm doing, and a big part of me is, but I'm fighting to protect my son from destroying his life. If I'm wrong, I can accept being looked on as a schmuck, but if I'm right—"

"You are not right!"

"But I may be, and you can't prove I'm wrong unless you—"

"Unless I what?" Leon bellowed. "Oh, my God! You ask me to lend you twenty-five thousand dollars for *this*?!"

Leon stared at his son, aware of what he was doing but

powerless to control himself. "Freddie, do you really think that Maria would take my money and give up Kevin?"

Fred snapped his fingers. "Like that!"

"And I say she'll throw the money in my face, just like Camille did!"

Had not Leon been confident that Maria would prove herself to be a person of integrity, he might have felt guilty about calling to invite her to drop by for a visit. He could not believe that at his age he would feel nervous and excited at the prospect of meeting with Maria. Maria, on the other hand, had become frightened when her aunt Teresa told her that Kevin's grandfather was on the phone. She was sure some accident had befallen Kevin, or worse, that he had been kidnapped by his parents. She was relieved to hear Mr. Cox say that Sarah had knitted a sweater for Julio. "We know your sister is working, Maria, and we thought it would be nice if you came by to pick it up."

This actually was the truth and Leon wished that it was the whole truth. Maria, considering Mr. Cox's invitation as a positive sign, dared to dream that this could be a prelude to a more friendly relationship with all of the Cox family. Maria said that she would like to come but she was minding Julio. Leon tried to imagine how the scene would play out with a baby added to it and decided that although perhaps more bizarre, it would not change the outcome of their meeting.

"Bring the baby. My wife loves Julio, and she'll get to see if the sweater fits."

As soon as he said it, he realized that if Sarah took Julio into another room to play, she would be spared seeing him humiliate himself.

32

WHEN HE RETURNED to the hotel, Fred found Sharon saying a tearful and resigned good-bye to her son. Kevin's anger at his father had abated, and he was able to accept his father's offer to shake hands, but he could not accept his request for no hard feelings. Fred offered a suspect but sincere-sounding apology by explaining how the drugs had scrambled his brains and caused him to say things that he now deeply regretted.

"Kevin, do you think it'd be possible for you and I to spend a little quiet time together before your mother and I leave? I promise I won't try to tell you what to do with your life, and if you're worried that I might lose it again, like I did in the hospital, we can have our chat in the hotel coffee shop, a public place."

To ensure that Maria had enough time to get to Sarah and Leon's condo and hear his father's offer, Fred monopolized his son's time by engaging him in the warmest, friendliest conversation they had ever had. It made Kevin wary. He knew that conciliation and acceptance were not his father's goals. He had to have a second agenda hidden somewhere. For the moment he found it pleasant having a cup of coffee with his father and watching him try to behave fatherly. Kevin enjoyed hearing him say things like "You've got to be angry with me, son. I never once tried to find out how serious you were about Maria" and "When I think about how many times you became annoyed with your mother and me for not making the effort to learn which of the twins was which . . ."

Kevin particularly enjoyed hearing his father say things he

knew were meant to win him over: "Believe me, son, if I was your age, I probably would have fallen in love with Maria just as you did. She is really an extraordinarily attractive young woman."

Kevin expected that his father's calling Maria a woman was a prelude to a speech about the disparity in their ages. What he heard instead was a long but not uninteresting account of his father's many dalliances with young girls before he found the one he truly loved and wanted to marry. Kevin was surprised to learn that that one was not his mother but an Arkansas beauty named Emma Jean Covington. They had met at a summer theater when they were seventeen, fallen madly in love, and when the summer ended, corresponded for ten long and lonely months, waiting for the following summer.

"My parents disapproved of Emma Jean because she wasn't Jewish, but that didn't change the way I felt about her. I was in love, and Emma Jean and I decided that when we were eighteen, we'd elope." At this point, even though he felt his father was being baldly obvious, Kevin was hooked. Fred knew it.

To ensure that his father had enough time for his meeting with Maria, Fred told his story fully. He described how he and Emma Jean had planned to meet on her eighteenth birthday at the little church in Stockbridge, the site of the summer theater where they had met and fallen in love. He told, in elaborate detail, how he had managed to save enough money to pay for the rings, the minister, transportation, and a three-day honeymoon. He had mowed lawns and washed cars, and he actually admitted to stealing from his father's pants pockets and his mother's purse. Kevin thought, Unless my father is making this up, he has a human side that he's managed to keep hidden from me all of my life. Kevin was aware that his father was telling this story for some reason other than to enlighten or amuse him, but whatever the reason, Kevin was so genuinely interested in what happened to Emma Jean Covington that he asked, "So what happened? Why didn't you go through with it?"

Once again Kevin did not expect what he got. "Oh, but we did. We were married on the ninth of October, 1966, one month after Emma Jean turned eighteen and six days after I did." Kevin was now both interested and perplexed.

"How come I never heard about this? You and Mom never said either of you were married before."

Kevin now heard the second example of his father's humanness.

"Your mother was married before, too. When she was twenty, she married this older bachelor, an airline pilot, and when she found out that he wasn't a pilot or a bachelor, she had the marriage annulled. My marriage to Emma Jean didn't last that long, either. Emma Jean told her kid sister Lindy-Lou about the elopement, and her father, Lt. Col. William "Brute" Covington, threatened to ground poor Lindy-Lou for the rest of her life if she didn't tell him the address of the church. She told."

"But you said that you got married."

"We did. Brute Covington got to the church an hour too late, but he got to our honeymoon suite just in time, he thought, to save Emma Jean from losing her virginity by 'copulating with a dirty Jew bastard.' Those were his exact words. They might've been stronger if he'd known that the dirty Jew bastard had been copulating with his daughter for two whole summers."

Kevin thought, He must know that we're planning to get married. Is he threatening to call Maria a dirty something-or-other, or is he trying to be a good father and point out that I'm as big an idiot as he was? Kevin wondered if this story would have ended with an abortion had his father known Maria was pregnant. Kevin expected that at any moment he would hear words like "Son, you've got to give her up." Whatever the words were, Kevin was ready for them, but he was not ready for the waiter to walk up to the table with a cordless phone and ask, "Are either of you gentlemen Mr. Fred Cox?" Kevin thought at first that it was part of the act, but he knew it was not acting when he saw his father blanch on hearing that it was an urgent, emergency call from Mr. Leon Cox.

If her husband had not been in the bathroom moving his bowels, Sarah would have insisted he answer the doorbell and let Maria in. By permitting the little sweater she knitted to be used as an enticement to lure Maria to her home, she had unwittingly allowed herself to become an accomplice to a plan that was sure to break someone's heart.

"Sarah, is that the doorbell?"

Sarah reluctantly opened the door. On seeing this lovely young girl holding an innocent baby, Sarah had an urge to hand Maria the baby's sweater, say, "Sorry, my husband is busy right now," and close the door. Instead, Sarah warmly welcomed Maria and the baby into her home and held out her arms to Julio. The seven-month-old made a studied appraisal of Sarah and, satisfied that she looked trustworthy, leaned over and gave himself to her. Sarah offered Maria a "nice cold glass of iced tea" and raced off to the kitchen, where she could avoid looking into Maria's face, a face that, Sarah felt, was begging her to divulge the real reason that she had been invited to visit.

With Julio in her arms, Sarah added ice cubes to a pitcher of tea while listening impatiently for the sound of a flush that would herald the end of her husband's ill-timed call to nature. Sarah was grateful to Julio for sticking his hand into the glass of iced tea she had just poured, for by the time she had poured a second glassful, she heard her husband greeting their guest. It was obvious to Sarah that Leon had a crush on Maria. Through the years she had noticed that when her husband spoke to a woman he found attractive, his enunciation improved, and his language became flowery.

"Mrs. Cox and I are so pleased that you could come and visit, and I'm happy for the opportunity to see that little *shmendrick* again.

Reading Maria's questioning face, Leon quickly explained that *shmendrick* is a Yiddish term of endearment for cute little feller. While Leon and Maria chatted uncomfortably, Julio, who had been sucking on a small ice cube, took it from his mouth and carefully placed it down Sarah's blouse. Sarah shrieked, Julio started to cry, and Maria and Leon dashed into the kitchen to find out what the problem was.

Because everyone was so tense, the sight of Sarah fishing for the piece of ice started Leon chuckling. When Sarah retrieved the ice, Julio took it out of her hand and carefully placed it back in her ample bosom, where he thought it belonged. Leon erupted into full-throated laughter as he watched Sarah fish again for the melting ice cube. Maria, who was struggling to keep from laughing, was instantly sobered by a pungent odor emanating from her nephew. She immediately took the baby from Sarah and asked for a place to change his diaper.

Sarah and Leon watched guiltily as this very good soul expertly cleaned and diapered the happy, cooing baby. Leon felt his wife's eyes on him but knew that if he looked at her, he would weaken and become unable to do what he had promised Fred he would do. Sarah, aware of how uncomfortable her husband would be if she were present when he made the offer, asked Maria if she might take Julio to her room. "I have a few little *chachkas* that Julio might like to play with."

As Leon watched his wife carrying Julio from the room, he reached into his pocket and fingered the envelope that contained the twenty-five-thousand-dollar cashier's check. It made him shudder. Maria, noticing that he had shuddered, asked if he were all right. Rather than make a silly excuse, he decided to tell the truth.

"Maria," he began, "my wife did knit a sweater for Julio, but it is not the reason we asked you here."

Maria had imagined as much but was not prepared to hear the real reason.

"Maria," Leon said as lovingly as he could, "my grandson has told us how very much he loves you."

Leon had to turn away. There was no way he could say what he had to while watching Maria's trusting eyes start to fill with tears. He looked down at his hands and continued, "And, Maria . . . Kevin also told me how much you love him . . . and that's wonderful . . ."

Maria prayed that a dream-destroying *but* was not Mr. Cox's next word.

". . . but sometimes, Maria, this kind of love comes to people before they're capable of handling it."

Leon looked up from his hands and saw tears rolling down Maria's cheeks.

"And you think," she said, sobbing, "that Kevin and I are not capable?"

"No, I think that you are very capable of having a serious relationship with someone, Maria, but Kevin is very young, and his parents feel that he's not mature enough to—"

"Not mature enough?" Maria sobbed, tears welling in her eyes. "Mr. Cox, when Kevin told you that we loved each other, did he tell you anything else?"

Assuming that she was talking about sex, Leon fumbled. "No, no, he didn't tell me anything else. Kevin is a gentleman, and gentlemen do not discuss such things, but *of course* we assumed that you, uh, were intimate with each other."

While Leon was searching for a diplomatic way to continue, Maria, through sobs, presented his case for him. "Mr. Cox, you're trying to tell me that I should go away someplace and forget Kevin, but I cannot do this. I love Kevin and he loves me, and nobody can change that!"

Leon was so moved by Maria's sincerity that he could barely restrain himself from taking her into his arms. He wondered if Sharon and Fred, had they witnessed this powerful display of raw emotion, would have capitulated and given the young lovers their blessings. Leon considered not offering Maria the money, but he had such faith in her integrity that he decided to go forward. He couldn't wait to rip up the twenty-five-thousand-dollar check in front of his smart-aleck son.

"Maria," Leon said slowly, taking the envelope from his pocket, "I'm ashamed of my son for asking me to do this, and I'm ashamed of myself for agreeing to do it."

Fearing that the envelope contained a subpoena or something pertaining to Domenico and Immigration, Maria suddenly became rigid.

"Maria," Leon said, tapping the envelope, "I know what your answer will be, but Kevin's father has asked me to offer you twenty-five thousand dollars if you'll promise not to see Kevin anymore."

Maria stared at the old man in disbelief. "Is this a joke?"

Leon sheepishly opened the envelope and showed her the check. Maria looked first at the check in Leon's hand and then up at Leon, who was trying to smile.

"It's a cashier's check." He shrugged.

Maria started to shake as she searched for words to describe the hurt and disgust she was feeling. Leon knew that the look of betrayal in her eyes would haunt him for the rest of his life. His heart pounding, Leon stood motionless as he watched Maria race to the bedroom and retrieve Julio. The baby's face was primed to burst into tears, which it did when Maria strode defiantly up to Leon and spat at his feet. She then sneered at Leon, snatched the check out of his trembling hand, and bolted from the apartment. Sarah, who arrived in time to witness the operatic climax of the scene, looked to her husband. Leon looked away, hoping that she would have the decency not to point out that his misjudgment of Maria's character had cost them twenty-five thousand dollars.

Sarah clucked three times and spoke softly. "Leon, call the bank immediately and stop payment on the check." Leon, clenching and unclenching the muscles in his jaw, pulled a slip of paper out of his pocket, moved toward the phone, and angrily punched in the numbers. Sarah, knowing the number on the slip of paper, asked why he had dialed Freddie's hotel.

"Because," Leon barked angrily, "I want to tell him the wonderful news!"

"Leon, hang up! While you're talking with your son the girl could be cashing the check."

"Freddie Cox, please . . . How do you know he's not in his room? . . . Well, then ring the coffee shop and tell them that it's his father calling and it's an urgent emergency!"

Leon then turned to his wife and explained that if Maria is cashing the check, she had a perfect right to do so, adding, "I offered her a deal in good faith, and she accepted it!"

Sarah was furious. "Leon, we are talking about a good part of our savings!"

"No, Sarah," he said, a righteous tone now overlaying his sarcasm, "we are not talking about our *savings*. We are talking about our *honor*! Case closed!"

Before Sarah could offer twenty-five thousand good reasons why the case should not be considered closed, Leon heard Fred's anxiety-ridden voice.

"Dad, what happened?"

To avoid her censuring stare, Leon turned his back to Sarah and recounted to his gloating son the scene that had just been played out in his living room, omitting how Maria had spit at him. "So, Freddie," Leon continued, "without even a thank-you, she took the money and ran."

"Like a thief," Sarah could not help interjecting, "to the nearest bank, she ran."

Leon glared at his wife, who left the room mumbling, "Stubborn, stubborn!"

Sarah's empathy for Maria, which was considerable, all but disappeared when Maria spit on her husband's shoes.

Leon did not appreciate hearing from his son "You did a

good job, Dad, and I'm proud of you." Without saying good-bye, Leon hung up.

Kevin, hearing only his father's end of the conversation, wondered what good job his grandfather had done. From the uh-huhs and grunts and the smirky smile on his father's face, he could not guess that his father was listening to his grandfather's report on the success of their ugly plan to demean Maria. Kevin could not wait to hear the reason for the strangely humorless smile that now played on his father's lips.

"Kevin," he began, dabbing his mouth with a napkin, "I suppose you're wondering what that call was all about."

Kevin admitted that he was curious.

"Son," Fred began, "your grandfather just had a little talk with your friend Maria. Now before you jump—"

Kevin had already jumped. At the mention of Maria's name, he rose from his chair and demanded to know what right they had to contact his fiancée. Hearing his son refer to their former maid as his fiancée only strengthened Fred's conviction that he had acted wisely.

"I expected that you'd be angry with me, Kevin, but one day you'll thank me for what I did for you today."

His rage mounting, Kevin pounded the table and demanded, "What the fuck is this all about?"

"Kevin," he said calmly, "if you can manage to avoid using foul language in a public place and can keep your temper in check, I will tell you what this is all about."

Bursting to know what had happened, Kevin promised to control himself. Fred accepted Kevin's promise and forthrightly told him about the money Maria was offered and how eagerly she had accepted it. Then, just as forthrightly, Kevin, with one short, quick jab, broke his promise and his father's nose.

Kevin ran from the coffee shop without looking back to see the effects of his explosive jab.

Fred, holding a napkin to his nose, called out sharply, "Waitress, check, please."

33

KEVIN DID NOT realize how hard he had hit his father until he reached into his pocket for a quarter and yelped in pain. At this moment, however, his more intense pain was clearly the one he felt for Maria. Using his left hand to put the quarter into the slot and the pinky of his injured right hand to dial, he called Amalia's house. When no one answered, he assumed Maria had either not made it back from his grandfather's or had gone to McDonald's looking for Carla to comfort her. With mounting discomfort, Kevin called information, got the number for McDonald's, and learned from the manager that it was Carla's day off.

Thwarted and angry, Kevin threw another short right jab, this time at the blameless telephone. The pain in his hand now completely overshadowed the one in his heart. Within seconds the two excruciating pains that racked his being joined and sent their hapless victim to his knees. He cursed every member of his whole meddling family, then himself and his own god-damn stupidity, and finally a short, unsuspecting old man who dared to ask if he might use the phone. "You dumb fuck, can't you see that this booth is occupied?" He would like to have apologized, but by the time the pain had left, so had the old man.

Deciding that Maria might be home by now, Kevin thought he would try again. This time, by using his left hand exclusively, the dialing process was much less painful and infinitely more rewarding. He whooped for joy when he heard the phone being picked up on the very first ring.

Hearing the strange and, in her state, totally inappropriate whooping, Maria assumed that someone had dialed incorrectly. She informed the joyous nut that he had a wrong number and hung up just as Kevin shouted, "No, no, no, no, Maria, it's me!"

Kevin was stunned. He expected that Maria would be upset, but he could not imagine that she would hang up on him. Perhaps she didn't know it was him. With this spurious logic guiding him, he went through the excruciating ordeal of fishing another coin out of his pocket.

Before he finished dialing, Kevin remembered that he had said it was him calling. He was certain she wouldn't hang up on someone who called her by her name. While he was ruminating, Maria's phone started to ring, and Kevin heard it being picked up and slammed down. He was satisfied now that Maria knew who had called but, because of what his father had done, did not wish to speak with him now, or perhaps ever again. With his good hand, Kevin deposited another quarter and redialed. His hand was now so swollen and painful that if she refused, he would not be able to fish out another coin from the pocket of his tight jeans. "C'mon God," he prayed, "please make her talk to me."

By leaving the phone off the hook, Maria had rendered God powerless and ensured that Kevin's frustration would be complete. The annoying, mocking sound of the busy signal and the throbbing in his hand was now forcing Kevin into a choice: find an emergency trauma center and have his rapidly swelling hand attended to or go to Maria and risk having his hand explode in front of her. The decision was made for him when, because of the unbearable pain in his hand, he fainted dead away.

Sol Wolfe, the tiny old terrier of a man who a few moments earlier, had been called a "dumb fuck," by Kevin, courageously returned to see if the "meshugana" had gone and made the phone available for "decent people to use." Sol Wolfe stepped over Kevin's limp body, jockeyed himself into the booth, and before calling his daughter, dialed 911 on Kevin's behalf.

Kevin, starting to regain consciousness, felt something poke him in the ribs. "Hey, 'Mr. dumb fuck,' " Sol Wolfe asked, prodding him with his cane, "are you all right?"

As soon as Kevin sat up and convinced the old man he was

not dying, Mr. Wolfe, speaking with a thick Yiddish accent, told him that God had punished him for shouting obscenities at a man who was the Former President of Temple Beth Israel in Fort Lauderdale.

"But," he added, "because Sol Wolfe is not a vengeful man, I called the paramedics. Maybe they can let some air out of that balloon sticking out of your sleeve. My God, what did you do to it?"

Kevin looked at his hand, then at his wristwatch, and realized that he had been out for only a few moments. He apologized to the former president of Temple Beth Israel for cursing at him, staggered to his feet, and over the strong objections of the ex-president, made his way to a cab stand. He struggled into one of the four waiting cabs, only to be told by the driver that he would have to get out of his cab and into the first one in line.

Sol Wolfe, being an ethical man, waited for the paramedics and explained to them that, against his sound advice, the "stupid idiot with a hand the size of a melon drove off in a cab."

It was five long blocks from Amalia's house to the bus stop, and Maria, carrying her large, heavy suitcase, found it necessary to stop and rest every hundred paces or so. Maria was also carrying with her the memory of Kevin's pleading voice on the phone. It tortured her that she hung up on him each time he called. She told herself over and over, "It is best for him, and it is best for me, and it is best for our unborn child." She knew it was futile, but she prayed for some small miracle to happen.

One block from the bus terminal, Maria stopped to rest, and to the accompaniment of screeching brakes, the small miracle happened. A yellow cab had pulled up, and a sickeningly pale version of Kevin Cox stumbled out, grabbed Maria's suitcase, and using every last bit of strength that was left in his good arm, he swung the bag high in the air and onto the luggage rack atop the cab. He then turned to Maria and indicated that she get in the cab.

"Maria," he said forcefully, "you must talk to me."

With her eyes staring at the ground, she climbed into the cab. Only after Kevin settled beside her did she see his grotesquely swollen right hand. She broke her vow of silence and asked what had happened to it.

"I hit my father because I was angry at him for what he did to you."

Maria went deep into her reservoir and brought forth the last of her tears, but she would not allow Kevin to touch or comfort her.

During the short cab ride back to Amalia's house, Maria kept her eyes shut and tried to avoid looking at Kevin's injured hand. Her strong feelings for Kevin made it impossible to remain uninvolved, and without conferring with Kevin, she instructed the cabdriver to drive to the nearest hospital.

Kevin thought, She cares about me. . . . Maybe all is not lost.

In the emergency room, young Dr. Juan Ortiz was surprised to hear that the massive amount of damage to Kevin's hand was accomplished with one blow to someone's nose. While examining Kevin's hand, he asked jokingly, "Who's the bully who got fresh with your young lady?"

When Dr. Ortiz saw Kevin and Maria exchange glances, he assumed that he had guessed right. "From the looks of your hand," the doctor said, chuckling, "I'd say the SOB got more than he bargained for."

Kevin was tempted to shout, "My father was the SOB," but decided that since his fate was in Dr. Ortiz's hands, he would prefer that the doctor think of him as a gallant who defended his girl's honor rather than a violent, ungrateful son.

In less than an hour, Kevin's hand was x-rayed, his three fractured fingers reset and splinted, and his wrist and hand uncomfortably encased in a bandage that looked like a six-ounce boxing glove.

On leaving the clinic, Maria bought from a vending machine two sliced-egg-and-tomato sandwiches and two small cartons of milk. As they settled on a tree-shaded bench to have their snack, Kevin thought, Why would she bother buying food for me if she didn't still love me?

Kevin, who had been so anxious to ask Maria why she accepted the money, was now apprehensive about finding out. While he was thinking about how to word the question, Maria spoke. "Kevin, I know that you are thinking about the twenty-five-thousand-dollar check I took from your grandfather and wondering why I spit at him."

No one had reported to Kevin that Maria had spit at his grandfather, and it unnerved him. Somehow, punching his father in the face seemed a less violent act than Maria spitting in his grandfather's face. Trying not to be harsher with Maria than necessary, Kevin asked what his grandfather had said that would provoke her to spit in his face. He was partially relieved when Maria explained that she had not spit in his grandfather's face but on the floor, at his feet.

"Perhaps," she added, "if your father had the courage to offer me the money himself, I would have spit in *his* face. . . . Kevin," Maria continued hesitantly. "I know you have not told your parents about our baby."

Kevin nodded and saw in Maria a seriousness that worried him.

"Kevin," she explained, looking directly into his eyes, "if your father is willing to give me twenty-five thousand dollars to stop seeing you, then he is capable of doing even worse things."

To make Kevin understand, she knew that she had to keep her emotions in check and state, clearly and simply, what she felt.

"Your parents, because they are very rich and powerful, would find a way to stop me from having our baby."

"Maria, my parents don't have that kind of power. That's crazy!"

"I am not crazy. I did not hire a private detective to track you down." Maria, now starting to lose her composure, pulled an envelope from her brassiere and shouted, "And I did not make your sweet, old grandfather embarrass himself by offering me this dirty money to run away and hide from the man I love. These people did that! They are crazy, not me!"

Kevin, incredulous, asked how she knew that they had hired a private detective.

"My brother-in-law, Domenico," she shouted. "He said that this man called Aunt Teresa to find out if you were here, and that's how your parents knew about our plane."

Kevin shook his head in disbelief until he remembered the

reference his father made about selling the Toyota. "That's how he knew I got four thousand for it!" Kevin said, and slapped his head. "Damn! Maria, you're probably right about the private detective. But so what? So he found me. I got a busted hand, but we're still together."

"Yes, but if we stay together, your father will call Immigration and have Domenico deported. I know this! Kevin, go home, please," Maria pleaded. "Go back to them before they find out that I am pregnant. Maybe"—Maria now measured her words—"when I have the baby . . ."

Kevin winced, and Maria continued, ". . . they cannot stop you from coming to me, and, Kevin, if you want to know about the money, I did not take it and promise your grandfather that I will not see you again." Maria's tears broke through, but her voice remained firm.

"Kevin, until I am able to go back to work," she said, "this money will buy for the baby whatever it will need."

Kevin again started to speak, and again Maria silenced him. "I must do it this way. When the baby is born, your father cannot stop you from coming to me. I pray that you will want to come, and if you still feel that we should marry, I will be very, very, very happy to marry you."

Kevin was stunned and would have fought her ultimatum if he did not hear in her voice a tone that precluded any chance of negotiation. Maria's sad face, glistening with tears, triggered in Kevin an overwhelming need to hold her. Now weeping unashamedly, Kevin, with a powerful one-armed hug, was able to communicate to Maria that he accepted what she proposed. When Kevin trusted that he could speak without sobbing, he told her what she most wanted to hear—that he would love her always.

Because of his incapacity, Maria volunteered to accompany Kevin to their room and help him pack.

As she folded his clothes and placed them in his suitcase, Maria looked at Kevin reclining on the bed and realized that she had made a mistake in coming back to the room. After his ordeal with his father and the breaking and setting of the bones in his hand, she never imagined that Kevin would be thinking about sex, but that was exactly what he was doing. He suggested that before they parted, they make love one last time. Knowing that if she were to lie next to him and feel his body against hers, her resolve would weaken, Maria begged Kevin not to ask her again, and he reluctantly promised that he would not.

Before leaving the room, Maria sat next to Kevin on the bed and scribbled some numbers on the back of the envelope that held the check. She tried to calculate the date the baby would be born, using, as the time of conception, the fateful afternoon in Kevin's bedroom when he ran out of condoms and told her, "It was the very, very best ever!" Unless something unusual happened, like a premature birth, she was certain that their baby would be born in eight months. Maria felt a stirring in her breast and knew that it was time for her to leave. She dared to give Kevin a long and sensual good-bye kiss, and before Kevin could return the favor, Maria picked up her suitcase and left.

34

NEDRICK JONES had driven a cab for fifteen years and was amazed at how many people who rode in the back assumed that he was deaf.

On the taxi ride back to their hotel from the plastic surgeon's office where Fred had his broken nose reset, Sharon tried, without success, to convince him that going back to California and leaving his son behind was not a responsible thing to do.

Partly because of the Novocain shots in his nose but more because he felt that he had completely lost his authority as a father, Fred spoke softly.

"Sharon, a son who would break his father's nose no longer needs that father's help and guidance."

"Maybe," Sharon countered, "the help and guidance you gave him drove him to it. That was a stupid thing you did."

"That stupid thing, Sharon, is going to make your son see clearly what his little girlfriend was really after. Give him a couple of days and he'll be begging to come home."

"And if he doesn't *see clearly?*"

"Then J.J. flies down, slaps some handcuffs on him, and drags him home!"

"Nice going, Fred," she snapped. "First bribery and now kidnapping!"

At the mention of bribery and kidnapping the cabdriver's interest in his passengers perked up. But much to his disappointment, neither Sharon nor Fred said anything for a long while. Finally, Fred spoke.

"Sharon, I think we should talk. This may be the wrong time and the wrong place . . ."

146

Sharon focused on the gold drop earring in Nedrick Jones's right earlobe, drew a deep breath, and said, "Talk."

"Sharon, for the past few years I've felt that our marriage was stagnating."

"I guess our life hasn't been all that exciting, has it?"

"No, it hasn't, Sharon, and this being the case, I think we should talk about . . . my nose."

"What about your nose?"

"Don't be cute. The numbness is starting to wear off, and it hurts. You know that we're both talking about divorce, or aren't we?"

Sharon agreed that they were and without conviction brought up the idea of perhaps visiting a marriage counselor before taking the final step.

"Counseling at this juncture . . ." Fred said, pretending to consider the idea, "I don't know . . . You could ask Dr. Lowenthal what he thinks."

"I know what Dr. Lowenthal thinks," she lied. "He said that for certain couples counseling could be effective . . ."

". . . but not for us," Fred happily finished her thought. "Well, he should know."

"I would think so." Sharon smiled benignly.

Having agreed to the solution for their unhappiness, both Sharon and Fred breathed a his-and-her sigh of relief. Each was now free to pursue the woman they loved.

Nedrick Jones thought, The wife's not gonna believe me when I tell her how unemotional white folks are about splitting up.

Two blocks from their destination, Fred blurted out, "Sharon, is there some guy you're interested in?"

"No, Fred, there is no *guy* I'm interested in."

35

AFTER THEIR marriage-dissolving cab ride, the nastiness in Fred and Sharon's failed relationship had given way to pleasantness. This new attitude brought Sharon to a point where she could actually compliment Fred on his masterful, albeit expensive, handling of the "whole Kevin/Maria mess." In the middle of this atypical exchange, Kevin called to ask permission to come up and see his father. "Oh, my God!" Sharon shouted. "Yes, yes, come up, come up! I'm sure it'll be all right."

Kevin assured his mother that he had come to the hotel not to hit his father again but to apologize and to ask if they could buy a plane ticket for him. An ecstatic Sharon relayed Kevin's message to Fred, who grabbed the phone out of her hand. "You little shit," he shouted. "You busted my goddamned nose. Serves me right. I should never have taught you how to throw a jab. Come on up! We have a ticket for you!"

Kevin had no interest in hugging either of his monster parents, but until he could join Maria again, he would try to make the best of a disgusting situation.

When his mother opened the door, he used his broken hand as an excuse not to rush into her outstretched arms. Instead, he pecked her on the cheek. Sharon, concerned about Kevin's bandaged hand, asked how badly it was hurt. Kevin shrugged and said that it was just a couple of sprained knuckles. It was only after Fred boasted that his nose was broken in two places that Kevin announced proudly that he had actually fractured *four* of his fingers. Throwing in one extra fracture, he felt, might make his parents feel more guilt about the shitty thing they had done to him.

Kevin and his father, each sporting serious bandages, stood facing each other, Fred waiting for the apology Kevin had promised to make and Kevin trying to find a way to apologize for a punch his father richly deserved. He could find no way and settled for a simple and insincere "I'm sorry."

On the plane, Kevin sat directly across the aisle from his parents and thought, Something stranger than usual is going on with them. Why is my mother being so goddamned nice to my father? Why did she just tell the flight attendant to exchange his steak dinner for a steamed vegetable plate? Why would she keep asking him things like "Would you like another pillow?"

Kevin was convinced that his father was dying and his mother was making nice to ensure that she remained in his will.

Halfway through the trip, Kevin's parents became involved in a very serious and intimate conversation that he was sure pertained to him. Why else, he thought, would they keep sneaking looks at me?

Sharon, using Fred's argument that telling people upsetting things in a public place was insurance against overt antisocial behavior, prompted Fred to remind her that he got his nose busted using that same premise.

"This is quite different," she insisted. "He's not going to punch you for informing him of our decision. It's unfair to keep it from him."

"Would you have liked, Sharon, to have learned about *your* parents' divorce while flying in a plane?"

"Better than hearing it like I did, in nursery school from Rhoda Fields, whose blabbermouth father handled the case."

Fred finally relented, but preferred that Sharon tell Kevin. Sharon felt that psychologically it would be better if he heard it from his father. When neither could convince the other, they tossed a coin, and Sharon won.

Sharon was praying that Kevin not ask her any embarrassing questions. She knew that sooner or later Kevin would have to know that she had left his father for a woman, but until she was fully comfortable with the idea, she preferred not to tell him.

The seat next to Kevin was unoccupied. Sharon slipped into it and asked, "Am I disturbing you?"

"No, Mom," Kevin lied.

He would have preferred to ignore both parents, but he was curious to hear what his mother had to say. There was a very slight possibility that she and his father had reconsidered their position and were willing to admit they had been grossly unfair to him and Maria.

Sharon smiled sweetly and said, "Kevin, your father and I have come to a decision that you should know about."

My God, he thought, they're going to admit they were wrong!

"Kevin, you're father and I, after much soul searching, have agreed to separate."

Kevin shook his head and said, "Shit!"

"Shit? Is that all you have to say Kevin?"

Sharon was primed for some kind of emotional reaction from her son, but "Shit!" was not the one she expected or appreciated.

"Did my running off with Maria have anything to do with you two splitting?"

"It did not."

He was both disappointed and relieved to hear that he was not the cause. Disappointed because he would have liked to have been responsible for making his parents suffer for being totalitarians and relieved because, much as he despised them, he did not want it on his resume that he wrecked their marriage. To head off questions she was not ready to answer, Sharon volunteered, "These things happen." Using a wadded-up tissue to wipe phantom tears from her eyes, Sharon continued: "I still have great fondness for your father, and when you talk with him, I'm sure he'll tell you he feels similarly about me. It's really no one's fault. Couples sometimes just drift apart."

Kevin was a breath away from yelling, "Yeah, and sometimes couples are *torn* apart by people who don't give a shit for other people's feelings."

Sharon read the tears of rage in Kevin's eyes as being tears of empathy and tried to comfort him.

"Don't feel badly, Kevie baby, we'll get through it."

While she prattled on about how things will "work out for the best," Kevin, furious that his mother called him Kevie baby, calmed himself by thinking of ways he might make capital of his parents' breakup.

When Sharon paused, Kevin asked, "Will Dad be leaving the house?"

Sharon's face flushed. She was caught completely off guard. "Oh," she fumbled, "your father and I haven't worked out any of the physical details yet."

Kevin could sense his mother's discomfort, and it pleased him. He then asked the dreaded question that Sharon tried desperately to answer without sounding evasive.

"Mom, are either you or Dad involved with someone else?"

"Why do you ask, Kevin?"

"Isn't that why couples usually break up?

"I don't know about usually, but it's often the case."

"So, Mom, are you?"

"Am I what?"

"Involved?"

"What do you mean, 'involved'?"

"C'mon, Mom. Do you have another guy, and has Dad got a girl stashed somewhere?"

Sharon was happy to be able to answer Kevin's questions with total candor. "No, Kevin, I do not have 'another guy,' and as for your father, I think you'll have to ask him that question."

Kevin did not think it was necessary, and when Sharon asked why he thought that, Kevin brought the blush back to his mother's face. "Mom, does that Japanese teacher, uh, Ms. Yoshi, have anything to do with this?"

His mother stiffened, and he knew he had touched a raw nerve. Kevin enjoyed making his mother answer a question with a question, a technique he had used many times when their roles were reversed.

"Kevin, what do you mean, does Ms. Yoshi have anything to do with this?"

When Kevin saw his mother's eye twitch, he went in for the kill. "Dad is having a thing with this girl, isn't he?"

Sharon breathed a sigh of relief and demurely told her son that she was not aware of any *thing* going on between his father and Ms. Yoshi.

"Not aware? Did you ever take a good look at her, Mom? I'll

bet that ten seconds after that Japanese fox smiled at Dad, he started to pack his bags."

Sharon was dying to say, "I started packing mine in *five* seconds," but the mother in her took control and made her see that her son's losing both his girl and the use of his right hand in the same day were more than enough for him to handle. She assured him that until she and his father reached a final settlement, Kevin would continue to live in the house. Then, unthinkingly, Sharon added, "Dad and I will do everything we can not to disturb your life."

"Not to disturb my life?" Kevin exploded. "You and Dad just disturbed the shit out of my life, so what the fuck life are you talking about *not disturbing*?"

Without showing any emotion, Sharon unbuckled her seat belt, avoided the shocked stares of the passengers, and returned to her seat. Fred was thankful that the final exchange was directed at his wife. Had Kevin spoken to him that way, another nose would surely have been broken.

36

IT TOOK THE better part of three months and a program of supervised rehabilitation before Kevin regained the full use of his hand. His parents, who were now happily living apart and close to a divorce settlement, were delighted that Kevin agreed to let their personal trainer help with his rehab. While attending to the strengthening of his hand, Stoney Sheib prescribed a few extra exercises for Kevin's torso and in the process transformed a lithe, sinewy body into a powerful and muscular one.

Kevin had always thought that his parents' addiction to firming their bodies was one of their stupider indulgences, but now that he was going to be a father, he saw the sense to it. Living in a community where great gobs of money were thrown at people who have good bodies and good looks made him see the economic wisdom of trying to become one of those beautiful people.

As his mother had promised, Kevin continued to live in the old house. He had little contact with his father, who was racing around trying to raise money for a project involving the Japanese woman who, he was sure, had stolen his father from his mother. He was amazed how cavalierly his mother accepted this fact. The few times she had visited Kevin at the house, she seemed much too happy. He concluded that his mother had found Mr. Right.

Kevin spent a good deal of time in his room. It was the one place in the house where Maria's aura still existed. A day before his parents returned from Japan, she had carefully removed all traces of herself except for a small vial of perfume that had fallen into one of Kevin's shoes. When Kevin's longing for Maria was too strong to bear, he would sprinkle a drop or two of the flowery scent onto his pillow, close his eyes, and conjure up images of Maria.

For those first months after they were separated, Kevin and Maria would call each other two or three times a day. To keep his father from seeing the large phone charges and discovering that Maria and he were still in contact, Kevin would call from a phone booth, or Maria would call him when she knew his father was out.

To support herself, Maria had taken a job at McDonald's, working alongside her sister. At the end of the first week's work, Maria, shocked to find that she had used up half her salary talking to Kevin in California, insisted that they write letters every day and speak but once a week. Kevin had no fear that his father would discover Maria's letters; because Fred left the house hours before the mail arrived. Kevin would collect his precious letter every day and leave the rest of the mail in the box.

During the fifth month of their separation, two historic letters in the life of Kevin and Maria flew past each other at thirty thousand feet and were delivered on the same day. Kevin ripped open his letter and read:

My dearest, dearest, Kevin,

Te amo, te amo, te amo. I was asleep and dreaming that I was in your arms, and I felt you poke me. It was so real that when I opened my eyes, I was surprised to find that you were not in my bed. It happened again, a small, small poke. Kevin, my darling, our baby moved inside of my belly. See the smear on the top of the letter? That is where a tear of happiness fell from my eyes. Kevin, I cannot wait for our baby to poke you, and I cannot wait for you to kiss and hold his or her mother. I love you very, very much, my wonderful Kevin.

Your Maria

P.S. I am too excited to go to sleep, so I will give you some more good news. In my night school I got A's for English grammar, composition and one for oral comprehension. You know, when I started four months

ago, I did not know what oral comprehension was and
now look at me, I got an A in it. Te amo, Daddy.

At approximately the same time, Maria was reading:

I love you, Maria!
It happened! I did my first television commercial today.
It's for a new product, a combination shampoo, body
soap, and deodorant called Head to Toe. Boy, do I wish
you were here. I'm so clean you can eat off of me. I mean
it. I took about fifty showers. I got it right the first time,
but the director didn't like what the suds were doing. Just
for taking a shower and saying, "From Head to Toe, I'm
ready to go!," they're giving me fifteen hundred dollars.
It's weird. They pay me all that dinero to do something I
do every day for nothing. I want you in my bed right
now because I love you and I want you to smell me.

"King Kevin the Klean"

37

O N RETURNING to his office after a rest that his personal physician forced on him, Fred Cox found his staff happily occupied with the launching of his new project, *Hana and Her Great-grandmother*. A lively discussion ensued when Fred suggested the title. Quigley thought that *Hana and Her Great-grandmother* might be perceived as a satire on Woody Allen's *Hannah and Her Sisters* and pointed out that nobody had ever successfully done a satire on a satire.

Fred argued that it wasn't a satire, and Quigley argued back that the audience will think it is and stay away from the theaters in droves. Fred insisted that the public was not that smart. The title would stay, and he saw absolutely no need to defend his decision. He had thought of the title, Hana loved it, and that was enough for him.

When Battlin' Mike Zermat heard about *Hana G.* (as *Hana and Her Great-grandmother* became known in the industry), he immediately got in touch with Clarence Burroughs and offered to drop the unfair-practices suit he was about to file against Sky Productions if his client, Jason Hansen, was given the opportunity to write the screenplay for *Hana G.* Everyone in the office agreed that Jason had the talent for it, so an amount was agreed upon, and thanks to Marvin See, a deal was struck.

Fred's hardworking accountant had, that same week, made contact with Sebu Hayakawa. Mr. Hayakawa, of Hayakawa Industries, was "most eager" to become involved in a Hollywood film production, but not nearly as eager as Sky Productions was to become involved with Mr. Sebu Hayakawa. In the space of a few weeks, all the diverse elements were falling into place, and it appeared that Sky Productions would avoid having to face bankruptcy.

The final element fell in the afternoon that Fred arranged for Mr. Hayakawa to meet the mysterious, unknown actress who had been hired to play the title role. Mr. Hayakawa was too well bred to stare, but one look at Hana Yoshi made him forget his breeding.

Sebu Hayakawa had spent his life acquiring enough wealth to be listed in *Forbes* as the seventh-wealthiest man in the world.

Until he had accumulated his first billion, Sebu Hayakawa had given no thought of marriage or a family, but now that he was approaching his sixtieth year, he wished desperately to have a tall, handsome son who would inherit his money and someday live the life he had denied himself. Sebu was very aware of how he was perceived by women whose pleasures he had sought and bought all of his life. He knew that given his unprepossessing appearance, if he were to have any chance of siring a tall, handsome son, the woman he chose to be the child's mother must, of necessity, be tall, and to offset his inelegance, terribly, terribly beautiful. Hana Yoshi came into his life soon after he became obsessed with the idea of having an heir. Sebu, who thought of everything in terms of acquisitions, knew the moment Hana Yoshi walked into the room that he had to acquire her.

During a very special sushi lunch at Nobu's, Sebu Hayakawa, without the help of sake, became intoxicated by Hana's breathtaking beauty. That afternoon, a completely smitten billionaire agreed to take on the financing of *Hana and Her Great-grandmother*, with the secret hope that he would, ultimately, also take on Hana!

That evening, in Sharon's new two-bedroom rented condo, which miraculously had already been furnished to her taste, Hana described the meeting at Nobu's restaurant and how uncomfortable she was with Mr. Hayakawa's leering at her all through lunch. Sharon became very agitated as she listened to Hana speak. Sharon had heard enough horror stories about people like Mr. Hayakawa to guess what his agenda might be.

"Hana, darling," Sharon warned, "Mr. Leery-face doesn't

just want to get into the movies, he wants to get into your panties."

"Oh, I know"—Hana laughed—"but for the good of the project, I may let him get into my panties . . ." Before Sharon could voice her displeasure, Hana continued with her little tease, ". . . but I will not be in them. Sharon, you know that I never wear panties."

Sharon would not be placated. She wanted to hear from Hana exactly how she planned to handle this letching billionaire, and Hana told her.

"I will handle him the same way I handle the president of Sky Productions and most men who find me irresistible. I promise much," she chided, "but I deliver little."

"Hana," Sharon reminded her, "these are grown men you're dealing with. How long do you think they'll accept being teased?"

"I hope," Hana said, "until the movie is finished and we have the money to pay for our honeymoon in Hawaii!"

Hana hugged Sharon and danced her around the dining-room table, laughing a little too hard for Sharon's peace of mind.

Two or three times a week, Hana would lunch with Fred Cox either at Nobu's or at her home, where she would prepare very elaborate meals. To show her concern for his health, she learned how to make cholesterol-free omelets. Fred always left these lunches feeling disappointed and frustrated. He expected "desserts" other than the delicate fruit tarts that Hana offered. Fred's subtle advances ("Hana, why don't we screw the dessert, get naked, and jump into the Jacuzzi!") were now being rebuffed. Hana explained that their relationship was "entering a new phase."

"I am," she lied, "just as anxious for your body as you are for mine, but this cannot be until certain things happen."

Fred was desperate for those "certain things" to happen and asked what he could do to bring that about. Hana explained that time would make it happen. She then spoke honestly of her deep affection and respect for Mrs. Cox and why she could not develop with him "the kind of exciting and full relationship" they both wanted until he was "emotionally and legally free" of his commitment to Mrs. Cox. She stressed "legally" very hard to avoid giving Fred room to argue. Hana would allow Fred to kiss her amorously, but only at the door when they were saying good night. As soon as she felt his penis growing, she would pull away and make arrangements for their next lunch date.

38

THERE WAS a serious financial crisis swirling around the production of *Hana and Her Great-grandmother*, and solely responsible for the crisis was Sebu Hayakawa. His overpowering need to capture the heart and body of the film's leading lady and her reluctance to give herself to the billionaire benefactor forced Mr. Hayakawa to declare his intention of pulling out of the project unless, as he put it, "I am treated with proper respect."

Hana Yoshi was well aware that she held the life or death of this project in her hands. For longer than she thought was possible, she held at bay the two principle players who lusted after her. Each night, when she had fended off one of them, she would call Sharon and boast that she was still a "virgin."

Sharon, who appeared to accept it all lightheartedly, was, in actuality, steaming. She had not envisioned that this arrangement would go on as long as it had. The actual production of the film was months away, and Sharon would not have been at all unhappy if Sebu Hayakawa did pull his money out of the production.

Mr. Hayakawa's threat was not an idle one. At a private breakfast meeting with Fred Cox, he stated his case clearly. "If Ms. Yoshi feels I am not deserving of her, then I feel this movie is not deserving of my money. I will wait one more day for this situation to change!"

Ten minutes later, Fred Cox called Hana into his office and had one of the most uncomfortable meetings of his life.

"Hana," he began apologetically, picturing himself playing a pimp in a bad movie, "I suppose you're wondering why I asked you here this morning."

Hana shrugged and shook her head.

"Hana, my dear"—Fred fumbled as he tried to find an inoffensive way of asking a woman to be a prostitute for a night—"you might have heard it before but . . . our business—that is, the business I am in—which you have recently become a part of, can sometimes become a . . . how shall I put it . . . a dirty business. I guess you know what I'm getting at."

Hana knew exactly what he was getting at but enjoyed watching the man squirm and said naïvely that she had no idea. If it had been some bimbo starlet, Fred would have had no difficulty telling her that she would have to sleep with so-and-so if she wanted the job. He thought, Here I am, about to ask the woman whom I hope to marry to give that exquisite body of hers to that sweaty son-of-a-bitch banker whose father probably bombed Pearl Harbor.

"Hana, Mr. Hayakawa has come to me and—I don't know how to put this without embarrassing myself—and you . . ." Fred sucked in some air, wiped his wet palms with his pocket handkerchief, and continued: ". . . and he's threatened to withdraw his backing from our project unless certain terms are met. Oh, shit, I'm not going to beat about the bush. What he's asking is horrible, and I would never approach you with his suggestion if this project were mine alone, but it's as much yours as it is mine. In short, Hana, this project is history unless you agree to go to bed with the son of a bitch. There, I've said it, and I'm sorry, but that's the disgusting bottom line."

Hana knew just what she was going to do but would not volunteer the information.

"Fred, darling, this is so demeaning. As much as I want my great-grandmother's story to be told, I cannot do what this terrible man is asking. I would feel as my great-grandmother must have felt so many years ago."

"I understand completely," Fred said, trying to sound sympathetic, "and if you want me to, I will convey your decision to Mr. Sleaze later this afternoon, unless—"

"Unless what? Do you have an idea how we may continue without my having to give myself to Mr. Hayakawa?"

Fred admitted that he did not but added how devastated he was at the thought of losing the opportunity to make an important movie that had a good chance to be nominated for an

Academy Award. Hana then asked if it were possible to find another financier. Fred said that he would sure as hell give it a shot, but given the state of the industry and the tight money situation, he did not hold out much hope.

"How would you feel if I were to accept Mr. Hayakawa's offer?" Hana finally asked.

Fred's dilemma was palpable, and he embarrassed himself by hesitating too long. "I would feel cheap and horrible."

For a long while, Hana contemplated her nails. When finally she spoke, it was quietly and deliberately, and by the time she had finished, she had convinced herself and Fred that the road she had chosen to travel benefited the people she cared about most. Hana's arguments were compelling. With complete candor, she admitted to having had many sexual encounters in her life that were as meaningless as the one she now considered having with Mr. Hayakawa. She dared to invoke for Fred the memory of their first meeting.

"That afternoon when I invited you into my Jacuzzi," she admitted, "had no real emotional meaning for me. I did not know you as I do now, and I did it then for much less of a reason than I have now.

"I'll be honest. I became involved with you because you are an important producer who I felt might help me to achieve my goal. I want to work in films and someday, possibly, to direct." Hana read the look of deep disappointment in Fred's face and quickly added, "My original plan became less important the more I came to know you. I don't think I can ever repay you for giving me the opportunity to expose the horrors that were visited upon my great-grandmother by the men of an ugly, uncaring, sexist society."

Fred could not believe what he had heard. It all made such fucking good sense, he thought. Who am I to deny the girl I hope someday to make my wife the chance to strike a blow against all the exploiting pimps of the world? It was all Fred could do to keep from applauding. "Hana dear," he said taking her hand, "I am extremely touched by your honesty and I am eternally grateful to you for the selfless act you have volunteered to perform. My only fear is that your involvement with Mr. Hayakawa might somehow change how you feel about me."

"Fred," she assured him, "the feelings I have for you could never change. If anything, they are bound to become even stronger."

On her drive to Sharon's house that night, Hana debated how best to tell her friend that she had volunteered to rescue Sky Productions from bankruptcy.

Recalling how upset Sharon had been when she reported that Fred was making sexual demands on her, Hana concluded that no purpose would be served by telling Sharon about her upcoming involvement with Sebu Hayakawa.

39

Until she had fallen in love with Sharon, Hana Yoshi had never had any restraints on her sexual conduct. Tonight, however, she had prepared herself to deal decisively with any unusual or kinky requests that Mr. Hayakawa might make. She vowed to walk out of his apartment if she considered them to be too aberrant or humiliating, even if it meant losing his financial backing for the movie.

As Hana stepped off the hotel elevator and into Sebu's opulent suite, she could never, in her wildest imagination, guess what Mr. Sebu Hayakawa had planned for her that night. She had expected to find her date in pajamas and chaffing at the bit, but here he was, wearing a tuxedo and reflecting the soft, candlelit living room in his black patent leather shoes and his shiny black hair. Sebu Hayakawa then did something few Japanese gentlemen do. He kissed Hana's hand and told her, in Japanese, how honored he was that she had accepted his invitation to spend the night with him.

For the next hour, while they were served champagne and hors d'oeuvres by a beautifully costumed geisha, Sebu asked nothing of Hana but that she allow him to stare at her.

At dinner, Hana had her first experience eating of the infamous fugu fish. For the occasion, Sebu had flown in from Japan both the fugu and his own personal master sushi chef, Siduru, the only chef that Sebu trusted to slice up a fugu fish properly. So addicted was Sebu to the pleasures of dining on fugu that twice a month he was willing to take the small risk to his life. Hana was not sure whether it was the paper-thin slices of fugu she had eaten or the anticipation of what Sebu was going to suggest after dinner that made her heart race and her head spin. When the thumping in her chest became worrisome, she reported it to Sebu, who laughed and said, "Only people who are pure of heart react this way when they eat fugu, but not to worry, you will recover."

By the time dinner was over, Hana's heart rate returned to normal. Later, while sitting in the drawing room sipping plum brandy, Sebu, who had been very charming and jocular all through dinner, suddenly turned serious. He outlined precisely what his plans were for the remainder of the evening. He spoke first of his desire to have a male heir and candidly admitted that he did not expect that she would be immediately receptive to the role he wished her to play, but he pleaded that she not make up her mind until she heard all he had to say. Hana, with an almost imperceptible nod of her head, indicated that she was receptive to his continuing. Sebu explained to Hana that he had no desire to take unto himself a wife but admitted to being so taken with her beauty and bearing that he would not rule out the possibility of someday asking for her hand.

"Perhaps," he conjectured, "after you have birthed a baby, you will have thoughts other than the ones that you are now having."

Sebu then informed Hana what to expect for her efforts in providing him with a son and heir. For each unsuccessful attempt at becoming pregnant, he guaranteed she would receive, in advance, a quarter of a million dollars. If she were to become pregnant and present him with a daughter, she would receive a million dollars; if she presented him with a son, she would receive two million. If, after she had produced a daughter and wished to continue the arrangement until a son was born, the amounts would increase by a million with each birth. If, at any time during their contract, Hana wished to discontinue their relationship, she would be free to do so without penalty of losing any of the money she had already earned.

Hana sat dumbfounded as she listened to the outlandish offer being made by a man who, on first meeting, she considered to be offensively unattractive. With each increase he offered, his unattractiveness decreased proportionately. She calculated that she might make many millions before she ever became pregnant. Never having tried, she wondered for a moment whether or not she could bear a child.

Hana was in the process of accepting Sebu's extremely generous offer when he interrupted. "Of course, Miss Yoshi, the deal is not binding until you submit to a blood test and it is determined that you are free of the AIDS virus."

"I will not, Mr. Hayakawa, submit myself to such a test," she said sharply, "unless you do likewise."

Sebu was at first offended by her counterrequest, but after considering it, he concluded that she was a woman of rare courage and intelligence. It was at that moment he decided that he would do anything to keep this woman in his life permanently. He smiled, bowed, and agreed that he would be happy to do as she wished. Hana felt relieved on two counts: one, that she would be in no danger of becoming infected by a man who, in his lifetime, must have had his share of prostitutes; secondly, that she would not have to bed down with him until the results of the blood tests were known, which would take at least a day. During that time, she might reevaluate her decision to accept what had to be the most bizarre offer ever made by a man to a woman.

The surprises continued. Not only had Sebu flown in a master fugu chef from Tokyo; he had also arranged that for a large donation, an AIDS research fund would set up a minilab in his library. A doctor and two technicians were now waiting to draw and evaluate her blood. Hana suddenly felt that she was Alice and had fallen into a Wonderland in which a short Japanese Mad Hatter had taken charge of her life. She thought of Sharon, who she imagined was lying awake and waiting to hear a description of her evening with Sebu. Hana was brought back to the insane reality when a white-coated young physician, Dr. Melton Fine, announced that he was ready to proceed with the testing. Sebu graciously volunteered to have his blood drawn first. Everyone except Sebu Hayakawa was aware of the utter ridiculousness of conducting after-dinner AIDS tests in the penthouse of a high-rise hotel.

At five o'clock that morning, a very weary and annoyed young doctor announced, "Negative on both of you. You can go about your business."

Ordinarily, Sebu would have reacted to this rudeness by having the doctor's license revoked, but he was so relieved to learn that he was HIV-negative that he accepted it as a wonderful suggestion.

As Hana lay under the pumping, sweating, grunting flesh-ball of a man, she told him in answering grunts and in whispered Japanese that he was pleasuring her to the skies. Although she was in no way enjoying the interlude, Hana realized that it was not nearly as appalling as she had imagined it would be. Perhaps it was the fugu or the two hundred and fifty thousand dollars she was earning for six and a half minutes of mental and physical discomfort. She managed to keep the mental anguish to a minimum by conjuring up a memory of Sharon. Hana's reverie was shattered by elephant-like trumpeting that exploded from her partner as he climaxed. For the money he was paying, Hana charitably gave his male ego a boost by matching him bellow for bellow and shudder for shudder, simulating what he believed was a mutually shared orgasm.

The smile on Sebu's face and the gracious manner with which he presented her with his personal check for a quarter of a million dollars made Hana know that Sebu Hayakawa approved of her performance that night. As Hana dressed to leave, Sebu noted that it was stockings and not panty hose that Hana, with a dancer's grace, was easing onto her long, exciting legs. Hana was aware of Sebu's eyes on her as she wondered how many times she would have to perform before she became pregnant. Sebu, who appeared to be reading her mind, said, "My dear, I am leaving for Australia tomorrow morning, and I thought, to increase the odds of your becoming pregnant, if it is not disagreeable to you, I would like to repeat what we have just done. Of course, there would be no remuneration for this act except my humble gratitude."

Sebu, sensing Hana's disinterest, asked, "Did you not enjoy making love with me?"

"Oh I did," she lied. "I enjoyed it very much, but the hour is late and I am tired . . . blissfully tired and for that I thank you."

Reluctantly, he accepted her rejection and told her that he would return from Australia in two weeks, adding, "If, at that time, you have not had a positive response from our alliance, I will require that you be tested for fertility, and if all is as I pray it will be, we can continue to create my heir."

As they said their good-nights, Sebu presented Hana with a six-carat emerald brooch as a token of his appreciation.

Hana stretched out in the backseat of Sebu Hayakawa's limousine and examined her exquisitely cut green gem, wondering if Sebu would have presented her with a "larger token" of his appreciation had she bothered to choreograph for him a second, simulated double orgasm. Hana was dying to sleep in Sharon's bed that night and share with her the bizarre events of the evening but knew that she could never make Sharon understand why she had accepted Sebu's proposal. How could she? She herself could not quite accept what she had done. Tired as she was, Hana knew that her first priority that morning, after opening a new bank account, was to decide what, and how much, she could tell Sharon.

As she listened to the quiet hum of the car's motor, Hana conceded that she had made herself available to Sebu to obtain just one thing: untold wealth! The only kind of wealth that brought with it the power to defy convention. As she caressed her precious emerald, she vowed that she would amass enough of Sebu's untold wealth to one day allow Sharon and herself to live, openly and proudly, as a married lesbian couple. With that comforting thought, Hana closed her eyes and fell soundly asleep on the plush headrest of Sebu Hayakawa's Rolls-Royce limousine.

Fred, consumed with a rich blend of curiosity and jealousy, was searching for a diplomatic way of calling Hana and asking for a blow-by-blow description of her evening with Mr. Hayakawa. At ten o'clock that morning, Marvin See called with the news that $10 million had been deposited by Sebu Hayakawa into Sky Productions' account. Fred assumed correctly that the night before, in the penthouse of the Sanyito, Hayakawa Industries' new high-rise luxury hotel in downtown Los Angeles, Hana Yoshi had hit a bases-loaded home run.

_40_

T WO DAYS before Sebu returned from Australia, Hana was disappointed to discover that for the very first time in her life she had missed her period. She had been hoping to earn many more millions before becoming pregnant and for a split second wondered if there was some uncomplicated way to terminate the pregnancy. On learning of Hana's pregnancy, Sebu was both thrilled and disappointed. Thrilled to discover that he had the ability to impregnate Hana but disappointed to have lost the opportunity to make love with her again. Sebu's high moral standards would not allow him to pay to have sex with the future mother of his child while she was in a family way. Were he to treat the mother as a common whore, it would dishonor the growing fetus and the father who had conceived it. If, however, Hana should fall in love with him (a prospect for which he held little hope) and request that he make love to her without an exchange of money, then and only then would he do so. Fortunately for Hana, Sebu did not think it demeaning to the mother-to-be to present her with a four-carat diamond ring as another token of his esteem and appreciation. Hana argued, weakly, that he was being much too generous, but Sebu convinced her that her beauty deserved such generosity. For the next two months, Hana paid biweekly visits to her safety deposit box to place in it the latest of the many, many tokens of appreciation that Sebu Hayakawa insisted she de·served.

Hana knew, of course, that sooner or later she would have to inform Sharon of her pregnancy but could think of no gentle way to break the news.

How could I put it? she thought. "Sharon, darling, I have wonderful news. Because of a business arrangement I just made with Sebu Hayakawa, you and I are going to have all the things that we have ever dreamt about. Mr. Hayakawa is giving me tremendous amounts of money and jewels, and all I have to give him is the temporary use of my body to grow himself an heir. Isn't that wonderful?"

By the fourth month of her pregnancy she still had not found the right words, or the courage, to inform Sharon of her condition. Hana, who had always walked around in the nude, now complained of drafts and took to covering her slightly distended belly by wearing loose-fitting, beltless robes. No one but Sebu and her obstetrician knew of Hana's condition, and Hana intended to keep it that way. To further delay the inevitable, Hana volunteered to travel to Japan with the film's production staff and act as their interpreter while they did their preliminary location scouting.

The actual filming of the movie was six months off, and Hana planned to tell everyone that she would remain in Japan until the filming started, writing a book of memoirs. In truth, Hana had accepted an invitation to spend these last months of her pregnancy living in Sebu Hayakawa's beautiful home on Hakone Lake and was actually going to try and write something. She had hoped that in committing to paper the complete, uncensored story of her duplicitous life, which would include the improbable last three chapters—Fred, Sharon, and Sebu—she might unburden herself of the overwhelming guilt and self-doubt she had developed since learning that she was to be a mother.

When told of Hana's plans, Sharon became depressed, and the expensive Fendi pocketbook and silk shawls that Hana showered on her, instead of pleasing her, made her even more despondent. Sharon looked upon them as parting gifts. She thought, My little friend's not going to Japan to write any damned book; she's going there to dump me!

_41_

T HE PANIC IN Sharon's voice was so compelling that Dr. Lowenthal, who was usually unbending when it came to rearranging his rigid schedule, delayed a luncheon appointment with his young fiancée to accommodate his near hysterical patient.

An ashen-faced Sharon entered the doctor's comfortable book-lined office and without even saying hello started to unburden herself of the terrible secret she had kept hidden since she was thirteen years old. Speaking very rapidly, Sharon asked the doctor if he thought that a recurring dream that haunted her all her teenage years might have been prophetic. Using his most fatherly tone, Dr. Lowenthal asked to hear the dream. Sharon hesitated and then told how, when she was about thirteen, she dreamed she was lying naked on a red satin sheet next to Marilyn Monroe, who was also nude, and both were posing as Marilyn did for her famous calendar photograph.

"We really weren't doing anything bad, just sort of playing a game, like seeing how close our nipples could come together without touching. I had that dream a lot of times, and our nipples never touched, never ever, so I didn't think that there was anything wrong with me."

"And do you now think," Dr. Lowenthal asked gently, "that there *is* something 'wrong' with you?"

"I don't *think*, I *know*! I'm a mess! A fucking mess!"

Dr. Lowenthal had never before seen Mrs. Cox so deeply emotional and had never heard her use the word "fucking," even when referring to the sex act. He concluded that his

171

patient had finally, after months of marking time, made a most important breakthrough in her therapy. Although he thought he had a pretty clear understanding of what his patient had broken through to, he wanted to hear it from Mrs. Cox's lips.

"Mrs. Cox," he prodded gently, "why did you say that you're 'a fucking mess'?"

"Because I am!" was all that Sharon would volunteer.

Dr. Lowenthal decided to remain silent and wait for his patient to explain the revelation that she seemed to think she had had about herself. Sharon snatched three tissues from the Kleenex box that the doctor kept on his desk. She appreciated that Dr. Lowenthal always had Kleenex for his patients rather than one of the cheaper, non-pop-up brands. It somehow comforted her. She blew her nose into the three tissues and, with her red-rimmed eyes, looked straight into the doctor's sleepy blue ones. "Dr. Lowenthal, I'm a lesbian!"

Sharon knew well enough of Dr. Lowenthal's low-key approach and did not expect his jaw to drop, but she did expect a little more than a single legato blink of the eye, which, for all she knew, was natural and not a reaction to what she had just confessed. To give himself time to think of an appropriate response, Dr. Lowenthal slowly took off his gold-frame spectacles, wiped them carefully with a tissue, and smiled. "Mrs. Cox, having recurring dreams about Marilyn Monroe when you were a teenager may mean something quite, quite different."

Sharon felt like shouting her rebuttal but instead adopted an even more saccharine tone than Dr. Lowenthal's.

"How about if I had glorious, multiorgasmic sex dozens and dozens of times with a beautiful Asian woman and felt for her a love that I have never felt before for my husband or any other man? Would that mean something 'quite, quite, different,' too?"

Dr. Lowenthal put his glasses back on, nodded his head thoughtfully, and asked, "Did you dream this?" When Sharon cried, "I lived it!" Dr. Lowenthal produced the longest, most significant-sounding "Hmmmmmm" of his psychiatric career.

"Mrs. Cox," he said simply, "this is an extremely significant piece of knowledge you have discovered about yourself, but I'm afraid we'll have to stop now and continue this Thursday at your regular session."

Dr. Lowenthal, seeing Sharon's eyes pop and the blood drain from her face, sought to soothe her by explaining that he had stolen these twelve minutes for her from a most important appointment that he now had to keep.

"Mrs. Cox," he said as he ushered her to the door, "you have learned a very, very positive thing about yourself, and because of this dramatic breakthrough you can look forward to a significant acceleration of the therapeutic process."

Sharon, who had been feeling completely abandoned by everyone in her life who meant anything to her, now felt the ultimate abandonment—by the man to whom she had paid a small fortune to be her trusted friend and ally. Seething with frustration and anger, Sharon managed a crazy, twisted smile and said, "Thank you so very, very much for all your help and understanding!" Then, on an impulse, she turned and brought her knee forcefully into her doctor's unprotected groin.

As she ran from the scene, she could hear Dr. Lowenthal's constricted voice shout, "Ms. Marsh . . . Get me an ice pack and then cancel my lunch appointment."

In his long career treating repressed patients, Dr. Lowenthal had never experienced a more dramatic or painful break-through.

42

THE BLOW Sharon delivered to her psychiatrist's groin brought her only temporary relief from the pain she was feeling at the thought of losing Hana. As she drove home from her frustrating minisession with Dr. Lowenthal, she thought, Sharon, you're an idiot! How could you be so fucking naïve to believe that someone who really loves you could leave you for six months? Sure, she gave me all those lovely, expensive gifts because she's guilty about something. Fred used to do the same damned thing, only he did it with flowers and toilet water, and where the hell is she getting all that money from? She sure didn't make it teaching Japanese.

Sharon had meant to drive to her new home but suddenly found herself a mile or so from her old home in Bel Air. Fred had been on her mind the night before, and here she was, thinking about him again. Why? she asked herself. I know why. Hana and Fred are having a thing. How could I be so blind? The first time he laid eyes on her, he almost tripped over his tongue. I'll bet he's going to be in Japan while she's writing her memoirs. Sharon slowed the car as an image of a supersize box of tampons suddenly popped into her head. She had seen that box sitting on a shelf in Hana's bathroom for two months—unopened!

"Oh, my God! She's pregnant!"

Sharon quickly replayed in her mind all the small, seemingly unimportant things that led her to this inescapable conclusion. That rat, she thought. She hasn't complained about having PMS for months now. No wonder she didn't open that box. And the three breakfast dates she canceled? Why? Morning sickness. Of course! Sharon kept piling on evidence. Was it her imagination, or in the last month didn't Hana's face and skin seem to be more beautiful and glowing than ever? And why those flowing robes she insists on wearing because of nonexistent drafts?

Sharon pulled her car into the driveway of her old house and realized that she had driven here looking for the confrontation with her husband that they should have had months ago. She looked at her watch and knew that Fred would not be coming home for at least two hours, if he was coming home at all.

Sharon looked up at the white two-story colonial house and was surprised at how unemotional she was on seeing it again. She sighed as she remembered how much of herself she had invested in it and how once she had thought of it as the fulfillment of her life's dream. Her life had changed, and her dreams, except for the ones she had for her son, now centered on securing a life with Hana. Sharon felt that if she did not immediately confront Fred, she would explode.

With the front door key that she kept on her key ring, Sharon let herself into her old house and used the powder-room phone to call Fred's office. Elspeth answered and attempted to tell Sharon that Fred was in a production meeting, but Sharon cut her off and said there was a dire emergency at the house and that it was imperative that he come home immediately. To emphasize the seriousness of the situation, Sharon violently slammed the phone down before Elspeth could ask what the problem was.

When Fred arrived at his home fifteen minutes later and saw Sharon's car in the driveway, he assumed that some disaster had struck their son. With no fire trucks or ambulances parked there, Fred wondered what the disaster could possibly be. Kevin had been giving his father a hard time lately. He did everything he was asked to do, but with an ugly sneer on his face. His pat response to anything his father would say was, "Whatever you say, Dad."

It was only a matter of time, Fred felt, before Kevin erupted and either punched him in the face again or put an ice pick through his heart. He had actually called Sharon and warned her to expect some dramatic or violent act from their much too obliging, constantly sneering son.

Before Fred could get his key into the lock, the front door opened. "Hello," Sharon said solemly. Fred felt uneasy about being invited into his own house by a woman who seemed so different from the one he had lived with for nineteen years. Her hair was shorter and no longer the subtle shade of their former golden retriever, Nougat.

Sharon knew that if she did not say immediately what she had come to say, she would lose the courage to do so. Fred made it a little easier by being unfriendly.

"Sharon, I just ran out of a production meeting. Now, what's the dire emergency?"

"Hana Yoshi."

Fred's face turned white. Concluding that some terrible accident had befallen his star, he asked, "What happened to her?"

"You . . . you happened to her."

"What the hell are you talking about?"

"I'm talking about the affair you're having with Hana!"

"You know, Sharon, we're legally separated. "Whatever is or is not going on between Hana and me is none of your damned business."

"It is my damned business, Fred, and I'll tell you why if you just tell me whether or not you've ever slept with Hana."

Fred was so proud that he had slept with her that he readily admitted it. Sharon suddenly felt relieved. She had been secretly hoping that it was Fred and not some stranger.

"Fred," she said, sighing, "I suppose you expect me to congratulate you."

"Why would I expect you to congratulate me for sleeping with Hana?"

Kevin, coming home from school early after ditching a lecture on safe sex, steered his bicycle into the driveway and on discovering his mother's and father's cars parked there, turned and coasted around to the back of the house. He had absolutely no interest in seeing or talking to either of his parents but was curious to know what they might be discussing. Whatever it was, he knew that it could have some impact on his life. He sneaked up the back stairs, raced down the bedroom corridor, and secreted himself at his listening post on the landing of the front hall stairway. He had missed very little of his parents' conversation because it had been interrupted by a phone call from Elspeth. Kevin heard the tail end of the phone conversation.

"Elspeth, just listen to me, will ya?" Fred barked. "Tell Mr. Hayakawa that I'll be at his office in thirty minutes. Yes, yes, everything is fine here. Just a little family business that we're about to wrap up."

In years past, Sharon would have been thrilled to know that her husband was meeting with a billionaire. But now it was just an annoying interruption, and as soon as Fred hung up, Sharon continued:

"I was congratulating you, Fred, not for sleeping with Hana but for making her pregnant."

From the look of utter confusion on his face, it was obvious to Sharon that Fred was unaware of Hana's pregnancy.

"Well," Sharon mumbled angrily, "it seems that she hasn't told *anyone* of her condition."

Kevin was shocked and amused. Finally, he and his father had something in common. Both were making babies and were upsetting the shit out of his mother.

"Sharon, if Hana is pregnant and I am the father, that's none of your business. And why did you call my office and say that there's a dire emergency at home? Unless you're thinking of trying to change the settlement, this is my home, and I'd appreciate your not barging into it whenever—"

Before he could finish, Sharon tossed her key angrily onto the glass coffee table.

"You know you have no moral or legal right to meddle in my private life, Sharon, but since you're here, I think I should tell you that *if* Hana is pregnant with my child, and I hope to hell she is, I would ask Hana to marry me in a minute and move right into this house with me."

While Fred had been making his big declaration of intent, his mind was trying to recall the circumstances under which he could have impregnated Hana. They had not been together for months now, and most of their sexual encounters had been oral or masturbatory. He tried to recall the times that they had had the kind of sex that would produce a child. He could recall only two, and each time Hana insisted he wear the condom she provided. Still, he preferred to think, one of those condoms could have been defective. He pushed from his mind any thought that Hana might have been with another man by remembering J.J.'s comforting words: "You are the only man in Ms. Yoshi's life."

Sharon listened patiently while Fred stated his case, one that surprised and unnerved her. She had no idea of the depth of Fred's feelings for Hana and wondered now if Hana was aware of them. If she was, why had she not shared that information with her?

"Fred," Sharon offered when he had finished, "I don't think there's much chance that Hana will accept your marriage proposal or move in here with you."

"Sharon, what the hell makes you such an expert on what Hana wants or does not want."

Not wanting to miss a single word of this exchange, Kevin hunkered down and put his ear between the white enamel posts of the banister.

"For one thing, Fred, she hates the decor in this house. And yes, Fred, she knows that I decorated it."

"Sharon," Fred countered coolly, "I thank you for telling me all this. When the time comes, I'll tell Hana that she has my permission to change the decor."

"And," Sharon asked sweetly, "will you also give her your permission to change her sexual preference?"

Kevin grabbed his forehead and pressed it hard.

Fred was livid. "Sharon, that is the lowest! What the hell are you trying to do?"

"I am trying, Fred, to tell you that Hana is a lesbian, and because she is, there is little chance that she will marry you or any other man."

Kevin cupped his face in his hands and let out a silent scream. Fred swallowed hard as he pondered his next question. Finally, he got up the courage to ask, "How the hell can she be a lesbian? I've slept with her dozens of times."

"And so have I, Freddie, so have I!"

Fred sank into a chair as Kevin sprung to his feet. Neither Fred nor his eavesdropping son were ready for Sharon's next pronouncement.

"Hana and I are planning to be married."

Fred was speechless, but Kevin, who had all kinds of anger

boiling in him, had much to say. He darted out onto the landing and shouted, "Boy, what an idiot I was to listen to you two!"

Fred and Sharon almost jumped out of their lives when they heard the voice of their son roaring down the stairwell. Fred, attempting vainly to act the father, asked, as sternly as a man who feared a second heart attack could, "Damn it, Kevin, have you been eavesdropping?"

"And lucky I did or I would never have known that my mother and father are both screwing the same woman. You know, you're both so full of shit!"

Sharon was not ready for this to happen, certainly not this way. Kevin, choking back tears, continued to attack.

"How the hell can you tell me how I should live my life when you don't know how to live yours! You're both sick!"

Kevin turned and ran back up the stairway. He was halfway down the hall to his room when he heard his mother shouting.

"Kevin! You come back and apologize! You have no right to speak to me that way."

Fred started up the stairway but knew that all he would get from Kevin would be more truth and abuse, and so he retreated back into the living room.

Fred could not fully absorb the fact that the woman who had shared his bed for almost nineteen years was a homosexual. How could it be? Sharon looked, sounded, and behaved as femininely as any heterosexual woman he had ever known. As he looked at the back of her newly bobbed hair, he did not see a trace of the lesbian that she admitted to be. Without turning toward him, Sharon asked softly, "What are you planning to do?"

"About what?" Fred asked innocently, his head spinning.

"About the child, of course." We have to talk about that, don't you think?"

"Sharon, it would behoove you to stop thinking of Kevin as a child but as an adult—a heartless one but an adult nevertheless."

"I am *not* talking about Kevin," she said disbelievingly. "I was referring to the child that Hana is carrying."

Fred shook his head violently, as if trying to clear from it all unfocused thoughts. He then assured Sharon that if there was such a child, it was not any of her business.

"Hana is very much my business," Sharon reminded him, "and anyone she may be carrying."

"Right now," Fred said, looking at his watch, "Kevin is your business, and if you'd like to talk with him, please do so; otherwise, you're free to leave."

Sharon considered going to her son, but before she could decide whether she was strong enough to go through another painful scene, Fred announced that he was leaving for an important meeting. Feeling that someone should talk to Kevin, Sharon volunteered to do so. Fred nodded and fled. As he drove off to Sebu Hayakawa's office, he wondered what other small surprises the Gods had planned for him that day.

Sharon stared at the family oil portrait hanging slighty askew above the fireplace and fought off her natural urge to straighten it. She studied the phony smile on Kevin's face and remembered the day Signor Davincicola had them pose for the colored Polaroids and how five-year-old Kevin refused to smile. After much cajoling, threatening, and the offering of bribes, Signor Davincicola had to settle for Kevin gnashing his teeth. The artist promised that as long as he could see the teeth, he would be able to "paint on a real, good, natural smile around them."

Sharon looked from the painting to the stairway and realized that if, when Kevin was five, she was not able to convince him that it was fun to pose for a portrait, how much chance did she have now to convince him that he should be happy his mother found true love with another woman. Sharon walked to the foot of the stairs and fulfilled her promise to talk to Kevin by shouting up the stairwell, "Kevin, I hope you can hear me. I'll call you when we're all a little less emotional."

Kevin, who was packing his bags, heard everything his mother said except "I love you, Kevin," which she whispered as she left the house.

Kevin finished packing his bags, then went to his set of the *World Book of Knowledge*, a present he had received on his tenth birthday and had used but once to look up the lifetime batting average of Eddie Murray. When he found that it wasn't listed, he vowed never to use the stupid books again. And he didn't, until a few months ago, when he hid all his valuables between its pages. Kevin gathered up his airline ticket and all the fifty- and hundred-dollar bills he had stashed there and phoned for a taxi. While he waited, he considered the pros and cons of leaving a note for his parents and concluded that it would be in his best interest to do so. He wrote:

Dad,

Please do not sic your private eye on me again. I will write or call soon to let you know where I am. Maybe by that time you and Mom will know more about where you are, too . . . and I'm not being sarcastic. I'm sorry I yelled at you and Mom, and I know if I stayed here, I might do it again, and I don't want to. Tell Mom that I want to think about what she told us about herself before I write her. If any checks come in from my Head to Toe commercials, hold them until I send you an address.

Kevin tortured for a bit about how to end his letter and decided that signing it "Love, Kevin" did not compromise his feelings or his integrity.

43

SHARON FINGERED her car phone nervously and finally tapped in Hana's number. Fearing that Hana might not be receptive to a visit, she hung up before it rang. She needed desperately to hear Hana say that it was stupid of her to deduce from an unopened box of tampons that someone was pregnant. After the abuse heaped on her by her only child, Sharon needed an open-armed welcome and a reassuring hug from someone who loved her. Sharon was exuberant when she saw Hana's Bentley in the driveway, so exuberant that she crashed into the car's rear bumper loudly enough to bring Hana to her bedroom window.

The sound of bumpers bumping and the urgency with which Sharon strode from her car to the front door informed Hana of Sharon's state. Hana, who was about to shower, quickly slipped into one of her new, billowy robes and raced to the door. She behaved just as Sharon had prayed she would. Hana stretched out her arms and gave her the warm, loving hug she could have gotten from no other person in her rapidly shrinking world. She appreciated that Hana held her in this tight embrace for a long time and was giving her the option of when to break out of it.

While they hugged, Hana decided that today she would tell Sharon of her pregnancy. When they parted, Hana brushed a tear from Sharon's cheek and told her how happy she was to have this unexpected and most welcome visit.

Sharon was on the verge of describing in detail the way her son discovered that his mother was gay but realized that to report it honestly she would have to tell about how Kevin overheard her discussing with Fred the possibility that Hana was pregnant and that Fred was the impregnator. While Sharon debated whether or not to ask about the tampon box, Hana suddenly threw open her robe and presented her nude body for Sharon to inspect. Sharon stared at it as Hana waited for an opinion. When none was forthcoming, Hana asked if Sharon had noticed any changes in her body since the last time she had seen it, and Sharon offered that her breasts seemed a bit fuller and her belly a little rounder. Hana looked down at her stomach, nodded sadly, and announced that she was carrying a baby. She begged Sharon's forgiveness for not confiding in her sooner and then started to sob.

"I am so ashamed . . . I am so ashamed."

Sharon had never seen Hana cry and was deeply touched by this rare display of unbridled emotion. Sharon took Hana in her arms and found herself saying, "Hana, dear, there's no need to be ashamed."

What Sharon really wanted to say was, "Hana, how could you do this to me? Not only did you go to bed with a man, but you allowed yourself to get pregnant!"

Sharon knew that she would ultimately ask Hana to name the son of a bitch who knocked her up, but at the moment, it was not possible for her to sustain her anger, especially under the developing circumstances, which now included Hana's putting her lips to Sharon's and her hand on Sharon's buttocks. For almost a full hour, the two women pleasured each other and then lay in each other's arms, each reconfirming that the other was the only one in her life who truly mattered. Believing this to be so, Sharon felt reasonably comfortable in asking her friend if Fred was the man responsible for her condition, and Hana, feeling safe in Sharon's arms, answered, "Well, you might say that Fred is responsible."

Hana felt Sharon's body tense and hastened to explain that it was Fred who encouraged her to be pleasant and accommodating to Sebu Hayakawa. "Fred made it very clear to me that Mr. Hayakawa was ready to withdraw his backing of the film unless—"

"Unless what? Unless you let that bastard fuck you?"

"Sharon, you're being very cruel and unnecessarily crude!"

"I may be crude and cruel," Sharon admitted, "but I never fucked a guy to do another guy a favor."

Hana sat upright in bed. "I was not fucking. I was assisting."

"Oh," Sharon asked ingenuously, "is *that* what you were doing?"

"Yes," Hana argued, "I was assisting a very lonely, desperate man to sire an heir."

Hana then went on to inform Sharon of Mr. Hayakawa's extraordinarily generous offer and his very gentlemanly comportment all during the negotiations and right through to conception. Hana made a special point of telling Sharon that she was able to conceive on the one and only night she spent with Mr. Hayakawa.

"Truthfully, Sharon," she added, "if it were not for you, I would not have been able to accept his hands touching my body." Sharon arched an eyebrow, and Hana explained, "I kept my eyes shut tightly and imagined that the hands touching me were yours."

When Sharon looked into Hana's face and saw there abject sadness and a plea for understanding, she folded Hana back into her arms and apologized for ever doubting her love. Hana suddenly rolled over on top of Sharon and started to giggle uncontrollably and through the giggles shouted, "It's perfect! . . . It's perfect!"

Sharon had no idea why her friend was giggling or what was "perfect," but she enjoyed seeing Hana happy and was satisfied to wait until Hana laughed herself out before asking what had provoked this explosion of joy. Hana was still laughing when she asked, "Sharon, would you like to be my *hisho-nakama* at Hakone?"

"I won't commit until you tell me what the heck you're talking about."

Hana finally pulled herself together and outlined, in detail, all that Sebu Hayakawa had offered, including the important stipulation that until the birth of his heir she live in Japan, at his house on Hakone Lake.

"He has recommended, Sharon darling, that because he will be away on business for much of my confinement, I hire someone to be my personal *hisho-nakama*, which means companion-secretary."

Sharon's reaction was immediate and positive, but she feigned indecision and asked kiddingly, "How big a house are we talking about?" On hearing that it was the most luxurious one on an idyllic volcanic lake, Sharon shook her head sadly and sighed. "I guess for six months I can stand it." Sharon laughed, grabbed Hana's hand, and announced, "Hana, my sweet, you got yourself a *hisho-nakama* mama . . . or whatever you said!"

44

As HE DROVE to his appointment with Sebu Hayakawa, the memory of Sharon's voice and matter-of-fact manner with which she admitted to having slept with Hana haunted Fred Cox. Also etched into his memory was the picture of his son standing defiantly on the stairway and accusing him and his mother of being sick people. All of his life Fred Cox had tacitly accepted homosexual men and women as a fact of life. During his years in the industry, he had worked beside, and socialized with, many people whose sexual preferences differed from his, and he never once considered himself to be prejudiced or intolerant of those people, but suddenly, as he stopped for a red light, an uncontrollable fury overtook him and he screamed at the top of his lungs.

"GODDAMN DYKES!"

An elegant middle-aged woman who was crossing the street shouted back, "GODDAMN BIGOT!"

Fred Cox sat stunned until the impatient driver of a ten-ton truck began honking.

Fred floored his accelerator, sped across the intersection, and mumbled to himself, "I'm a schmuck. I pick two broads to give my heart to, and both of them turn out to be lesbians. How'd I manage that?"

Fred drove in silence for a while, thinking about what Sharon had told him. To dismiss the small but gnawing doubt that his wife was lying about her involvement with Hana, Fred dialed Hana's number. The phone was picked up on the first ring. Fred was not surprised. A third sense told him that Hana was waiting for this call. He *was* surprised, however, to hear her laughing wildly.

"I'm happy you're in a good mood, Hana, because I have something very important to ask you."

The giggling stopped, and Fred plunged right in. "Hana, dear, this is a bit awkward for me, but I must know whether your refusal to go to bed with me these last few months was because you're not interested in me personally or . . . in men in general? And if that's true, why did you get pregnant, if you *are* pregnant. And if you are, am I the father?"

Fred slammed on his brakes and skidded to a stop when he heard Sharon's voice.

"No, she is not interested in you or any other man, and yes, she is pregnant, and no, you are not the father, and if you don't believe me, you can ask her yourself. Hana, it's Fred! He has some questions for you."

Coincidental with his slamming the phone down violently, Fred experienced a pain in his chest that was in some ways similar to the one he had right before collapsing in his parents' garage. My pills, he thought, I forgot to take those stupid pills. No, Elspeth handed them to me during the production meeting. So what the hell's this pain in my heart? It suddenly came to him that it was not unlike the heartache he felt in his senior year in high school, when he caught Benny Ginzer screwing his girl Marcie.

Fred's thoughts were interrupted by Elspeth, calling to remind him of his appointment and to inform him of a letter that had just come for him from Mr. Hayakawa. Fred readied himself for another blow to his heart.

"Go ahead, Elspeth," he said, sighing. "Open it and read it. If it's good news, tell me. If it's not, lie and say it is."

Elspeth, recognizing the tone of despair in her boss's voice, was reluctant to read something that might add to his anguish. She tore open the envelope, speed-read the contents, and breathed a sigh of relief.

"Good news, boss, and I'm not lying. You may even consider it *great* news."

Even fair news would be a welcome change today, and Fred asked that she read it to him.

" 'Dear Mr. Cox,' " Elspeth read. " 'I have just examined your estimated budget for *Hana and Her Great-grandmother*, and I feel strongly that it is not a realistic one.' "

Fred interrupted to say that it did not sound to him like a good-news letter.

" 'In my humble estimation, nineteen million dollars is not an adequate budget for a motion picture of quality, and I am therefore enclosing a check for an additional two million five hundred thousand dollars.' "

This was the first time that Fred had ever received additional money for a project without having to beg for it. Suddenly there was no pain around his heart.

By the time Fred rolled into the underground garage of the Hayakawa Industries' skyscraper, he had pretty well blotted from his mind what an abject failure he was as a husband, father, and lover and focused instead on what a good producer he was. Fred felt a burst of positive energy and could not wait to exchange low bows with the man who just threw his beleaguered Sky Productions another two and a half million dollars.

As Fred was ushered into Sebu Hayakawa's richly appointed office, Sebu bowed one time and started the meeting without waiting for Fred to return his bow. "Whatever we say here during the next minutes is for your ears and your ears only."

Sebu Hayakawa's demeanor was so deadly serious that Fred flashed back to the old war movies and imagined that he was about to be asked to spy for Japan against his own country. What he actually heard was at least as disturbing.

"Fred Cox," he began as he stared unblinkingly into Fred's eyes, "I have decided that we will not make *Hana and Her Great-grandmother*."

"But you just sent me a—" was all Fred got out before Sebu continued.

"A check for two and a half million dollars. Yes, I am aware of that, but it will be used not to make *Hana And Her Great-grandmother*, but *Ginko and Her Great-grandmother*."

The prospect of losing his backer frightened Fred into behaving like one of the obsequious, ass-kissing sycophants he had always abhorred.

"So what you're asking, Mr. Hayakawa, is that we change the character's name from Hana to Ginko?"

"I am not asking, Mr. Cox. I am insisting that it must be done or I do not continue with the project."

"Oh, Mr. Hayakawa," Fred groveled, "it's done! Say no more. Ginko it is! *Ginko and Her Great-grandmother*. You know something, Mr. Hayakawa, I like Ginko better. *Ginko and Her Great-grandmother* has three G's in it. Nice alliteration."

Once again, Sebu interrupted Fred and advised him to temper his enthusiasm. "Do not rush to accept a proposal that had not yet been presented."

Fred pressed his lips tightly together and nodded. Sebu again emphasized how important it was that Fred discuss this with no one. Certain that he was going to learn of Sebu's involvement with money launderers or drug dealers, Fred was relieved to hear Sebu say that the screenplay was being rewritten and the title role recast. Fred assumed that Sebu knew that the best movies are made from carefully written and rewritten screenplays, but he could not imagine why he would not want Hana to star in it. Her tests proved that she was as beautiful on screen as she was in person.

"Hana is carrying my baby," Sebu said proudly, "and I require that she give full attention to his birth."

Mistaking the anguished look on Fred's face as one of puritanical shock, Sebu hastened to add, "I have a great and deep affection for Ms. Yoshi, and as soon as she develops a like affection for me, I intend to make her my wife. That is why the screenplay must be rewritten. The story may remain as it is, but the names of the people and the villages must be changed. *Ginko and Her Great-grandmother* must be presented as a fiction."

Fred paid little attention to what Sebu said after learning that he was not the one who had impregnated Hana. The pain in his chest returned as his head filled with disturbing images of Hana doing all the exciting, sexual things with a fat, sweaty billionaire that she had once performed with him. He thought, First they grab our real estate and businesses, now our women! In his misery, Fred did not stop to remember that Hana was Japanese.

Fred awoke from his masochistic meandering when he heard Sebu ask why he had such a pained expression on his face. Fred smiled and thought, When this schmuck finds out that his wife-to-be and my wife-that-was are lovers, he'll have the same pained expression on *his* face!

"The pain? Oh, I bit my tongue." To keep himself from

saying what he was thinking, Fred actually did bite his tongue. "Uh, you were saying, Mr. Hayakawa?"

Sebu was not accustomed to repeating things, and his annoyance was apparent.

"To protect my son and heir from carrying the stigma of being the great-great-grandson of a graceless, murdering whore"—he sighed—"the film must be presented as fiction."

Before Fred could think, he heard himself saying, "No problem."

Sebu nodded and stared at Fred thoughtfully as he considered how to ask Fred an indelicate question.

"Mr. Cox," he began, "I am about to ask you something that you may consider indelicate but I assure you that your answer is of great importance to me."

Fred put on his most concerned face and asked, "How can I be of service?"

"Your wife," Sebu asked politely, "what is her name?"

"Sharon! There, that wasn't so difficult, was it?" Fred joked. "Now is there anything else I can help you with?"

"Yes, there is, Mr. Cox," Sebu continued without acknowledging Fred's small attempt at humor. "You and she are divorced, are you not?"

"We're in the process," he corrected.

"I ask you this "because Hana has requested that I employ Sharon Cox to act as her secretary-companion. What I wish to learn from you, who know this person intimately, is about any flaws in Sharon Cox's character that would make it unwise for me to accede to Hana's wishes."

The pressure in Fred's chest lessened as he decided to withhold from Sebu the knowledge that he was hiring Hana's lover.

"Sebu," Fred began with devilish glee, "I can honestly say that if I had to choose a companion for Hana, I can't think of anyone more perfect for the position. You can rest asssured, Sebu, that Sharon Cox will serve Hana very well."

It took the entire drive back to his office for Fred to sort out all the dichotomous feelings that were dizzying his brain. He pulled into his parking space and sat in his car contemplating the stenciled sign on the garage wall in front of him: Rsrved. Pres. Sky Prod's. He spoke to it.

"Damn right! President of Sky Productions, that's who's parked here!" Fred, with the wisdom he learned at his father's knee, counted his blessings. He was rid of a wife and mistress who never really loved him, had a heart that needed a lube-and-valve job, and had reared a son who temporarily wished him dead. "Yes," he mumbled, "your life is back on track, boychik."

45

KEVIN, CARRYING three suitcases, came out of the house and shouted for the cabdriver to open his trunk. Kevin estimated that barring unforeseen traffic snarls, he had just enough time to get to the airport and catch his plane. As the driver, a muscular, five-foot Mexican-American, loaded Kevin's bags into the trunk, Kevin offered him an extra twenty dollars if he could get him to the Delta Airlines terminal in twenty-five minutes. The driver gave the ubiquitous "No problem!," slammed the trunk shut, slid onto his wood-beaded car seat, pressed the buttons of his Casio wristwatch, and announced, "Twenty-five minutes, starting now! Jump in!"

Kevin jumped in, shouted, "Whoa!," and jumped out again to intercept the stout mailwoman who was trudging up the steep driveway toward the house. Kevin grabbed the two rubber-banded packets of real and junk mail from her and explained, as he always did, that he was saving her the climb. It was a ritual Marnelle had come to accept and enjoy, particularly when Kevin received one of those letters that made him slap it hard against the palm of his hand and shout, "Way to go, Marnelle!"

This time Kevin received two letters, one thick with the exciting new photos that Maria had promised and for which he had been waiting impatiently. He was tempted to tear open the envelope but instead sprinted back to the cab, jumped in, and rode off to what he believed was his destiny. He turned and sadly watched the house where he and Maria conceived their baby recede in the distance.

As they drove onto the San Diego Freeway, Kevin looked

down at the envelopes he was holding and decided that he would wait until he was seated comfortably on the plane before he read the letters and examined the latest photos of Maria, which, she warned in her last letter, he must not let anyone see.

The thought of seeing Maria posing naked and pregnant was too much for Kevin to resist. He tore open the envelope and laughed when he saw that they were the photos Maria had promised. His mind suddenly cleared itself of all that had gone through it that day.

"Looks like a bottleneck up ahead. Could be an accident or a stalled car. I don't know if we're going to make it in time."

"Sir, we have to make it!" Kevin pleaded.

The desperation in the young man's voice, his offer of a twenty-dollar bonus, and the fact that he respectfully addressed him as "Sir" all contributed to the driver's resolve to get to the airport on time. He immediately blew his horn and waved a white handkerchief out the window. By some dexterous slaloming, he snaked his way across two lanes, and to the accompaniment of screeching brakes and cursing truck drivers, he exited the next off-ramp. By using his considerable knowledge of little-known city streets, the driver brought Kevin to the Delta terminal with minutes to spare.

The tourist section of the Delta Airlines flight to Miami was full, and Kevin found himself sandwiched between two elderly Jewish women who were traveling together but had chosen to sit separately. The stouter of the two explained why she had to have an aisle seat.

"I don't want to be a pest and have to climb over someone every time I have to go. And my sister, Mrs. Leila Schift," she prattled on while pointing to the woman sitting in the window seat, "she gets so nauseous if she can't look out of a window. I don't understand it, but if it keeps her from getting seasick, I say let her look."

During the first leg of the four-and-a-half-hour flight to Miami, Kevin was to learn more than he had to know about the taciturn Mrs. Leila Schift and her garrulous, weak-bladdered sister, Mrs. Benjamin Pechter. Mrs. Pechter explained that her sister Leila's husband, Solomon, "he should rest in peace," passed on nine years ago, but Mrs. Pechter's husband, Benjamin, "thank God," was still with her. "Although," she whispered, "he's not always with himself." She grimaced, nodded, and barely spoke the word "Alzheimer's."

Kevin knew that if he attempted to look at his precious photos of Maria, Mrs. Pechter was bound to ask if she could have a look. When he opened the other letter from Maria, Mrs. Pechter asked, "From your lady friend?"

Kevin nodded, and Mrs. Pechter asked her name and did he have a snapshot of her in his wallet. Kevin knew he could silence Mrs. Pechter for the rest of the flight if he showed her the photos of Maria. He smiled at the thought but told her, "Maria's her name, and I don't have a picture of her."

"I'll bet," she said, nudging him gently with her elbow, "that she's a beauty."

Acknowledging that Maria was very beautiful brought Kevin another nudge from Mrs. Pechter. "And why shouldn't she be? A handsome fellow like yourself . . ."

Had the seat-belt sign not been turned on in anticipation of mild turbulence, Kevin would have escaped to the toilet and examined his precious photos. He thanked Mrs. Pechter for her kind words and very deliberately angled his back toward her as he unfolded one of Maria's letters. Mrs. Pechter immediately understood his body language.

"Read, read," she said apologetically. "I wouldn't talk to you anymore until you finish reading."

Mrs. Pechter was true to her word. While Kevin read his letter, she did not talk to him, but she did talk past him, to her noncommunicative sister, Leila, who continued to stare out the window. Somehow Kevin was able to tune out Mrs. Pechter, who was describing, in detail, the new weight-loss program that her "daughter the nutritionist" had developed for a new obesity clinic in Orlando.

Maria's letter to Kevin, besides being filled with reaffirmations of her deep love for him and the painful longing she had to feel him close to her, contained all kinds of engrossing information that included, among other things, a near run-in with his grandfather.

I was in the elevator, waiting to go to Dr. Alvarez's office for my checkup, when your grandmother and grandfather came into the elevator. Your grandmother was looking down, but your grandfather looked right at me and did not recognize me. I could not believe it. I thought it was because of my big belly until I heard him say to your grandmother that he was not going to let anyone talk him into a catarack operation. (I know I did not spell catarack right but I am too tired to look in the dictionary.) He didn't see me because he couldn't see me. I feel sorry that he has cataracks. I wonder if he's still angry at me for spitting on his shoes. Oh, Kevin, I want to see you so much. The doctor said it could be soon. If you can be here at the end of next week, I think you would only have to wait for a few days before the baby comes. I will not be so frightened if you are with me in the delivery room.

"I'm on my way!" Kevin said out loud.

Mrs. Pechter asked Kevin if he was talking to her, and he said that he was talking to his letter. Mrs. Pechter found that very amusing and repeated it to her sister. "He's talking to his letter. See how love can make a boy crazy!"

Kevin was so engrossed in reading Maria's letter that he did not notice that the seat-belt sign had been turned off. By the time it registered, a half-dozen passengers were lined up in the aisles, delaying his opportunity to privately view his photos. He climbed over Mrs. Pechter, who informed him that she could go but would wait till the line was smaller.

The smile he developed when he read of Maria's love for him broadened when a young mother and her two-year-old daughter finally emerged from the toilet they had commandeered fifteen minutes earlier.

After relieving a fairly full bladder, he dug the photos out of his pocket, flipped through them, and whimpered each time he looked at one that featured a seminude Maria in all her burgeoning, breathtaking glory.

Kevin, still frustrated by the lack of time he had to look at his precious photos, calmed himself by remembering that within a few hours he would be looking at Maria and her beautiful body in person.

When Kevin returned to his seat, he found Mrs. Pechter sitting in it. On seeing Kevin, she immediately stood up and moved out into the aisle to allow Kevin to slide back in. She resumed speaking even before he had a chance to settle himself and rebuckle his seat belt.

"Are you, by any chance, related to Leon and Sarah Cox who live in Miami Beach at 441 Esplanade?"

Kevin was startled by the question and hesitated while he weighed the advantages and disadvantages of admitting that he was their grandson. Mrs. Pechter solved his dilemma by telling him that he looked just like the Cox's grandson, Kevin, who used to visit them, adding, "You've gotten so much taller, and I wasn't sure it was you until I looked at the bag under your seat. You'll have to forgive me for snooping, but the tag had the name Cox on it, and I put two and two together . . ."

Kevin admitted he was Kevin and then, on an uncontrollable impulse and without thinking of the consequences, began unburdening himself by telling Mrs. Pechter every conceivable thing she could possibly want to know about him. By using Mrs. Pechter as a surrogate for his parents and grandparents, Kevin experienced a dizzying sense of liberation and invulnerability. Mrs. Pechter pursed her lips on hearing that Kevin was not coming to Florida to visit his grandparents but to marry his girlfriend, Maria, and to assist in the birth of their baby. Before his better judgment returned to censor his actions, Kevin found himself thrusting Maria's photos under Mrs. Pechter's nosy nose and proclaiming, "That's her!"

Mrs. Pechter took one quick look at the provocative photo, shoved it back into Kevin's hands, and started to make choking sounds. In between chokes, she spit into a tissue and muttered, "Shame on her and shame on you!"

Kevin thought that Mrs. Pechter's spitting was a symbolical gesture meant for him, but Mrs. Schift knew that her sister was having an asthma attack. Mrs. Schift suddenly came to life. She rang for a flight attendant and asked Kevin to change seats with her so that she could tend to her sister. Armed with her bronchial inhaler, Mrs. Schift helped her sister abort a major attack. When all had calmed, Kevin heard Mrs. Pechter mumble, "The nerve of him . . . showing me his dirty pictures."

Maria's beautiful nude poses being characterized by Mrs. Pechter as dirty pictures made Kevin feel stupid and unworthy. He was so upset at betraying her trust that he growled and slapped his forehead hard enough to make himself wince. The flight attendant who had just arrived to assist Mrs. Pechter smiled sweetly at Kevin and asked, "Young man, are you having a problem?"

"Yes, he's having a problem," the still-wheezing Mrs. Pechter answered for him, "and it's a problem that my sister and I would rather not be sitting next to. Miss, could you please find other seats for us?"

The flight attendant politely informed Mrs. Pechter that there were no seats available. Undaunted, Mrs. Pechter suggested that she look for two young men who would be willing to swap seats. "Nonsmoking!" she ordered, "and one should be a window seat!"

Rather than delve into the specific nature of the problem, the flight attendant decided that it would be less disruptive if she moved Mrs. Pechter and her sister. Being very pretty and personable, the flight attendant had no trouble convincing two college-aged men that by changing seats they were doing her a personal favor.

To avoid looking at the two sisters as they collected their shopping bags, Kevin stared out the window. He could hear Mrs. Pechter muttering, "His grandparents should know the kind of filth he shows to people!"

To discourage questions about the incident from the two men who moved into the vacated seats, Kevin put his head down and pretended to sleep. He pretended for less than five minutes before actual sleep overcame him.

For most of the flight he remained in this blessed state and dreamed of Maria. The most vivid dream was of her parading naked down the aisle of the plane and beckoning for him to join her. In frustratingly slow motion, he took off all of his clothes and started down a mile-long aisle. He was just about to join Maria in the toilet when he heard a distant voice say, ". . . in preparation for landing at Miami Airport . . ."

At the baggage-claim area, Kevin, who was not aware that he had screamed out "Don't land, I'm naked!," was sure that Mrs. Pechter had told every passenger in coach about Maria's photo. Why else, he thought, would they be looking at me as if I were some sort of weirdo?

46

Before he had met up with Mrs. Pechter, Kevin had decided that he would not contact his grandparents until after Maria had the baby, but now that Mrs. Pechter was a factor, he would have to change his plans. The woman was obviously a world-class gossip, and it was unlikely that she would not tell her neighbors the news about the Coxes' grandson marrying a pregnant *"shiksa."*

Kevin, figuring that he would have time to make a call before his bags arrived at the carousel, decided that before his grandparents heard Mrs. Pechter's version, he would phone and tell them the truth.

His grandfather did not seem a bit surprised to hear that it was Kevin calling. They had barely exchanged hellos before his grandfather asked, "Kevin, what's this I hear about you showing filthy pictures on the airplane?"

"Grandpa, how did you hear?"

"Grandma got a call a couple of hours ago from a neighbor. She said you showed her filthy pictures of a naked pregnant girl who you were going to marry. I told Grandma that Mrs. Pechter was crazy, but she said the girl's name was Maria. Kevin, is this true? Are you in Florida?"

"No . . . I mean, yes, I'm in Florida, but I didn't show her filthy pictures. Grandpa, did this woman call you from an airplane?"

"She said she was over the Grand Canyon, so she must have been in an airplane. Kevin, is Mrs. Pechter crazy or is—"

Kevin saw his baggage coming down the chute and excused himself with the promise that he would take a cab to their apartment and explain everything.

With the cabdriver's begrudging permission, Kevin kept the interior light on during the entire ride to his grandparents' condo, enabling him to examine meticulously every beautiful inch of every one of the extraordinary photos of Maria. When the cab stopped and the driver announced that they had arrived at 441 Esplanade, Kevin, who had been staring, longingly, at a soul-melting photo of Maria cradling her full, round belly, shouted, 1609 Marlin Circle!"

When the driver insisted that Kevin had said 441 Esplanade, Kevin exploded. "I made a mistake! Take me to 1609 Marlin Circle and HURRY!"

Kevin's heart sank as the cab arrived at 1609 Marlin Circle and he found the Sisneroses' house completely dark. He told the driver to wait while he checked to see if anyone was home. He rang the bell a half-dozen times, then ran around to the back of the house and banged on the kitchen door while calling the names of all the members of the household. When the driver offered to drive him back to the condo, Kevin knew that he did not want to do that. Expecting that Maria would soon come home from a movie or from the walk she and Carla took every night, Kevin paid the cabby, dragged his bags out of the trunk onto the lighted porch, and decided to wait for Maria there.

Leon Cox sat in front of the television set and pretended to be interested in a panel discussion on the future of the economy. Sarah also pretended not to be worried that something terrible had happened to Kevin. Every few minutes, without moving his head, Leon would sneak a look at his wristwatch. After observing this ritual for a while, Sarah finally spoke.

"You know, Leon, not that I'm worried, but it couldn't hurt to call the Highway Patrol and see if there were any taxi accidents."

"Sarah, if it'll ease your mind, why not?" Leon said without admitting that he had been consumed with that possibility for almost an hour.

Leon called the Highway Patrol and the three major cab companies that service the airport. They all reported that there were no accidents involving any of their vehicles. Leon hung up and started back to the television but suddenly shouted, "I'm so dumb." He picked up their phone book and waved it in frustration. "Sarah, what's his name?"

"What's whose name?"

"The uncle! You know, Sarah, Carla's uncle, Pedro Sisneros. What's his name, damnit?"

Sarah shrugged and said, "Pedro Sisneros!"

"Thank you!" he said, and went about looking up Pedro Sisneros's number.

Sarah thought it "idiotic" for him to drive all the way to the other side of town to a house he had phoned five times without getting an answer, but her remonstrations fell on deaf ears. Along with his eyesight and reasoning powers, Leon's hearing was diminishing at an alarming rate. Only his ability to be unbending remained remarkably intact. Sarah started to fear Alzheimer's when he pulled the car jerkily into a gas station. Had he forgotten, she wondered, that he'd filled the tank yesterday? And why was he spending so much time talking to the cashier? Did he forget, too, that he was in a hurry? When Sarah questioned his reason for stopping, Leon fixed her with a stare and barked out a conversation-stopping "Shush!"

An amazed Sarah realized that Leon had done something that in their long marriage she had never been able to convince him to do. Ask for directions.

As Dr. Gina Alvarez led Maria to the examining room, she tried to assure an apologetic Maria that her sister was right in bringing her to the office for an examination.

"Even though your due date is a week off," the doctor explained, "what your sister described on the phone could have been labor pain."

As she mounted the examining table, Maria insisted that she absolutely could not deliver the baby until Kevin was with her. Dr. Alvarez assured her, "Your husband will have plenty of time to get to the hospital. First babies take a notoriously long time to be born."

Hearing the word hospital threw Maria into a near panic. "Garlic!" Maria suddenly cried out. "Those cramps Carla called about were garlic pains."

Dr. Alvarez looked skeptically, and Maria rushed to explain. "At midnight, I went to the refrigerator and ate a small salad with a lot of garlic in it. Garlic always gives me cramps; tell her, Carla."

As she spoke, Maria was suddenly doubled over by a pain of seismic proportions. When it subsided, she said, panting, "It was the garlic."

Dr. Alvarez weighed the disadvantages of allowing Maria to go home and found none. Her patient's emotional state would certainly be helped, and even if she were starting actual labor, it was unlikely that the birth was imminent. Dr. Alvarez took Maria's hand and told her that she could go home with her sister and not to worry. The doctor allowed that the pains could have been brought on by indigestion but warned that it was altogether possible that real labor pains could start at any time. As Carla was assisting Maria off the examining table, Dr. Alvarez instructed her to call immediately should Maria's water break. Just then, Maria's water broke, and as instructed, Carla called out, "Doctor, Maria's water broke!"

Without making one wrong turn or cursing the other drivers on the road, Leon steered his reliable fifteen-year-old Chrysler directly to Pedro Sisneros's house.

Kevin's excitement on seeing a car drive up was short-lived. Under other circumstances, he would have been happy to greet his grandparents warmly, but all he could muster was an amazed "What are you two doing here?"

"We came to say hello, Kevin."

"You see, Kevin," Leon explained, "your grandma was very worried when you didn't show up after you said that you were coming right over, and frankly, I was a little worried, too."

"A little worried? Grandpa called the Highway Patrol to find out if maybe you were in an accident."

"Sarah," Leon admonished, "it's not a contest to see who was more worried. The important thing is that Kevin is all right. Of course, Kevin, you could have called. We were a little upset after Mrs. Pechter called from the Grand Canyon."

Kevin apologized and started to explain about Mrs. Pechter, then realized he could save a thousand words by showing one picture. He chose a photo that was the least likely to offend. It was of Maria smiling sweetly as she tried to keep her belly from peeking out of her dressing gown.

Kevin heard an actual gulp escape from his grandmother when she looked at the photo. She refrained from commenting until her husband had a chance to see what she had seen. Leon peered at it and said, "Looks like she's ready to pop!"

"She's due next week, Grandpa."

Still reeling from looking at the seminude photo, Sarah asked, "Kevin, do your folks know that they're going to be grandparents?"

"I don't intend to tell them," he explained, "until after the baby is born, and if you're wondering, Grandma and Grandpa, why Maria took that money—"

"It's not so hard to figure," Leon rushed to answer. "She took it for the baby. No wonder she spit on my shoes."

Outwardly, Sarah appeared accepting of Kevin's becoming a father; internally, she was a mass of grandmotherly concern and confusion, wondering what God's position might be. Ever the pragmatist, Sarah dropped her theological musings to ask Kevin where Maria was. Kevin listed the possibilities as Sarah shook her head. "Why would Maria go out to a movie or for a walk when she's expecting you? Or isn't she expecting you?"

Kevin admitted that she wasn't.

"This is what happens when you try to surprise people," Leon reprimanded. "You end up sitting on a porch waiting like a shtoomie."

Sarah berated Leon for calling his grandson a fool and asked Kevin, as offhandedly as she could, if he happened to know the hospital Maria was planning to use. Much as Sarah tried to disguise the significance of the question, it was blindingly clear to Kevin that his grandmother, who knew about such things, was telling him that Maria might be at the hospital delivering the baby.

Without uttering a sound, Kevin pulled a miniature address book from his back pocket, opened it to the first page, and shouted, "Salk-Reisman Memorial Hospital, 222 Jefferson Drive. Grandpa, we can go in your car. Do you know where that is? We should call first. We need a phone. Grandpa, you don't have a phone in your—? No, you don't. Maybe we can break into the house, they wouldn't mind."

Recognizing that there was a distinct danger of Kevin's hyperventilating, Leon suggested that they drive to a gas station and call the hospital.

"Calm down, boychik," Leon advised as he picked up one of Kevin's bags to carry to his car "There'll be plenty of time to be nervous and crazy, so don't start that part until you have to."

Kevin grabbed the bag from his grandfather and started to toss it back onto the porch.

"Grandpa!" he shouted. "Forget the bags."

"Kevin, you leave the bags here, someone'll steal 'em!"

"SCREW THE BAGS! Sorry, Grandpa. We'll take 'em."

On the way to a gas station, Sarah could not believe the words she heard coming out of the mouth of her teenaged grandson.

"I don't want to miss being in the delivery room. I want to be with Maria for the whole thing. I've been reading a lot about it, and I saw a great program showing a baby being born. The doctors and parents were saying how great it is for the father to be there with the mother and the baby and to cut the umbilical cord. I don't want to miss any of that."

Kevin's words had moved Leon to tears, but his stoicism did not allow him to brush them from his eyes. His vision was clouded enough by his cataracts, and Sarah knew he was in trouble when he made no signal to turn into the gas station ahead. Kevin's yelling, "There it is Grandpa!," jolted the old man into turning sharply into the service station. He missed the sloped access, jumped the curb, and brought the car to rest a foot from the phone booths. Acting as if all the bumping and lurching were normal, Leon announced, "There's your phone, son!"

Kevin dialed the hospital and was immediately put on hold and forced to listen to some annoyingly nondescript orchestral music. He was about to hang up and redial when the operator returned and informed him that neither a Maria Degrut nor an Evita Lopez-Gomez had been admitted to the hospital.

Had Pedro Sisneros and Leon Cox owned answering machines, on this one evening each would have received multiple messages from Kevin, Fred, Sharon, and J.J. Quicky.

It was Sharon who unwittingly triggered the flood of calls. In

desperation, she had called Fred to ask if he had any idea how
she could get in touch with Kevin. She felt that before flying off
to Japan that morning with Hana, she should contact her son
and try to say some sort of civilized good-bye to him and,
whether or not he believed it, to tell him that she still loved
him. All Fred could tell Sharon was what J. J. Quicky had told
him:

"The only logical place to look for a man as much in love as
your son is in the arms of his girl."

Between labor pains, which were now coming every fifteen
minutes, Maria concentrated on imaging Kevin's sweet face
and trying to will him to know where she was. The last time
they had spoken, they had agreed that he would fly to Florida
three days before her due date and live with her at her Uncle
Pedro's. She had called him many times this day and not found
him in. His father had answered twice, and rather than chance
that he would recognize her voice, she hung up without saying
a word. She still lived in mortal fear that Fred Cox had the
power to disrupt the lives of Domenico and her dear sister.

Even though Maria was one of four women in the maternity
ward, she felt alone and deserted. While she was being
prepped by kindly, overworked nurses, her family was en-
sconced in a room down the hall, waiting for an event that the
doctor could not guarantee would happen that night. Maria
had told everyone—nurses, ward boys, and her fellow expectant mothers—that her "husband" was flying in from Los Angeles to be with her in the delivery room. Maria started to cry
when the head nurse came into the ward and told her again
that her husband had not yet called.

"I'm sure your husband will be here in plenty of time," the
nurse reassured her. "You just concentrate on your breathing,
and we'll send him up the minute he arrives, Mrs. . . ." The
nurse glanced at the identification bracelet on Maria's wrist and
read, "Maria Cox. May I call you Maria, Mrs. Cox?"

At that moment, Maria, experiencing a sharp labor pain,
shook her head wildly and moaned, "No, no! *Mrs. Cox*! Call me
Mrs. Cox!" She then sobbed loudly, "KEVIN! I WANT KEVIN!"

47

Sᴇʙᴜ Hᴀʏᴀᴋᴀᴡᴀ did not process the reception of bad news very well, and he was especially upset when it came unexpectedly. To wait nine months and then learn that he had fathered a girl would have irked him terribly. To avoid such a disquieting moment, Sebu Hayakawa insisted that Hana submit to amniocentesis. On learning that she was carrying his son and heir, Sebu rewarded Hana with a flawless three-karat, diamond and became even more attentive to her physical comfort and well-being.

It was for this reason that Fred found himself in the unenviable position of riding backward in one of Hayakawa Industries' luxurious stretch limousines and looking into the faces of his soon-to-be ex-wife and her pregnant lover. At the request of Sebu Hayakawa, who had important business meetings in Japan, Fred Cox had agreed to personally escort Hana and her secretary-companion to the airport, where Sebu's private jet was waiting to fly them to Tokyo. During the ride to the airport, Fred and Sharon, each manning one of the limousine's three car phones, continued to call the Sisneroses' home and Kevin's grandparents. After each unanswered call, Sharon would question whether flying off to Japan without telling her son was a proper thing to do.

"When he was young, I was so careful to let him know I was leaving the house, and here I am leaving the country without telling him."

Fred, more concerned about catering to the needs of his billionaire benefactor, counseled Sharon that her flying to Japan at this time was the absolute right thing to do.

"Sharon," he said in his low, sincere register, "Kevin is your son—you are the only mother he has. There will come a time, and I think it will be very soon, I really do, when he'll realize that you are the one person in the world who cares about him like no other. At that time, he'll seek you out wherever you are, and when he does, remember that you'll be only one day away, or less than a day if Sebu makes his plane available to you, and I don't see why he wouldn't."

Fred, for the first time, looked to Hana for corroboration, and because their agendas were the same, she agreed that Fred was making good sense.

As Fred watched Sharon and Hana board Sebu's plane, he felt suddenly as if he were in a remake of *Casablanca*. He was Humphrey Bogart watching two Ingrid Bergmans go off together to start a new and exciting life without him. Had Fred not had another focus of interest, he might have emotionally fallen apart at the realization that in the part of life that his parents always preached was the only one that truly mattered, he was a complete failure. He stayed with this discomforting thought only until the jet started to back its nose away from the gate. He then allowed for some very insistent distractions to filter back into his head. Leading the list was a dinner meeting later that evening with his casting director, Paula Petroff, and the lovely Chong Sook Kim, the leading candidate for the role of Ginko in *Ginko and Her Great-grandmother*.

48

ON THE DRIVE back to the Sisneroses' house, Sarah, trying hard to accept a situation of which she disapproved, asked Kevin a series of grandmotherly questions that directly led to finding Maria. It began innocently, with Sarah asking him if he had chosen a name for the baby. Kevin, pleased that his grandmother showed signs of being interested, told her that they had not really decided yet but had a couple of names they liked a lot.

"If it's a boy, Maria wanted to call him Kevin, Jr., but I told her that in our religion I didn't think it was allowed to name a baby after his father."

"It's allowed if the father is not living," Leon offered officiously. "A Jewish baby can only be named after a dead person. What other names are you considering?"

Kevin was not expecting the reaction he got when he informed his grandparents that Maria liked the names Simone for a girl and Simon for a boy. Kevin pronounced the names as Maria had, with a Spanish accent, which made both names sound out like "See-moan." Kevin, who was sitting in the backseat, looked into the rearview mirror and saw his grandfather smile.

"Did you know, Kevin," Sarah asked, "that Grandpa's father was named Simon?"

Kevin was not sure whether he did or not, but from the look on his grandmother's face, he knew that it would be politically advantageous to say that he did. As soon as he said, "Of course I remember," he did remember that his father had told him that the family name was once Kakaffsky and that Simon Kakaffsky had changed the family name to Cox. Because of the way that Maria pronounced the name Simone, it had never occurred to Kevin that his great-grandfather's name Simon and "Seemoan" were the same name.

Leon rolled the name around on his tongue and agreed that "Simon Cox was a fine name for a child."

"SIMON COX!" Kevin suddenly screamed, "THAT'S IT!"

Leon jammed on his brakes and shouted back over his shoulder, "Who's arguing? Simon Cox is fine . . . I said I liked it. What's all the screaming?"

Sarah knew exactly why her grandson had gone berserk and nodded knowingly as an excited Kevin explained that Maria must have registered under the name of Cox, not Degrut or Lopez-Gomez.

Leon's suggestion that they call the hospital to check was loudly vetoed by Sarah. "Leon," she insisted, "you'll do like you did before, get directions and drive straight to the hospital . . . only this time let Kevin drive."

From the moment Dr. Alvarez uttered the words "For a first baby, this is most unusual," Maria, between labor pains, kept insisting that she didn't want it to be unusual.

As she was wheeled down the hall to the delivery room, she pleaded, "I want it to be 'usual,' like you said it would be! You said the baby would not come for hours and hours and hours. You must not let the baby come until Kevin is with me. Dr. Alvarez, please stop the baby from coming!"

Paying no attention to a prominent No Parking sign, Kevin drove his grandfather's car right up to the front entrance of the hospital, jumped out, and shouted, "If I don't come out in a couple of minutes, Grandpa, park the car and come in with Grandma."

Because Maria had beseeched her family to do everything in their power to help Kevin find his way to her, Uncle Pedro, to humor his niece, volunteered to station himself near the information desk, promising that as soon as Kevin walked into the hospital, he would whisk him to her side.

Uncle Pedro was facing the lobby door when Kevin came

through it. On recognizing each other, they shouted the other's name at the top of their lungs and frightened a security guard and all the people in the reception area. Pedro ushered Kevin into a waiting elevator and on the ride up to the fifth floor informed him that Maria was still in labor.

With Kevin in tow, Uncle Pedro steered him down the corridor and into the maternity ward where he had last seen his niece. As Kevin stepped into the ward, he was greeted with shouts of "He made it!" "That must be Kevin!" "She said he'd be here!" "They took your wife to the delivery room!"

With each painful contraction, Maria, who had been screaming Kevin's name, now screamed it with such intensity that attending nurses all rushed to attend her. With all of the strength she could gather, Maria violently shoved aside an unsuspecting nurse who was blocking her view of the door where the heroic figure of Kevin, in a sterile green hospital gown, was standing in silhouette.

The sight of Maria with her knees up, struggling to give birth, was overwhelming. Kevin stood transfixed as he watched Maria, laughing and crying, stretch out her arms toward him. He had seen this scene dozens of times in movies and television shows, but it was the first one that starred someone he knew personally. He rushed into Maria's arms, and they embraced and held each other until the next labor pain struck. Then, suddenly, with superhuman force, Maria punched Kevin in the chest and let out a soul-wrenching scream. Carla rushed to support her sister's back and urged her to breathe. Along with her breathing, Maria managed to scream and curse at Kevin in two languages while praying silently for God to forgive her for cursing and sinning. When the pain subsided, Maria apologized to Kevin for hitting him in the chest and ingenuously explained, "The labor pains are very painful."

The first time that Maria cursed at him and blamed him for being responsible for all the unbearable pain she was suffering, Kevin mumbled an apology and started to leave, but each time the pain subsided, she told him how much it meant to her that he was there with her.

During the long vigil, Kevin stayed at Maria's side and opted not to move to the foot of the bed and observe what Dr. Alvarez was describing to the visiting interns.

It was not until Maria said, for perhaps the tenth time, "I am so happy, Kevin, that you are here with me to watch our baby be born," that he realized that he had no intention of actually watching his baby be born. He had planned to avoid the actual process by watching Maria's face. Kevin knew that he was involved in a once-in-a-lifetime experience, and it bothered him that he was behaving like a frightened teenager. He just could not bring himself to look at Maria's vagina, which Dr. Alvarez was periodically monitoring for increases in dilation. He suffered with this upsetting feeling of revulsion through two more intense labor pains, the first ones that Maria was able to get through without cursing at anyone but the pain itself. When Kevin heard Dr. Alvarez announce it would be an hour at the most, he knew what he had to do. He kissed Maria lightly on her wet, salty lips and told her that he had to go to the men's room. As he bolted from the delivery room, Maria shouted after him, "Don't go now, Kevin. I need you!"

Kevin had not intended to go to the toilet, and until he used it as an excuse to leave the room, he was not aware of how desperately full his bladder was. He found a toilet directly opposite the waiting room, where he saw his grandparents and the Sisneroses, all waiting eagerly for news of Maria. They spotted him, but to avoid peeing in his pants, he simply waved and shouted, "Nothing yet!"

Frustrated with Kevin's cursory bulletin, Leon followed Kevin into the toilet, but before he could ask about Maria, Kevin, who was at a urinal sighing with relief, shocked his grandfather by asking if he could have the keys to the car. The old man glared at his grandson and was a breath away from lecturing him on being responsible when Kevin said that he had to get something from the trunk. Ashamed that he had doubted his grandson, Leon handed Kevin the keys and told him that he had parked the car in front of the hospital, in a red zone.

"For an occasion like this," he boasted, "I'll pay the ticket with pleasure!"

It took Kevin less than three minutes to urinate, wash his hands, run down to the car, retrieve his video recorder from the trunk, run up the five flights, and struggle into a new sterile gown. Kevin entered the delivery room panting and sweating and was frightened by how quiet it was. Carla, who was wiping Maria's brow, told him that he had just missed Maria's most painful contraction yet.

Kevin apologized profusely to Maria, who nodded. "I'm glad you missed it. I said some things that were not nice."

Kevin hid his video recorder behind his back and wondered how Maria would feel about his taping their baby's entrance into the world. Given a choice, he would have preferred not to be an eyewitness to the actual scene. He thought, however, that seeing the event through a lens and in black and white might make it tolerable. And, he reasoned, it's something that someday I might want to show to my parents. He stopped to wonder if they would be at all interested to know that he was about to become a father. He decided that whatever they thought now did not matter. Someday they might appreciate that he thought of them at this moment, much as he appreciated Carla's chronicling for him, in still photos, the last days of Maria's pregnancy. He brought the camera from behind his back and showed it to Maria, who nodded her approval.

When the actual delivery was announced as having begun, a trembling Kevin quickly stationed himself in a far corner of the room and stared at the back of Dr. Alvarez's head. He held his video recorder at his side, trying to find the courage to focus his camera on the event. When Dr. Alvarez moved her head to one side, Kevin caught a very brief glimpse of Maria's pelvic area and instantly became light-headed. He knew that if he were to continue seeing things like that, he would very likely pass out. For Maria's sake he wanted to remain conscious and in the room. He considered keeping his eyes shut for the remainder of the birth process but gathered courage from Maria, who, after a painful contraction, managed to give him a reassuring smile. To capture that smile, Kevin brought the camera up to his eye, and this, involuntarily, solved his dilemma. By looking through the eyepiece, he saw nothing but blackness. Great, he thought, I'll leave the lens cap on and listen to the birth instead of watching it. He would have continued to peer intently at nothing had not Carla told him that he had forgotten to remove his lens cap. Kevin ripped it off and joked, "Hey, I wondered where everybody had gone."

The first image Kevin saw through his viewfinder was of Maria in close-up, resting on her pillow and readying herself for her next big effort, which came while he was taping it. He widened the shot to include Carla, who was supporting her sister's back and relaying the doctor's orders to breathe and bear down. Kevin did not stop to analyze why, but as he became absorbed in the challenge of documenting the most important event of his life, his nausea miraculously disappeared. He moved quickly and efficiently to different corners of the delivery room, looking for the best angles to capture the agony and ecstasy in Maria's heroic face as she went in and out of contraction. At one point, when her struggle became too upsetting for him to bear, Kevin lay down on the floor at the head of her bed and shot a series of close-ups of the legs and feet of Dr. Alvarez and the attending nurses and interns. He then ran to the opposite end of the room, isolated Carla in an extreme close-up, and recorded her empathetic reactions to the pain her twin sister was enduring.

Kevin had just loaded a new cassette and was taking yet another shot of the clock on the wall when the doctor announced, "The baby is crowning." Without hesitating, Kevin moved with the rest of the staff to the battle station, where, through the viewfinder he saw, protruding from Maria, a cap-like crown of wet velvety black hair. A sense of rapture overcame him, and he could no longer abide the impersonality of watching the miracle of birth in black and white through a two-inch eyepiece. Kevin brought the camera to his side and allowed himself the awesome privilege of seeing the miracle in person and in living, breathing color.

He stood immobilized from the time the baby's head became fully visible to the moment its mucus-covered body propelled itself into the world and signaled its presence by letting out a heartrending cry. Carla burst into tears and smothered Maria with kisses. Unblinking, Kevin remained riveted to the floor, staring first at a smiling and spent Maria and then at the baby, who dangled upside down from the doctor's hands. When Dr. Alvarez announced that Maria had delivered "a healthy, beautiful baby girl," Maria looked anxiously over to Kevin for his reaction to fathering a daughter. From the width of his smile and the joyous sound in his voice as he sang out, "HEY A *GIRL*! WAY TO GO MARIA, WAY TO GO!," she knew that she had fallen in love with the right man.

Kevin Cox strode into the fifth-floor waiting room, raised his video camera to his eye, and proudly announced to all the Sisneroses and his grandparents that Maria had given birth to an eight-pound, twenty-inch baby girl by the name of Simone. Through his viewfinder, Kevin recorded in two languages a veritable orgy of embracing and congratulating. The celebration came to an abrupt halt when Sarah looked directly into the lens and ordered, "Kevin, stop already with the camera and call your parents."

49

IT WAS FIVE-THIRTY in the morning when Fred returned to his home in Bel Air from his dinner meeting with his casting director, Paula Petroff, and Chong Sook Kim. Chong Sook Kim was not only his number-one choice to play Ginko but the one person who might help him put out the smoldering torch he was still carrying for Hana Yoshi. Chong Sook, like Hana, was an inordinately beautiful woman, but unlike Hana, she seemed to be truly interested in him. As for playing the role of Ginko, neither he nor Paula saw that Chong Sook's being Chinese, and not Japanese, presented any real problem.

During the course of the evening his casting director had made many wise suggestions, the best of which resulted in Fred's spending time alone with Chong Sook. Paula conveniently remembered a late-night appointment and asked Fred, "Do you mind terribly seeing Miss Kim home?"

On the way to her modest apartment on Olympic Boulevard, Fred and Chong Sook learned that they had much in common. Each was lonely and nursing slow-healing wounds from an unrequited love. Chong Sook made it clear that the last thing she was looking for was any kind of emotional involvement, and Fred admitted that he, too, had promised himself to steer clear of anything that remotely resembled a serious commitment. What amazed Fred was that after being invited up to Chong Sook's apartment for a cup of coffee, he and Chong Sook actually did sit around and drink coffee, and pour out their hearts to each other.

At dawn, in gratitude "for being so very kind and understanding," Chong Sook cooked for Fred the most delicious waffles he had ever tasted.

At the door, she kissed him on the cheek and said, "Mr. Cox, whether or not I get the part in your film, it is my hope that we can continue to be friends."

Fred was hoping that the ringing phone that greeted him as he entered his house was Chong Sook calling to ask him to return to her apartment to cement their friendship. With that thought in mind, Fred answered the phone with an abnormally cheery "Helloooo!"

The smile on his face froze.

"Dad?"

Fred demanded to know where he was, and Kevin told him that he was in Florida and then said that he had something very important to tell him. Fred, sure that he knew what the very important something was, blurted out, "You and the girl went and got married, didn't you?"

Today Kevin was ready to forgive anything, even his father's referring to Maria as "the girl."

"No, Dad. Maria and I did not get married yet, but a few minutes ago she gave birth to our baby girl, and I cut the umbilical cord."

Fred did not speak for an uncomfortably long time. He was waiting for the adult parent in him to surface and instruct him on how to feel and what to say. He finally found his voice and said something that Kevin had never imagined he would ever hear from his father.

"How's Maria? I mean, how's she doing?"

"Maria and the baby are both doing "fantastic," Kevin said, and then quietly thanked his father for asking. In an attempt to build an emotional bridge, Kevin, even though he was not being totally honest, said, "We named her Simone, after Simon Kakaffsky!"

The Hayakawa Industries private jet was two hours west of the Hawaiian Islands when the pilot received an urgent message requesting that his passenger Sharon Cox call Mr. Cox in room 557 at the Salk-Reisman Memorial Hospital in Miami Beach, Florida. The flight attendant brought a portable telephone to Sharon's seat, awakened her gently from a pill-induced sleep, and informed her of the message. Since the ugly confrontation with her son, Sharon had been having frequent and disturbing dreams of Kevin dying in some bizarre way. Her most recent and horrifying nightmare was of Kevin bungee jumping off a cliff and tape-recording his own crash after the rubber cable snapped. As she read the message, she assumed that the "Mr. Cox" was Fred and that he had flown to Florida to be with Kevin, who lay dying in a room at this Memorial Hospital. As soon as the phone rang, Sharon asked the hospital operator for Mr. Cox in room 557. When Kevin answered and said, "Hello," Sharon asked, "Fred?"

"No, Mom, it's Kevin."

In the shortest, happiest phone call Sharon had ever had in her life, she learned not only that Kevin was alive and was still calling her "Mom" but that he was happy to hear from her. Sharon would remember for the rest of her life the next few words from her son's mouth.

"Mom, I'm sorry I said those dumb things to you. I apologize. And Mom, I know you look too young to be a grand-mother, but I must tell you, you have a very beautiful grand-daughter who I think looks like you."

There were thousands of miles separating Sharon and her son, and except for the time she carried him in her womb, she had never felt closer to him.

B EFORE MIRIAM married J.J. and joined J. J. Quicky, Inc., the company was a one-man operation working out of a modest bungalow in West Hollywood. Within five years, with Miriam as comptroller, the company had become a national organization, with offices in Los Angeles, New York, and Dallas, employing two dozen skilled private investigators. It was acknowledged that J. J. Quicky Enterprises, Ltd. had more complete and accurate data on people's lives than any private investigatory organization in the country. It was Miriam who realized that the company's comprehensive case files were excellent source material for a television series. With J.J.'s blessings, she contacted an old friend and sex partner, the president of DBS Cable, David B. Sterling. He was happily surprised to discover that Miriam's series idea was a good one but saddened to learn that this onetime uninhibited nympho had become a born-again monogamist.

The day after Miriam Quicky and David B. Sterling had their initial meeting, Elizabeth "Liz" Layton, the bright, pretty, twenty-four-year-old vice president in charge of development and acquisitions at DBS, received a manila envelope containing a dozen cases from the *Files of J. J. Quicky*.

While scanning the cover pages of the files, Liz's eye caught the name Cox. When she discovered that it was a file on the Fred Cox family, she settled back to read it. She was eager to learn what had happened to handsome Kevin Cox, the first boy she had allowed to get to third base and who, two years later, dumped her to run off with a Spanish maid.

When she had finished, Liz stared at the Cox folder and

questioned the morality of invading the privacy of people she knew personally just to get a television show on the air. Her ethical dilemma lasted only as long as it took to raise the question, and she hastily scribbled a note to her boss:

David,

Congratulations! You have come upon excellent material for the making of a successful anthology. The opening segment of the show would deal with the messes in which people, by design or accident, find themselves, and the second part would show how, where, and what these people are today—a kind of *Whatever Happened To.* I look forward to your comments.

Liz

David B. Sterling, impressed with Liz's synopsis, requested that she develop the project but recommended a title less cliché than *Whatever Happened To.*
Liz memoed back immediately.

David,

In place of *Whatever Happened To,* how about *Then and Now?*

David Sterling was sufficiently intrigued by the characters in the *Then* segment of the Cox file to read their updated bios for the *Now.*

1. *FRED COX:*
   Became engaged to CHONG SOOK KIM in Taiwan during filming of *Ginko and Her Great-grandmother.* When the movie opened to poor notices and worse business, CHONG SOOK broke their engagement and moved out of his house. She moved in again two years ago, when a musical version of his old film, *Acrimony, Alimony and Nougats,* became a smash hit on Broadway.

2. *LEON AND SARAH COX:*
   Paid weekly visits to KEVIN and great-grandaughter until their deaths at eighty-seven and eighty-five, respectively.

3. *SHARON COX:*
Worked as secretary-companion to HANA YOSHI for two years. Flies to Florida often to visit her grandchildren. Always accompanied by HANA and her son SEBURU.

4. *DR. DICK COX:*
Sued for medical malpractice and had his license revoked. Recently married one of the litigants, MRS. BARBI FELD-MAN, and changed his name. Is presently working in Tecate, Mexico, as chief medical consultant for Saludos Salud, a posh, new detox facility for the ridiculously rich and obsessive. The facility is solely owned by Dr. and Mrs. Richard Kakaffsky.

5. *HANA YOSHI:*
Married and divorced SEBU HAYAKAWA and retained custody of son. Was officially married to SHARON COX in a formal ceremony at a church in San Francisco.

6. *SEBU HAYAKAWA:*
Soon after his wife admitted to being a lesbian, he acquired the services of three attractive mistresses and set up expensive homes for them in Tokyo, Sydney, and Malibu.

7. *KEVIN AND MARIA COX:*
Now living with their three children, seven-year old SI-MONE and month-old twins SARAH and LEONA, in Orlando, Florida, in a comfortable, lightly mortgaged, five-bedroom house. KEVIN presently directing television commercials for McDonald's and Disney World and MARIA doing tutorial work (teaching English to Spanish children). KEVIN's last extended contact with his father was during father's recent open-heart surgery.

David,
You know, of course, to protect the real people, we'll change their names . . . and to protect our chances of success, we can also change their stories.
I recommend that we go forward.

Liz